ZANE PRE

THE
PAGES
We
FORGET

Dear Reader:

Anthony Lamarr made his debut as a Strebor author with *Our First Love*, which I found compelling once I discovered that it centered around the lives of two brothers, one who suffers from agoraphobia, and their bond. They eventually fall in love with the same woman. Now he returns with another type of love story.

June is a famous singer-songwriter who's caught up between the man who ruined her life a decade earlier and a musician who helps to boost her career to success. Whom should she choose? *The Pages We Forget* is a poignant read that features original lyrics from June that are included in her CD of the same name. Get ready for these passionate pages that will warm your heart.

As always, thanks for supporting the authors of Strebor Books. We always try to bring you groundbreaking, innovative stories that will entertain and enlighten. All of us truly appreciate your love and support.

Blessings,

Zane

Publisher
Strebor Books
www.simonandschuster.com

ALSO BY ANTHONY LAMARR
Our First Love

ZANE PRESENTS

THE PAGES *We* FORGET

A NOVEL

ANTHONY LAMARR

SBI

STREBOR BOOKS

NEW YORK LONDON TORONTO SYDNEY

Strebor Books
P.O. Box 6505
Largo, MD 20792
http://www.streborbooks.com

ISBN 978-1-59309-568-0
ISBN 978-1-4767-5884-8 (ebook)
LCCN 2014936769

First Strebor Books trade paperback edition December 2014

Cover design: www.mariondesigns.com
Cover photograph: © Keith Saunders/Keith Saunders Photos
Interior illustration: © abstract/Shutterstockimages.com

10 9 8 7 6 5 4 3 2 1

Manufactured in the United States of America

For information regarding special discounts for bulk purchases, please contact Simon & Schuster Special Sales at 1-866-506-1949 or business@simonandschuster.com

The Simon & Schuster Speakers Bureau can bring authors to your live event. For more information or to book an event, contact the Simon & Schuster Speakers Bureau at 1-866-248-3049 or visit our website at www.simonspeakers.com.

For Clarence "Jody" Adams III
"If you were here…"

*In her first passion woman loves her lover.
In all the others, all she loves is love.*

—George Gordon Byron

This story is a work of fiction. The real Hampton Springs Hotel was built by railroad pioneer J.W. Oglesby and not the fictional character John Bacon. The town that developed around the hotel in the novel does not exist except in my imagination.

Still, what a beautiful place it is.

"The Pages We Forget"

(lyrics and arrangement by June)

Yesterday's songs,
some live forever.
Their rhythm and their rhymes
still playing melodies in our minds.
A story behind each
of a love we both promised to keep.
So many, many years
of lonely nights filled with tears.

CHORUS:
Our eyes tell stories
of how we used to be.
Memories locked inside
never to be free.
And now, after all this time,
we pass like we've never met.
Neither wanting to remember
the pages we forget.

The years have healed the pain.
We've learned to love again.
Until that moment in time,
when again we feel the rhythm
we hear the rhyme
slowly start to beat.
Then those chapters of our lives
start to repeat.

CHORUS

And now, after all this time,
we're still feeling the rhythm
and hearing the rhyme.
Will we ever remember?
Why don't you want to remember
the pages we forget?

Chapter 1

His touch ruined her life. It had been more than ten years since she last felt his touch, but June remembered that night like it was last night. She could still feel their bodies touching for the first time. His trembling lips. Her love enveloping him. Him surrendering to her. Nothing escaped her memory of that cool April night. She could still hear the rain playing pitter-patter against the window. Smell traces of his Eternity cologne on the green comforter. Feel his love inside of hers. She didn't forget anything about the night they first made love. Not even the tears in his eyes as he tiptoed out of the room while she pretended to be asleep.

It had been ten years, two months and sixteen days, to be exact, since she gave herself to him, and seldom did a day pass when she didn't find herself reliving all or some part of that night. The memories didn't always replay in sequence. Sometimes they began as he took her in his arms while posing for their prom pictures, or two hours later when he opened the bedroom door at Mildred's Bed and Breakfast Inn. And sometimes at the very moment he surrendered to her. But mostly they began at the beginning with her staring out of her upstairs bedroom window at his house next door. Then Keith, alluringly debonair in a sky-blue and white tuxedo, strode out onto the wraparound porch with his gushing parents, Reverend and Lucy Kaye Adams, right behind him. He stopped at the bottom of the four steps and patiently posed for pictures with his mother and then his father before getting into Reverend Adams' navy blue Lincoln Town Car and backing out the graveled driveway.

"Here he comes," she shouted to her mother, who was in the next room putting film in the camera. She grabbed her pearl white clutch and white shawl off the bed and hurried out of the room. "Ma, come on!" She stopped at the top of the stairway and fidgeted with the spaghetti straps of the sky-blue gown, meticulously adjusting the opaque wrap until it draped perfectly. "Ma!"

"I'm ready," Kathryn yelled and rushed in the hallway. She stopped in her tracks. "Oooh, my baby. You are so..."

The doorbell rang.

"Ma, it's him," she shrieked. "He's here!"

"I'll get it," Kathryn announced and started down the stairs.

"And I'll wait here." She still felt butterflies whenever he came near, even after a twelve-year courtship that began the first time she saw him. His parents had driven from New Jersey to Hampton Springs so he could spend the summer with his grandparents, who lived next door. Her heart started racing and her legs began wobbling the moment she saw him get out of his parents' car that day. She felt that same dizzying sensation as she waited for him at the top of the stairs. To stop her knees from knocking and her heart from racing, she took a deep breath and held it.

Kathryn opened the front door. "Good evening, Mrs. Thomas." Keith greeted her with a regal bow of the head before stepping inside.

"Is Junie ready?" Lucy Kaye asked as she and Reverend Adams rushed to beat each other inside, almost knocking Keith over during their haste.

"Wait until you see her." Kathryn closed the door, trying her best to contain her excitement.

Keith watched her descend the stairway. His eyes glazed over. She exhaled.

"Kathryn, she's beautiful," Lucy Kaye gushed. "Oh, my babies."

He met her at the bottom of the stairway. "You look good." He reached for her hand, his eyes conveying more than his lips could express in that moment.

"Good?" she hesitated.

"Better than good," he corrected himself, trying to find the words that wouldn't sound inappropriate in front of everyone. "You are beautiful."

"Thank you. And I must say that you are quite handsome."

Lucy Kaye nudged Kathryn giving a knowing wink. "They're going to be the best-looking couple at the prom."

"Turn around," Reverend Adams told them, "so we can get a picture of you together."

Keith put his strong, yet gentle, arms around her, and they both smiled as the cameras flashed. "Okay, I want you to change sides." Reverend Adams took a look at the pose, shaking his head in his displeasure. "No wait. Keith, why don't you let Junie stand in front of you?"

"Come on, Dad. That's enough pictures." Keith took her hand in his and led her out the door.

Outside, the scene, the moment, everything was perfect. It felt surreal. She paused to listen to the song of the redbirds as it floated melodically on the gentle breeze. It was a twilight symphony heard often in these parts. Majestic magnolias framed the yard and the ornately detailed Victorian house. The magnolias permeated the air with their pungent perfume. The sky, already painted in hues of faded blues, became even paler against the brilliance radiating from June and Keith.

The neighbors gathered in the yard. Mrs. Croft, who made the white lily corsages and boutonnieres that perfectly complemented their attire, fettered into the yard like her feet were shackled. Mr. and Mrs. Whitehurst, Coach Rickards, Mrs. Blue Hen, holding her four-year-old grandson's hand, Mrs. Rosa Lee and her sister and brother-in-law, Mrs. Fannie Lou and Deacon P. H., and every member of the seven families who lived on Bacon Street were present. Inez, her best friend, and Inez's date, Nathaniel, a young man from Perry, were pulling in the driveway. Mrs. Whitehurst, Inez's grandmother, was already passing around Polaroids of Inez and Nathaniel. This was a proud moment for all of them. Three members of the Bacon Street families would soon be graduating from high school, and they knew that together they'd done a good job rearing these three exemplary young people. It showed on their gladsome faces and echoed in their jubilant laughter.

Inez, dressed in a lavender silk gown, got out of the burgundy Bonneville. Her fingers spoke for her. "You're beautiful, Junie."

She signed back, "So are you."

"Reverend, get one of him opening the car door for Junie," Lucy Kaye suggested, taking her by the hand and guiding her down the steps and across the mulch-covered walkway.

"Mom, don't you think that's—"

"Do what your mother says," Reverend Adams told Keith.

"Turn around, Junie." Kathryn was already positioned to take the photo that Lucy Kaye suggested. "Smile for the camera."

She turned slightly so that she and Keith were facing both her mother's and Reverend Adams' cameras. As she turned, she glimpsed his face. He was smiling, beaming, laughing almost.

Almost in that instant, the same unpredictable and unannounced way they began, the memories ended, but not before picking away the scab of a wound that would not heal.

June's life was over after that night, but she didn't stop living. Not at all. She left for college two months later. Within a year of leaving town, she hit it big. Really big. But that didn't surprise the folks in Hampton Springs. They always knew she was going to be the one who put the once famous North Florida community back on the map.

When June was eight, she strolled into the kitchen one Sunday morning as Kathryn was dicing an onion to go in a bowl of potato salad for Mt. Nebo's first Sunday fellowship. She announced her new career plans. She no longer wanted to be a doctor when she grew up. "I'm going to be a star," she foretold.

"What kind of star?" Kathryn asked without bothering to look back at June, who was wearing an afro-puff wig too big for her head, a pair of two-inch-heeled bare backs that were three inches too long, and a yellow and white ruffled skirt that fitted like a maxi-dress.

"The kind in the movies," June answered, grabbing a wooden spoon off of the counter. "I'm gonna be like Diana Ross." She sashayed around the counter, snapping her fingers to get a rhythm. She turned to her mother, who still hadn't looked around. "Cause wherever my man is," she belted with a voice well beyond her years. "I'm his forever..."

The jar of pimentos fell out of Kathryn's hand and the sound of breaking glass brought her first performance to a sudden halt. Kathryn couldn't believe her ears. It was the first time she, or anyone else, had paid attention to June's captivating voice. "Don't stop! Keep singing," Kathryn cheered her on.

"'Cause wherever my man is, I'm his forever more," June sang. Then she turned to her mother and said, "That's all I know."

"Junie, when did you start singing like that?"

"You promise you won't get mad?"

"Mad about what?"

"Well, last night after you told me to go to sleep, I slipped back up so I could finish watching this movie on TV with Diana Ross in it called *Lady Sings the Blues*. You ever seen it, Ma?"

"Child, I done seen that movie more times than I can count. Now go on."

"Well, I really liked it and I decided I wanted to be a singer like Diana Ross and the lady she was playing, Billie... Billie something."

"Billie Holiday," Kathryn informed her.

"Yeah, that was her name. Anyway, after I finished watching the movie, I started practicing."

"You started practicing last night, and you already singing like that? Move over, Miss Ross! My girl's on her way!"

June knew it and her mother did, too. She was going to be a star like she said she would. And it wasn't because she had what Lucy Kaye, Mt. Nebo Baptist Church's choir director, described as a blessed voice after hearing her sing later that day. It was more than mere talent or even desire. It was something else. Something preternatural. No one understood what made her so special, but everyone recognized that she was.

Me, her first album, released when she was nineteen and a sophomore at the University of Florida, proved how special she was with worldwide sales in the millions. That was followed by two other platinum CDs, two movies, both box office hits, and a multimillion-dollar promotion contract with a leading cosmetics line. The world loved her and watched her every move.

Junie Thomas became June, one of the entertainment industry's brightest stars. As she sat in the parlor of her lakefront mansion in Grosse Pointe playing Joy, the black enameled Baldwin piano she received on her thirteenth birthday, she quietly sang a song from her upcoming CD, *The Pages We Forget.* "Our eyes tell stories, of how we used to be. Memories locked inside, never to be free. And now after all this time…" She paused and studied the piano's keys. "We pass like we've never met. Neither wanting to remember the pages we forget."

This song was special because she wrote it for Keith. Well, not exactly for Keith, but about him. She didn't know if he listened to her music, saw her films or even glanced at the magazine and tabloid covers she often graced as he went through the supermarket check-out lanes.

June stopped singing and peered out the window at the two men applying a fresh coat of paint to the exterior of the house. One of the men, a blond-haired, blue-eyed reincarnation of Paul Newman, was looking at her. She knew from the look on his face that he was excited about seeing her in person. He stopped painting and smiled at her. June straightened the sash on her white satin robe and then adjusted the hairpin that held her hair in an upswept twist. She smiled invitingly at the young man. Although his wide-toothed smile was nothing like Keith's timid smile, she was reminded of the last time she had seen Keith smile—the night before he ran away. No one saw or heard from Keith after he left except for his parents, who received an occasional letter or a brief phone call every few months. He made them promise to keep his whereabouts a secret and that they wouldn't come after him.

Three years passed before he came home again and then it was to attend his father's funeral. Kathryn called and told June that Reverend Adams had passed away as she prepared to perform in front of a sold-out crowd. She could not go on afterwards, so she canceled the show and caught the next flight to Tallahassee, which departed at four-thirty that morning. A few minutes after sunrise, June was speeding along the two-lane stretch of highway between Tallahassee and Hampton Springs.

Only a stone's throw from the marshy coast of Florida's Big Bend, Hampton Springs' destiny could have easily been like those of its nearby neighbors. The coastal fishing villages of St. Marks and Apalachicola were havens of born and bred fishermen and their families struggling to make a living plucking oysters, shrimp, blue crabs and mullet from the gulf and inland bays. However, the sulfuric spring that gushed what was once believed to be medicinal waters out of a small enclave near Rocky Creek reversed the town's fate.

B & G Railroad owner John Bacon, who suffered from rheumatism, stumbled on the springs during a 1913 hunting and fishing trip in Taylor County's bountiful pine forests which were filled with deer, raccoons, squirrels, quail, and wild hogs. The creeks overflowed with bream, catfish, and speckled trout. After bathing in the spring and sipping its bitter brew, Bacon proclaimed himself healed of the stiff joints and muscle swelling that had nearly crippled him. Within a year, he constructed a magnificent 45-bedroom resort, the Hampton Springs Hotel, on the site. Then he placed colorful advertisements on his trains and in stations around the country touting the spring's healing waters, the forests' abundant wildlife and streams, and the fresh Florida air. The hotel's mineral-rich bathing pools began luring wealthy guests from across the country, many of whom settled in the area.

When the hotel burned down in March 1952, most of the town's three hundred residents were wealthy white landowners who made their living selling timber to the pulp and saw mills in nearby Perry and by harvesting and selling turpentine to medicinal distilleries.

June's family and the other six black families who lived on Bacon Street inherited their lavish homes and enough land to buy their dreams when Old Man Bacon died in 1956. He bequeathed most of the property to the indentured black servants who still resided in Brown Quarters, a shantytown of shotgun houses behind the hotel. This benevolence gave them a chance to rewrite their lives and their children's lives.

June longed to see her hometown after the two-year whirlwind of appearances and touring that followed the release of her first CD and the recording of her second. She pulled out a Newport as she counted down the ninth mile of her thirty-two-mile journey. She wasn't sure what made her purchase the pack of cigarettes because she didn't smoke, but she'd instinctively walked in a store at the airport and asked for a pack of Newports.

"Long or short?" the clerk asked.

"Short, I guess."

"Box or soft pack?"

"Box," she answered. "I also need a lighter."

The clerk, who looked to be in his early forties, stroked his long curly hair behind his ear and stared over his wire-framed glasses at June as he rang up her purchase. "That'll be four dollars and seventy-nine cents."

She handed him a five-dollar bill.

"Out of five," he said, and counted out twenty-one cents. He hesitated before handing her the change. "Are you...?"

"No." She hurried her answer, hoping to halt the conversation before it continued.

"You could've fooled me because you look exactly like her," he remarked, looking closer. "Did you know she was from 'round these parts?"

"I may have read that somewhere," she replied, taking the change out of his hand. "Thank you."

He nodded and watched as she walked out the store through a terminal full of pointing fingers and curious glances. She turned and headed toward the Enterprise Rent-a-Car counter.

An hour and five cigarettes later, she steered the Toyota Camry into a cramped parking space in front of her mother's downtown bakery. She had not been home in almost two years because she had been busy recording and promoting her first album, which she immediately followed up with the recording of her second album, *Feel My Love*. Still, she didn't expect the whole town to turn out simply to see her. The majority of Hampton Springs' 824 residents were gathered inside the bakery, next door in Inez's Beauty Salon, outside along Willow Street's wooden covered sidewalks, and in the shade of the moss-covered oaks and dogwoods that lined the street. No one had to tell the town folks June was on her way home. They knew she would be there as soon as she heard about Reverend Adams. Some came clutching yellowed scrapbook and grade-school photos, while others brought copies of her first album, *Me*, for her to autograph. The entire town was happy to see her. Everyone…except Keith.

It was early the next morning when she saw him. She was sitting in her old bedroom staring out the window when a black and white Toyota Corolla pulled into the Adams' driveway. Her heart stopped. She pressed her face against the window to get a better view of him. She gasped when she saw the forlorn look on his face as he got out of the car. "Ma!" June rushed out the room and almost fell running down the stairway. "He's home, Ma! He's home!"

Kathryn ran out of the kitchen just in time to stop June from running out the front door. "No!"

"What?"

"You can't just run over there, Junie," Kathryn advised and closed the door.

"Why?"

"Because of everything that's happened."

"But..."

"No buts, Junie! You can't rush this. You've got to wait for him. Give him time."

June stared into her mother's eyes. "I can't, Ma. I've been waiting three long years. Three years that feel like a lifetime. I can't wait any longer. I have to see him now!"

"I know how you feel and I know—"

"Do you, Ma? Do you really know how I feel?"

"Junie, I'm trying to understand."

"How can you, Ma? He was the first man I ever loved! The first one I made love to. And after I made love to him, he disappeared. He didn't say good-bye. He didn't say anything. He just left. Has that ever happened to you, Ma? Because if it hasn't, you can't begin to understand how I feel!"

June reached for the doorknob, but Kathryn stood firm. "No, that's never happened to me," she tearfully replied. "But I'm your mother, and every time you hurt I hurt. My heart broke too when he left, and my heart is breaking right now because I see how much you're still hurting. But please, Junie, trust me on this."

June reluctantly consented. During the next two hours, she paced back and forth through the living room and trampled up and down the stairway. In between the pacing, she kept staring out the windows hoping to catch another glimpse of him. She couldn't wait any longer. While Kathryn wasn't looking, she dashed out the front door, down the steps, across the yard and through a gap in the azalea hedges separating their yards. Kathryn heard the door open and rushed out of the kitchen. It was too late. "Junie!"

Keith didn't see June coming up the walkway when he opened the screen door and walked onto the porch. When he did see her, it was like seeing a ghost. He stood frozen.

June stopped at the bottom of the steps. "Hi," she said nervously, looking directly into his eyes, hoping they would tell her what she knew he wasn't going to. "I saw you when you got in this morning, but Ma told me I should wait until you got settled before I came over."

His face turned stolid. Without saying a word, he turned and bolted back in the house. June ran up the steps and tried to snatch the screen door open, but he had already latched the door. She stared through the screen at him as he hurried through the living room and up the stairs toward his bedroom.

"Why? Why won't you talk to me?" she yelled as he disappeared up the stairway.

She didn't cry the morning he first ran away and she had not cried once since then. No matter how much it hurt, she wouldn't let herself cry because she couldn't be sure the tears would stop falling if they ever started. So she played it safe and never consciously questioned why he left. Or why he refused to see or talk to her. But now, after seeing his face again and looking into his deep, despondent eyes, she could no longer make herself forget what happened that night. She remembered touching him. Then slowly undressing him. Making love to him. She remembered everything. Even the words she'd tried so hard to forget: *please don't*. As much as she wanted to, she couldn't forget those two words. "Please don't" echoed down the stairway, through the living room and onto the porch as he walked out of her life again.

Scared that Keith might not show up for his father's funeral, June and Kathryn decided it was best for her not to attend. So, June flew back home to Detroit that afternoon, promising herself she would never interfere in his life or attempt to contact him again. Her tears started falling that day seven years ago.

June wiped a tear from her eye, then turned and looked at one of the three framed pictures of her son, Trevor. There was Keith's smile again. Trevor's eyes were his, too. So was his straight black hair and caramel complexion. They could pass for twins.

"The years have healed the pain and we've learned to love again," she sang and watched her fingers caress Joy's keys. In her mind, she wiped away the tears she had seen in Keith's eyes that morning ten years ago. "Until that moment in time, when again we feel the rhythm, we hear the rhyme, slowly start to beat. Then those chapters of our lives start to repeat."

She remembered how hard it was to let go, to simply give up on the life she was supposed to share with him, but she did it. She made the painstaking decision to go on, to live, even though the life she would be living would not be her own. She couldn't forget him though. Not the smile on his face as they backed out of her driveway that night. Nor his telling eyes. His touch. Once, when she couldn't recall the sound of his voice and the silence had become too unbearable, she phoned his mother back in Hampton Springs and asked her to make a three-way call to him, so she could hear his voice.

"Remember, you can't say anything, Junie," Lucy Kaye reminded her as Keith's phone rang. Lucy Kaye didn't know what happened between the time Junie and Keith backed out of Kathryn's driveway and the next morning. But she already knew that whatever happened, June and Keith were keeping it between them. And she knew what Keith had said about telling anyone his whereabouts. "If it was left up to me, I'd give you his phone number and address."

"I understand, Mrs. Adams." The phone continued to ring. *Please be home. Please be home,* June repeated in her mind when he didn't answer after five rings. *Please.*

Finally, a wavering voice answered, "Hello?"

He sounded the same. His voice still gravelly. She wondered if he looked the same. Was his hair long or short? Was it still straight and jet black? Did he ever grow the mustache he always wanted? Did he learn to smile again? Hearing his voice wasn't enough now. She wanted to see him, but seeing him was out of the question.

"Ma, I'm sorry I forgot to call you back the other night," he said, "but I got a little busy."

June wanted Lucy Kaye to ask him what he was busy doing. Did some friends drop by? Was it his girlfriend? Did he have a girlfriend? Did he go over to her place? Did they go out to dinner? Did they watch a movie? Listen to music? What did she look like? Was she pretty?

"I'm rewriting a story for a nature magazine, and the editor needs the rewrite plus a few more photographs by next week," he explained. "So, that's been keeping me busy."

"Well, let me know when the magazine will be out so I can pick up a copy at the supermarket," Lucy Kaye uttered, trying to lengthen the conversation for June's sake, if not her own.

"You probably won't find it in Hampton Springs. It's a regional magazine, so I'll have to send you a copy," he said. "Now tell me, are you calling just to say hello or are you still trying to get me home for the Fourth?"

"I was calling to see how my baby's doing," she answered. "But I really would like to see you next month. So why don't you come on home and see about your lonely old mother? It's been five years."

"I can't promise you anything, but I'll see what I can do," he said. "So..." he started to say but suddenly stopped. "Ma?"

He knows I'm on the phone, June told herself. *He feels me. He knows. I have to say something.* She opened her mouth to say his name but nothing came out. She tried again and still nothing. "Hello," she finally mumbled.

"Ma, who was that?"

Lucy Kaye didn't answer immediately.

"Ma?"

"That was Kathryn," Lucy Kaye responded. "She just walked in."

"Then, I better let you go," Keith said. "I'll call you next week."

"All right," she replied piteously. "I already know you're going to eventually say no, but please think about coming home for the Fourth."

"I will," he said.

Afterward, June apologized to Lucy Kaye. She didn't know what made her say something while Keith was on the phone. It had not been her intention because she remembered the promise she made to herself. She had already broken it by having his mother call him.

That was two years ago.

June looked up from the piano keys and stared at the gold and platinum records lining the parlor wall. She looked at the framed magazine covers: *Rolling Stone. Ebony. Esquire. Vibe. People. Cosmopolitan. Essence. Vogue. Redbook. Good Housekeeping.* Even, *Time* magazine. She'd done good for herself, had nearly everything she wanted.

She felt the compelling urge to say his name, which she rarely allowed herself to do. "Keith," she whispered and glanced around to make sure she was still alone in the parlor. It felt good. And since there was nobody around to hear her, she said it again. And again. But this time she played a few keys on the piano and crooned each letter and every sound associated with his name. "K... Kei... Keith. Keith."

She closed her eyes so she could see his face. She looked in his eyes and felt his fingers touch her. She felt his lips tremble when she kissed him. Then she heard the door close the morning he left her in bed pretending to be asleep. "Why?" she asked and then waited for his reticent eyes to answer her.

His eyes refused to disclose the answer she sought.

"If You Were Here"

(lyrics and arrangement by June)

When I'm with you,
there's no place I'd rather be
'cause you fulfill my every need,
though you're only in my dream.

CHORUS:
You've made my life so happy,
and I'll always want you near.
But what would I say,
if you were really here?

You let me touch the sun,
hold the moon in my hands.
And when I fail to be my best,
you always understand.
I've never felt this way,
because you've never let me down.
When you hold me in your arms,
you turn my world around.

CHORUS

You're always there for me,
when I'm feeling sad and blue.
To have you here forever,
there's nothing I wouldn't do.

I'll never let you go,
never let you walk away.
Without you here with me,
I couldn't make it through the day.

CHORUS

But what would I say,
if you were really here?
I'd hold you real close
and whisper in your ear,
I love you,
if you were here.

Chapter 2

June craved sunrises like a hungry baby craved its mother's milk. And God could not have created a more beautiful dawning than this one.

There's no way, she thought out loud as she stood on the ice-covered wooden dock. She watched as the first rays of sunlight waltzed across the sky before skipping across the frozen lake.

Snow had fallen for two days, blanketing the wooded estate with more than twenty-two inches. She was standing in the same spot Tuesday when the storm bore down on the area. Alex had tried to talk her into staying inside. "You can watch from the window," he told her as he climbed out of bed behind her. "The weather advisory said not to go outside unless you have to."

"I have to." She slipped an oversized wool sweater on over her knee-length flannel gown. Then she put on a pair of long johns. "And since you're up, why don't you fix me a cup of cocoa while I finish getting dressed."

Alex walked over to the window and stared out into the dismal night. The storm had touched down an hour earlier, with trailing gusts strong enough to knock a four-foot limb off the giant sycamore outside. The limb fell on the balcony and scratched the window, almost breaking it. That's what woke them up.

"Junie, there's no way I'm letting you go out there," Alex said.

"Will you hand me my boots?"

"You're not listening to—"

"Yes, I am," she said, looking up at him. "I hear you, loud and clear. But you already know..."

"Junie, you're going to freeze." He handed her the snow boots. "It's below zero."

"Alex, I don't have time for this. It's already after six. If you hadn't bothered my alarm clock—"

"I didn't touch your clock."

"So, why didn't it go off?"

"Maybe you forgot to set it."

"I forgot to set it? Don't go there, Alex."

"Well, maybe you did. Shit, you're not infallible."

"Watch it, Love. You're getting upset when you don't have to." June calmly took a few breaths, giving him a quick smile. "I'm not mad about it. I was just saying. Now, can I get that cup of cocoa?"

Alex left the room without saying another word. June began stringing the knee-high boots. She put on the green and beige scarf Lucy Kaye crocheted and gave her last Christmas, draping it around her long, slender neck twice.

Alex was waiting at the back door with a covered mug of cocoa in one hand and her down-filled overcoat and gloves in the other. He placed the mug on the table by the door and helped June put the coat on. "When you come back in here with pneumonia, don't come crying to me."

"If I did get sick, trust me, you would be the last person I'd come crying to."

"Do I detect an attitude?"

June entered the security code to turn off the house's alarm system.

"Well, do I?"

She opened the door.

"Junie!"

"You did, but I'm sorry."

"You know something? You're starting to wear that word out."

"Then I'm not sorry! Is that better?"

"Yeah," he answered and then turned and walked away. "Lately, everything is okay as long as you are the one doing it."

June hesitated for a moment. Alex was right. She had become such a bitch. Everything he did or said bothered her. At times he could be overbearing and he was always too nurturing. He watched over and cared for her like a doting father would his first newborn. But it was those same traits, the ones she used to call his strengths, that she leaned on after Keith ran away. He helped her find her way back. Lately, however, she'd become short with him, intolerant. She hoped that soon she would be able to tell him everything that had transpired without his knowledge over the past few weeks. She had an appointment with Dr. Wylie Thursday. She figured she would explain everything to Alex after the appointment, when she could assure him there was no reason for him to worry. She hesitated, wanting to apologize, but there wasn't time. Morning was fast approaching. She slipped the leather gloves on and pulled the coat's hood tight around her head. Then, with the cocoa in one hand and using her other hand as a face shield, she stepped into the frigid darkness. She pushed her way through the sixty-eight-yard barrage of wind and snow that gnawed like ants through the layers of heavy clothing. She made it to the dock in time to see the sparse remnants of what was surely a brilliant sunrise above the impenetrable overcast. That was Tuesday.

But this morning, Thursday, could not have begun more quietly spectacular. Sometime during the night, the snow had stopped falling. She'd stayed up late talking to her mother on the phone and then she spent about an hour and a half skimming through the script, *For His Love*, a psychological thriller about a young woman coping with the anguish she felt upon witnessing her soon-to-be husband rape her sister. June had fallen in love with the story and purchased the rights to the screenplay. She decided to produce the film through her and Alex's company, White Flowers Entertainment. She also planned to star in the film, set to begin production in three weeks. The cast was assembling for a table reading in six days and she wanted to be up to par when she started rehearsing with Zoe Ross, the actress who would play her sister. June's two previous movies had done well. They were hits at the box office and she received good reviews for her acting. Despite the films' success and her success as a recording artist, she saw herself as a budding thespian, so she surrounded herself theatrically with professionals, like Zoe, whom she'd asked personally to costar in the film. She laid the script down and went to sleep around midnight.

By dawn, the gray clouds had drifted northward and the scathing wind had subsided. Stars crowded the night's dusky canvas. The waning moon hung low, illuminating the area in a translucent glow. The air was light and crisp. The faint wheezing of her breathing and the squishing of stepped-on snow punctuated the quietude. A very visible flicker of light began to burn on the horizon. That's when she closed her eyes and tried to hear the silence.

She remembered her father telling her she could hear God in the silence. "If you close your eyes and listen closely, you'll sense His presence in the playful chatter of the redbirds, in the rustling leaves, and in the splendor of the wind's soaring aria. But, to really hear Him you have to find a way to shut the rest of the world out and hear only the silence," her dad, Henry, told her one morning twenty-three years ago. She had only missed a handful of sunrises since. Eight thousand, five hundred and thirty-four mornings of watching, waiting and listening. It wasn't always easy to shut out the rest of the world, but somehow she managed to find a way. Whenever she was away from home or in the city for a concert, recording session, interview or premiere, she specifically requested an eastward-facing room with a balcony high above the city streets. And she always had a window seat in case day broke while she was traveling.

Alex never understood her craving for sunrises, but he'd come to learn over the past ten years that they were as essential as oxygen for June. It was her fascination with sunrises that brought them together two weeks after she arrived at the University of Florida. They met in the hallway of the music building. Alex, a junior majoring in music, had gotten up before class to post an audition notice on the student bulletin board. She was taking a shortcut through the building on her way to the football stadium.

Music Producer/Songwriter looking for
talented singer for demo recordings.

"What kind of songs do you write?" she walked up behind him and asked.

The box of tacks flew one way and the handful of notices he had left went the other way. "You scared the shit out of me!"

"I'm sorry." She laughed. "I thought you heard me when I came in the door."

Alex stared suspiciously at her as he bent over and picked up the tacks and collected the notices.

"Why are you looking at me like that?"

"Because," he mused, "I'm wondering what you're doing walking around campus by yourself this time of morning?"

"I'm going over to the stadium," she replied. "Am I supposed to be scared?"

"I would be if I was a woman. You have all kinds of nuts hanging around campuses like this."

"Are you one of them?"

"You tried me with that question, but that's okay." Alex stood and looked at June. "So what's up with the stadium? Are you going to exercise?"

"Walking there is the exercise. I'm going to watch the sunrise."

Alex grinned. "To watch the sun rise?"

She nodded her head, puzzled at his amusement to her ritual. "So tell me, what kind of songs do you write?"

"All kinds, but mainly ballads. Some dance grooves."

"Are you any good?"

"Am I any good? Actually, I'm better than good. You're looking at the next Babyface. How come you ask? You sing?"

"Some."

"Some? What's some? I mean, are you any good?"

"I do okay," she answered. "Actually, I'm pretty good, if I do say so myself."

"Can I hear for myself?"

"Right here?"

"Why not here? This is the music building."

June was nervous and it wasn't because she was afraid of singing in front of people. She'd been singing in Mt. Nebo's adult choir since she was nine. It was something about the way he looked at her that unnerved her. "What do you want me to sing?"

"It doesn't matter," he answered.

He writes ballads, so I'll sing something slow, something sweet and Whitney sounding, she thought. She looked up at Alex, grinned and half-covered her face with her hand. "I'm embarrassed."

"Don't be," he said. "I can't sing a lick."

"You better not laugh." She closed her eyes to find her comfort zone, but she felt his penetrating stare. His stare had her wondering. In her mind, she didn't think he was imagining what she looked like in a pair of tight-fitting jeans instead of the two-sizes-too-big jogging suit she wore. Her eyes were a little puffy after a late night of studying, but she was sure he wasn't staring at her for that reason, either. Her hair was braided back in one big plait that was starting to unravel, but the way she felt him staring at her, he was looking for something else. Something inside of her. And she felt him prying, searching deep.

"I've been searching..." she sang in a delicate falsetto. "Waiting. Hoping." She paused for a second before she belted out, "Boy, I've been praying."

She had him. Her voice was the perfect instrument. Passionate. Big. Colorful. Unique. He was mesmerized.

"For the Heavens to lead you back to me," she sang. "So I'm still wishing. Still waiting. Still needing you here with me."

"You're beautiful," Alex blurted out. "I mean you have a beautiful voice, and we really need to hook up!"

Two days later, in his cramped studio, a bedroom he transformed in his apartment in the university's student ghetto, she laid the vocal tracks to "Something Special." He wrote the mid-tempo dance groove the day he met her. The song secured her a label deal. Its original release date was postponed for three months until after Trevor's birth. But, eight months after recording the song, it skyrocketed up the R&B and pop charts and became her first number one hit.

Together they made each other's dreams come true. She became an international singing sensation and he became one of the top music producers and songwriters in the business. It wasn't long before Hollywood called. June signed an exclusive two-picture deal with a major studio, which included a provision that allowed her to choose the director of her first film. Naturally, she chose Alex, who'd directed several of her music videos. They became Hollywood's new royal couple after the success of *If At First*, a romantic comedy about a young couple who bitterly file for divorce after twenty-six days of marriage and then fall madly in love again after meeting on a blind date a year later.

It wasn't long before June wanted to dim the media spotlight that focused on her every move. She cut back on her work schedule and made fewer personal appearances in order to spend more time being Trevor's mother and Alex's lover.

June opened her eyes and basked in the tranquil beauty of the wintry scene as daylight chased away the impervious darkness. The intoxicating serenity was exactly what she needed to help her relax. She was confident the lab results would confirm that the persistent abdominal pains she'd been having for the past two months were nothing more than ill-timed menstrual cramps. She felt the tension and anxiety mounting. In a few minutes she was going to have to go back inside, pretend to be interested in Alex's small talk as they got dressed before sitting down to have breakfast with him and Trevor. She imagined how the conversation would take shape. He would spend breakfast briefing her about the morning's staff meeting and an afternoon luncheon with the studio executives who were financing *For His Love*. She hadn't come up with a good enough excuse to miss the meeting and luncheon, but she had to keep her appointment with Dr. Wylie. She was hoping that after the appointment she would be done with the secrecy and lies and things could get back to normal between them.

She was still trying to concoct a reason, any reason, to steal away from him for a couple of hours when he asked, "Are you ready?" Alex drank his last swallow of orange juice. He filled the eight-ounce glass with water and emptied it again. "We've got a busy day ahead of us."

"I know, but you go on ahead." June nudged Trevor's knee underneath the table. "I'll drive because I have a conference with Trevor's teacher this morning."

"When did this come up?" Alex turned to Trevor, who was eating the last slice of cinnamon toast. "I don't recall hearing anything about a parent-teacher conference."

Trevor shrugged his shoulders as he turned and stared questionably at his mother.

"I answered the phone when she called," she tried to explain, "and I guess it just slipped my mind. I'm sorry that—"

"Sorry again?"

Annoyed by Alex's mocking, June got up from the table and marched out of the morning room, a small glass enclosed patio off from the kitchen. "Trevor, I'll be right back. Be ready!"

Trevor turned immediately to Alex and jokingly asked, "Dad, what's wrong? Did she wake up in diva mode?"

Alex laughed. "For the past few weeks she hasn't been able to turn it off." He got up from the table, put his suit jacket on, then walked over and stood behind Trevor. "So why did your teacher need to schedule a parent-teacher conference? And how come I'm the last one to find out about it?"

Trevor turned completely around in the chair before answering, "I don't know. This is my first time hearing anything about it. For real."

"I believe you," Alex said. "I've got a meeting this morning that I can't reschedule, so I'm going to have to miss the conference. But I'll pick you up after school and we'll come on home and do a little ice fishing. How does that sound?"

"Sounds good to me." Trevor got up and followed Alex through the kitchen and down the long hallway that led to the garage entrance.

"Trevor, I want you to do something for me today," Alex said.

"What, Dad?"

"I want you to keep an eye on your mother."

"Is she sick?"

"I don't think so, but she's not her usual self."

"Is she ever?"

"Watch it," Alex scolded Trevor. "You know, you're really getting to be a little smart ass."

"I was just teasing, Dad. Chill."

"Trevor, are you ready?" June yelled as she came down the stairway.

"Yes, ma'am!"

"Do you have on your coat and gloves?"

"I'm putting them on now," he replied and took his Minnesota Vikings coat off the rack next to the door.

Alex pressed the intercom button next to the door and told Mrs. Freda, their housekeeper, to let Willie and Joe know they didn't have to drive Trevor to school or pick him up. He turned to Trevor and reminded him of his favor. "Don't forget what I told you." Alex took his black leather, three-quarter-length jacket off the rack and put it on over the charcoal Teres McClen suit tailor-made for his long, slender, yet muscular, frame. He ran his finger inside the snap-collar of the gray cotton shirt to loosen it a bit. "Keep an eye on her." He opened the door to the garage.

Trevor picked up his backpack and followed Alex into the garage. "Dad." Trevor walked over to Alex, who was unlocking the door of his black Cadillac Escalade. "What time are you going—?"

"Get in the car, Trevor!" June walked into the garage. She put on a black leather coat over her royal blue knit tube dress. She pressed a button on her keychain to unlock the doors of the silver Mercedes S500 sedan. "Alex, I'll be there as soon as I can."

Alex acknowledged her with an insipid nod. He turned to Trevor and answered, "I'll pick you up around three." He reached inside the Escalade and activated the garage door opener.

June had already started the car and was looking in the rearview mirror when Trevor got in and buckled his seatbelt. As soon as the garage door cleared, she backed out. Mr. Jake, one of the estate and house's five caretakers, had already plowed the snow out of the half-mile long, winding driveway. Two of the caretakers, Willie and Joe, handled security at the estate and doubled as June and Trevor's personal bodyguards. Freda and Carla took care of the house.

Neither Trevor nor June said much as they pulled out of the gated driveway onto icy Jenkins Boulevard and headed south. June stared ahead at the slush-covered road, while Trevor stared in the side-view mirror at his father, who drove a short distance behind them.

"You can turn the radio on," June said and glanced over at Trevor.

"That's okay," he declined. The Escalade's right blinker came on as they neared the intersection of Jenkins Boulevard and Woodard Street. Trevor turned completely around in the seat and waved at Alex, who blew the horn and waved. Alex turned onto the four-lane highway that led to East Jefferson Street and downtown Detroit.

As soon as Alex turned off, Trevor asked, "What does Mrs. Langford want to see you about?"

June, pretending not to hear him, leaned closer to the steering wheel and gazed cautiously out the lightly tinted windows at the road, narrowed by the piles of plowed snow.

Trevor knew she was pretending not to hear him, so he asked again, "Ma, what does Mrs. Langford want to talk to you about?"

Her face stiffened, her lips drew tight, and her eyes scatted back and forth searching for something, anything, to divert her attention from the question he was asking. "I hate driving in this kind of weather," she mumbled to herself.

"Ma!"

Acting like she'd been daydreaming, June turned to Trevor and asked, "What did you say?"

"What does Mrs. Langford want to talk to you about?"

June turned on her right blinker and slowed as they neared Beal Academy, a prestigious private school populated by the children of Detroit's most affluent celebrities, business and industry leaders, and political players. She glanced over at Trevor, who was getting somewhat impatient waiting for her response. "She didn't call," June admitted. She immediately turned her attention to the school's two security officers who were visually scanning cars as they turned into the cobblestone driveway.

"Then how come you told Dad that?"

"I needed an excuse to get away for a few hours this morning."

"What for?"

"There's something I need to take care of."

"And you don't want Dad to know about it?"

"No, I don't. That's why we're going to keep this between us. He doesn't have to know. All right?"

Trevor, feeling a little apprehensive about keeping secrets from his dad, reached in the backseat and grabbed his backpack as the car approached the entrance of the red brick building, formerly a Catholic monastery built more than a century ago.

"Trevor?"

"What's the big deal, Ma? It can't be nothing too important or Dad would already know."

June stepped on the brake and the car skidded a few yards, almost hitting the two parked cars in front of her. The car crashed into the embankment of snow on the opposite side of the driveway. Trevor unbuckled his seatbelt and pushed June's arm from across him; she had instinctively thrown her arm in front of him when the car began sliding. A tall, redheaded woman, the mother of two of Trevor's classmates, hurried out of her parked Lexus and ran over to June's car.

"Are you okay, Mrs. Thomas? Trevor?" the woman opened the passenger door and asked.

"We're fine," June answered. "I forgot how slick this driveway can get."

Trevor got out of the car and was about to close the door when he remembered what his father had told him. He knew something was bothering his mom and that it had to be something serious, because he couldn't remember seeing her so distracted. He turned around and leaned back in the car. "Ma, are you going to be okay?"

June forced a smile. "I'll be fine. Now hurry on inside before you catch a cold."

"I don't get a kiss?" he asked, a bit surprised.

June leaned over and kissed Trevor on the cheek.

"I love you, Ma."

"I love you, too. Now go on inside. I'll see you this afternoon." Trevor backed away from the car and June drove off. She looked in the rearview mirror and saw Trevor standing on the steps of the school worriedly watching her. "Everything will be okay in a few more hours," she promised his reflection in the mirror before pulling out of the driveway and heading toward Dr. Wylie's office in Eastpointe, where her best friend and stylist, Leatrice, would be waiting for her.

Leatrice was her confidant and the only person other than Dr. Wylie, a gynecologic oncologist, and his staff who knew about the biopsy June had undergone a week ago. June underwent the procedure while Alex and her manager, Bernard, were in Los Angeles making last-minute preparations for her Oscar night performance of her Best Original Song nominee, "Letting Go." The song was from one of the Best Picture nominees, *The Lost Day*. June suggested that Alex take Trevor along because she would be busy doing research at a psychiatric institution in Lansing to prepare for her upcoming film role. Alex, Trevor and Bernard flew out to California late last Thursday. The next morning, June, disguised in a short brown wig, dark shades, and a high-collared suede jacket, checked into the surgical center across the street from Dr. Wylie's office. Leatrice was there with her, believing strongly that the ovarian tumors discovered three days earlier would turn out to be benign. June's appointment to go over the biopsy results with Dr. Wylie was set for Monday morning, but Sunday night she called him at home and canceled. She told Dr. Wylie she'd been watching an old episode of *Touched By An Angel* about a young woman who had been diagnosed with cancer. Angels Monica and Tess came to the woman's aid but neither brought a cure. They offered only words, "God loves you." Those three words seemed to be enough for the woman because she gratefully accepted the inevitability of her end like it was a delightful homecoming. Until then, June had been optimistic, completely assured of the results. Now, she wasn't quite ready. So, when Dr. Wylie asked what day she wanted to come in, she told him she'd call and let him know. After hanging up with Dr. Wylie, she couldn't help thinking about how her life was already over. How she died once. But, she wasn't about to die again. She adamantly declared that everything was going to be fine. It had to be. So, later that night, she called Dr. Wylie and reset the appointment for Thursday.

June had driven the sixteen miles between Trevor's school and Dr. Wylie's office before she realized she was in Eastpointe. Her appointment was at eight. It was already eight-fifteen when she put on her right-turn signal and slowed down to navigate into the parking lot. Two men were busy clearing snow from the lot and sidewalks. She immediately spotted Leatrice standing under the covered walkway near the entrance of the building. It was hard to miss her in the full-length gray mink coat and matching headscarf that covered only the roots of her nearly waist-long dreadlocks. June pulled into the parking space next to Leatrice's car, and Leatrice walked over to meet her.

"You're late," Leatrice scolded as soon as June opened the door.

"I told Alex I had a conference with Trevor's teacher," she answered and stepped out of the car. "So I ended up having to take Trevor to school. How long have you been here?"

"About thirty minutes."

The glare off the snow was blinding, so June put on her blue-tinted shades before starting toward the entrance. "What excuse did you use when you called in?"

"My car wouldn't crank."

"Now, you know he's not going to buy that. You have a two-month-old BMW."

"He doesn't have to," Leatrice replied and flung her arm around June. "When we leave here today, we can tell him the truth about everything. Right?"

"Right."

The building security guard, who was used to June's specially arranged early morning appointments, unlocked the lobby door for June and Leatrice. "Good morning," he said as he opened the door for them.

"Good morning, Greg," Leatrice replied. June greeted him with a grateful smile. They took the lobby elevator to the second floor. When the elevator door opened and they stepped out, June almost immediately felt the angst she'd felt Sunday while watching the rerun of *Touched By An Angel*. She hesitated, closed her eyes and inhaled deeply.

"Don't worry," Leatrice said. "It's going to be all right."

June exhaled. "I hope so."

"Trust me."

Leatrice's words were comforting, but they could not restore the assurance she'd felt earlier. Now, standing at the door of Dr. Wylie's office, she was suddenly engulfed in a paralyzing wave of fear. She could not turn the knob and open the door, so Leatrice did. She could not sign in or even respond when the receptionist told her Dr. Wylie would be right with her. From the moment Leatrice opened the door and they walked in until she took a seat in the waiting area, all June could do was study the receptionist's ruddy face for any expression or sign that would foretell the results of the biopsy.

"She knows," June thought out loud.

"Who?" asked Leatrice as she thumbed through a magazine.

"Her," June whispered and nodded at the receptionist. "Do you see how somber she looks? It's because she knows."

"I don't think she looks somber," Leatrice said. "She looks like she's smiling to me and that's a good sign."

"You call that smiling?" June unbuttoned her coat and stretched. "Ooh, my body feels so tight."

"That's because you're nervous." Leatrice continued looking through the magazine.

"Shouldn't I be?"

Leatrice stopped on a full-page ad for Dark and Lovely's new line of hair colors.

"Well, shouldn't I?"

"I want to try this color on you," Leatrice said and pointed to the model's auburn locks. "I think it'll look good on you. What do you think?"

"How can you sit here and talk about hair color when I'm—"

"Good morning," Dr. Wylie said, walking into the waiting area.

"Hi," Leatrice replied. She nudged June, who simply sat there, unable to speak or move. "I'm sorry we're late, but the roads were worse than—"

"Tell me now," June blurted out. "Is it yes or no?"

Dr. Wylie adjusted his wire-framed glasses and started to say something but then paused. He sat down beside June.

"It's yes. Isn't it?" she repeated, trying to force the answer from him. The commiserating look on his face answered her question. "Then it's true. I have..." She couldn't bring herself to say the word.

"Dr. Wylie?" Leatrice clutched June's hand. "Is it?"

He nodded and said, "Although we found the cancer at a fairly late stage, there's still a lot we can do. If you come into my office, I can—"

"Not now," June tearfully declined. "I'll…I'll call you later."

"June, I feel obligated to tell you—" Dr. Wylie tried to explain, but June was too far gone to hear a word he said.

"Please don't. Not now." June stood and buttoned her coat. "I have to go. Alex is waiting on me." She fumbled around in her coat pocket for the keys. "Thank you," she said and started toward the door. "I'll call you."

Dr. Wylie turned to Leatrice, who was shaking her head in disbelief. "I think you should call Alex and try to keep June here until he gets here."

"Is she going to…?" Leatrice's eyes misted.

"No," he answered reassuringly. "As I was trying to tell her, there's still a lot we can do. But right now, you should call Alex."

"He doesn't know."

Dr. Wylie looked puzzled. "She told me she was going to tell him right before the biopsy."

"Well, she didn't," Leatrice said. "I better go. She may need me."

"She does," Dr. Wylie advised. "Please don't hesitate to call me if you need me."

June was getting on the elevator when Leatrice walked out of Dr. Wylie's office.

"Junie," Leatrice called. June acted as if she didn't hear her. Leatrice hurried toward the elevator, but the doors closed in her face. So, she ran toward the stairway at the other end of the hallway, pushed the door open, and rushed down the flight of stairs. June was coming off the elevator when Leatrice pulled the stairway exit door open and ran into the lobby. "Junie!"

June stopped but didn't turn around to acknowledge Leatrice, who hurried toward her. She stood there with a simper on her face, staring out of the lobby's tinted glass panes at nothing in particular. But there was something about the expression on her face that bothered Leatrice. June didn't appear distraught like she had when she got on the elevator less than a minute ago. Gone were the teary eyes and the nervous twitch…both were replaced by a frothy sense of relief.

"Junie, are you all right? Should I call Alex?"

"I'm fine," she answered and started toward the revolving doors. "Leatrice, so you think that auburn color would look good on me?"

Leatrice was stunned by June's surprising demeanor.

June turned to Leatrice and asked, "Well, do you?"

"Yes." Leatrice stammered, trying to adjust to the sudden change in June. "So what do we do now?"

"We better get to the staff meeting before it's over. I swear I don't feel like hearing Alex's mouth."

"Junie, I'm talking about the biopsy results."

June looked Leatrice straight in the eyes. "I don't know what I'm going to do," she calmly replied. "And right now, I don't want to think about it."

"But, Junie—"

"But nothing!" June marched off, but quickly turned back to Leatrice, meeting her confusion with a conviction in her eyes. "You may not know how it feels to have your life dangle on a thread in front of you, but I do. I know what it feels like to die, because I watched myself die before." June stepped into the revolving doors. "And I can't, no, I won't, go through that again."

Not again. Not again. Not again.

"It Must Have Been Magic"

(lyrics and arrangement by June)

Strangers;
That day you walked into my life.
Familiar faces, lonely hearts,
meeting each other,
though worlds apart.
We were strangers,
taking a chance with no doubt,
both wanting to know what love's about.

Friends;
Our thoughts we were willing to share,
both trusting and teaching the other to care.
Believing that dreams come true,
lost in a world that was so brand new.
We were friends;
Friends forever,
forever together.

Lovers;
All through the night you held me near.
You said you loved me but you didn't hear;
I thought it was true because hearts don't lie;
So how could you go without saying good-bye?
We were lovers;
You loved me 'til the break of day;
Then you turned and walked away.

Magic;
I remember playing like kids on a railroad track.
We circled the world; sometimes we made it back.
We lived in our world; we were all alone.
And in your arms, I built our home.
It must have been magic.
Heaven created a love like this;
and the magic's what I really miss.

Strangers
Friends
Lovers
It must have been magic.

Chapter 3

FADE IN:

A beautiful woman stares despairingly out the bedroom window of an old cottage into the moonless night. She remembers a time. A place. A man she used to know. She pulls her long, black hair back off of her face and then replays in her mind the dream that will not let her sleep. She can see him, feel him, and even hear him. But the words he says to her are lost in the silence of her fading dream.

Outside, the rain drizzles and plays pitter-patter on the window. It is music to her ears. Each drop that falls becomes a note in an all too familiar melody, even though ten years and two months have passed since she last heard his song. Ten long years and two months. Time has not healed the hurt.

"Yesterday's songs, some live forever," *she sings softly.* "Their rhythm and their rhyme, still playing melodies in our minds. A story behind each, of a love we both promised to keep."

She tries to find solace in the green comforter draped over her bare shoulders by pulling it tighter around her. She hopes that it will hold her together. Keep her from falling apart. But it can't stop her heart from breaking.

"So many, many years of lonely nights filled with tears."

She remembers kissing his trembling lips. Taking him inside of her. Surrendering.

"Our eyes tell stories," *her voice wobbles,* "of how we used to be."

She reaches for him, but his touch, like his tears, stings. Contuses.

"Memories locked inside, never to be free."

She stares through her tears at the door as it closes behind him.

"And now after all this time, we pass like we've never met. Neither wanting to remember—"

She tries to forget him, to remember this is just a song. The camera zooms in for a close-up as the woebegone look in her eyes betrays her. The dam breaks.

"Neither."

She's drowning.

"…wanting to remember…"

Not again. Not again. Not again.

"Cut! Cut!" Alex yelled to the thirty crew members working on the music video for the first single and title track of June's new CD, *The Pages We Forget.* One by one, the interchangeable parts that worked together to make the video come to life ceased.

The rain stopped falling outside the inn's window.

Bright incandescent lights replaced the moonless, starless night.

The music faded.

A lingering silence permeated the soundstage at Jam Sessions Studios in downtown Detroit as eyes moved to Alex, the director, wondering what the cause of the shortened take was about.

Alex stared dispassionately at June, who stood frozen on the studio set of the recreated Mildred's Bed and Breakfast. She gazed out the makeshift inn window, hoping to catch a glimpse of the man who walked out of her life ten years ago. Ten years and two months, to be exact. Alex wasn't angry with June, just a little broken-hearted and embarrassed. He was more than aware that the crew had heard and read about their troubled relationship while June was writing and recording the new CD. One tabloid announced they were getting divorced, even though they were never married. Another, more resourceful publication, reported she was leaving him for another man—her high school sweetheart who was the inspiration for her new CD. While this wasn't true, it wasn't entirely false, either.

The first song came to her in a dream. She had been sleeping soundly that night. In fact, she had gone through the entire day acting like nothing had changed, like Dr. Wylie's verdict had been the one she had graciously anticipated. The staff meeting was ending by the time she and Leatrice made it to White Flowers Entertainment's downtown production offices. However, she did attend the luncheon at the Renaissance Center with Alex, Leatrice, Bernard, in addition to John Madison and Lester Cogdell, both with Dreamland Studios. As she nibbled on a garden salad, she listened attentively to Alex and Bernard outline the revised production schedule for her new film, *For His Love*.

"Principal photography will begin in two weeks," Alex explained, "on location in Southfield. We're going to start shooting the exteriors at Simmie's house and then the Institution and downtown office exteriors. That will give us four full weeks of shooting before Easter."

"Are you still planning to take a four-day break for Easter?" asked Lester Cogdell, Dreamland Studios' CEO.

"We have to," Alex answered. "We promised our son we'd spend Easter in Florida at his grandmother's. It's been a while since we all went down together, and I think he'll be glad to get to Florida with all the snow we had here this winter."

"Junie," Leatrice whispered so as not to disturb the others' conversation.

June turned to Leatrice.

"Are you okay?"

June nodded and smiled, assuring her friend that everything was fine.

The rest of the day was uneventful, unsullied by the diagnosis. She told Alex that Trevor's teacher had only good things to say about his work. She went ice fishing with Alex and Trevor later that evening, and while hanging out on the frozen lake, she apologized to Alex for her earlier behavior. She was asleep and cuddled in Alex's arms when she finally reacted to the diagnosis. It started when Keith's voice jarred her awake.

"Some pages are best left forgotten, Junie," she heard him say. He'd whispered those words in her ear one morning as they watched the sun rise through the canopy of oak leaves and limbs that criss-crossed over Bacon Street. Now she was hearing them again. "Some pages are best left forgotten, Junie."

"What did you mean?" June thought aloud. She rolled over and tried to gather her senses. "Some pages are best left forgotten," she repeated.

Alex stirred and half-sleepily asked, "Huh?"

June remained motionless, knowing he would fall back to sleep if she stayed quiet. As she waited for Alex to drift off to sleep, she heard Keith say again, "Some pages are best left forgotten, Junie." June nestled in the sanctuary of Alex's arms, hoping to silence the haunting voice. But the voice would not be stilled. "Some pages are best left forgotten, Junie."

She had to get up and move before the voice woke Alex. She slowly lifted his arm from across her breast, easing toward the edge of the bed. Alex flung his arm over June's pillow and pulled it close to him. Three deep breaths later, he was sound asleep. June put on her slippers and tiptoed out the room.

The parlor was her special place in the tri-level, five-bedroom, six-bath house she helped design six years ago after her sophomore CD, *Feel My Love*, debuted at number one on the charts. The CD eventually sold more than four million copies. The 6,500-square-foot house, built on a steep grade that dipped downward to the lake, included a state-of-the-art digital recording studio, a giant family room with ten-foot-high pocketing glass doors that opened the room to a wraparound lanai with a pool and spa. There was even a guest cottage. But the parlor, with its high, coffered ceilings, stone arches and columns, was her personal retreat on the ten-acre estate. The dramatic touches, a rich marble fireplace and a flowing furniture arrangement that encircled the modest piano, created a relaxed, inviting ambiance.

Joy was waiting there for her. She closed the parlor door behind her and flipped on the light switch. She turned the dimmer until the artificial light of the crystal chandelier blended harmoniously with the moonlight shining through the half-hexagon of huge bay windows. "Some pages are best left forgotten, Junie," the voice whispered in her ear as she walked to the center of the spacious room. She pulled the piano stool out and sat down.

"Why do we have to forget?" June asked out loud to the voice in her ear. From where she sat, she could see the tip of the pear-shaped lake, but the dock was slightly out of view. The quarter-moon languished on the lake's round belly. A million twinkling stars, at least, were scattered across the sky. Out of the blue, the brightest star began to dance across the sky. "A shooting star!" June closed her eyes and wished, "Keith."

She gasped as the line was crossed. She was cheating on Alex. Wishing for Keith wasn't like thinking about him. Rarely a day passed when she didn't find herself thinking about him, or seeing his eyes in a crowd of admiring strangers, or feeling his presence when there was no one there but her and the memory of a night ten years ago. But since starting this new life with Alex she had not longed for Keith.

"Some pages are best left forgotten," she said again.

She had forgotten about the morning Keith told her that until a few minutes ago when the words stirred her awake. Now, she remembered that morning vividly.

The dirt was cool and moist from the morning dew. It clung to her bare feet and got stuck between her toes. A sulfur-tinged breeze drifted downward from the hotel grounds at the end of Bacon Street. She heard the Adams' front door close. There he was, trotting down the steps, across the yard, and out to the road. She turned around and pretended not to hear him coming. Without saying a word, Keith walked up behind her, put his arms around her, and joined her silent vigil.

June's fingers found Joy's keys and began playing the melody she heard the redbirds sing that morning.

She was back there, in his arms watching the first ray of sunlight flit across the sky. And the next and the next until shafts of light and darkness entwined like a crocheted tapestry. The light started to play with him. He playfully tried to escape from the light, but it bended and followed him. Flirted with him. Caressed the despondent frown from his face. He tried not to, but he couldn't hold it in. He giggled. He laughed out loud. She laughed, too.

"I wish you could see your face," she told him.

"Why? What's wrong with it?"

"Nothing," she answered, walking up to him. "Except, you're smiling and laughing. You know, the way you used to."

He coerced another smile. "I guess I'm smiling because we'll be leaving here in exactly two months. Can you believe it? In two months, we'll be leaving for college."

"And I can't wait," she said. "But I already know that I'm going to be homesick the day after we leave."

"Not me," he disagreed.

"You think that now, but wait until you leave."

"Believe me, Junie, I won't miss this place. As soon as I leave, Hampton Springs is history. Forgotten."

"How are you going to do that when our folks live here?"

"We'll come back from time to time to visit Mom, Dad, Mrs. Thomas and some of the others, but that's it. We'll never come back to live."

"Have you forgotten that you're next in line to be pastor of Mt. Nebo?"

"They'll find someone else when the time comes."

"I hear you talking." She touched his face and stared into his melancholy orbs as the sun rose. "We're about to start a new chapter of our life, but there's no way I'm ever going to forget this place or our lives here. You won't forget either. Why would you even want to forget?" She closed her eyes and waited to hear the voice in the silence.

That's when he whispered, "Some pages are best left forgotten, Junie."

June repeated the words Keith whispered in her ear as she recreated the melody of the redbirds. "Some pages are best left forgotten," she repeated. Then she sang the words. "Some page. Some pages are best left forgotten." There was something lyrical in his words. "Some pages are best forgotten." She improvised the words, replaying them like a broken record in the recesses of her mind. "Some pages we forget."

June stared out of the window as she continued playing the piano. "The pages we forget," she improvised. "The pages we forget." She stopped singing and listened attentively to the tune she was playing on Joy. *There's a song here*, she thought. *It's an old, familiar song that, upon hearing years later, you can sing every word and articulate each note like you heard it the day before.*

"Yesterday's songs, some live forever," she sang in a falsetto voice that flowed deliberately like molasses. "Their rhythm and their rhyme, still playing melodies in our minds." The lyrics seemed to come out of nowhere. "A story behind each, of a life." She paused. "Of a love we both promised to keep."

June had no idea Alex was standing outside the door listening. He'd woken up and realized his arms and bed were empty. Since it was too early for her to be out at the dock, he knew where to find her. But he didn't expect to come down to the parlor and hear her composing this yearning ode.

"So many, many years, of lonely nights filled with tears," she sang.

Alex reached for the doorknob but suddenly pulled back. He needed to hear more. Maybe, he figured, it was only a song that popped up in her head and nothing more.

She toyed with a line of lyrics that would become part of the song's chorus. "In our eyes, there's a story," she sang, pausing for a moment as she shook her head. "They tell stories of what?" she asked herself. "They tell stories about our love. No. That doesn't sound right. They tell stories of how we used to be."

June played the notes of the chorus and sang, "Our eyes tell stories of how we used to be." She paused again. "There are memories locked inside. Memories locked inside. Memories locked inside never to be free." She started at the beginning of the chorus. "Our eyes tell stories," she sang, "of how we used to be. Memories locked inside, never to be free."

June wasn't a songwriter, he was. As Alex listened, he slowly came to the realization that what he was listening to wasn't simply a song. It was too passionate. Too heartfelt. Too true. The lyrics and the music were coming from somewhere deeply personal and private.

"And now, after all we've shared," June continued singing. "We, we, we pass like we've never met. Neither wanting to remember, the pages we forget."

Alex couldn't stand to hear anymore, so he turned and walked upstairs, climbed back into bed, and tried to force himself to sleep. Two hours later, as soon as he'd dozed off, he heard June come into the room. He pretended to be asleep but lay watching as she walked into the closet and got dressed. She turned off the closet light and tiptoed out the room. When Alex heard the bedroom door close, he rolled over and looked at the alarm clock, which signaled morning was approaching. He turned the clock off and pulled the covers over his head.

The next sound Alex heard was their housekeeper knocking on the bedroom door. "Alex! Alex!" Mrs. Freda cracked the door and said, "Bernard's here and he seems a little anxious."

"I'll be down in a minute," he replied as he crawled out of bed. Mrs. Freda was about to close the door when he called, "Mrs. Freda!"

"Yes?"

"Where's Junie?"

"She's in the studio."

"In the studio?"

"She's been shut up in there all morning."

Alex looked at the clock. It was eleven-thirty. "Damn." Alex jumped up. "Why did you let me sleep this late?"

"Junie told me not to wake you."

"What?"

"She said you needed to rest."

"Tell Bernard I'll be right down." Alex walked into the bathroom to freshen up before meeting with Bernard.

Bernard was sitting at the desk in the library talking on the phone when Alex walked in. "What's up, B?"

Bernard signaled for Alex to wait while he finished talking to his assistant, Cheryl. "Pick us up here at six. And be on time. Our flight leaves at eight."

Alex sat on the edge of the desk and stared at the television. A show forecasting Oscar night was on E! Television. "Are you watching this?" Alex asked Bernard.

"It's a repeat. I saw it this morning," he answered. "According to E! and a poll on CBS's *The Early Show*, we're still the front-runner." He paused. "Cheryl, I'll check in with you later." He pressed the phone's end call button and then turned to Alex. "What happened this morning?"

"What do you mean, what happened?"

"Junie and Leatrice were supposed to meet with Chip so she could pick the gown she's going to wear Sunday, but Junie called and left a message canceling the appointment. I called here, but Junie told Mrs. Freda to hold all calls. I paged Leatrice to see if she knew why Junie canceled, but she hasn't called me back yet."

"I haven't talked with her this morning, so I don't know," Alex said and started toward the door. "She's been in the studio all morning."

"Really?" Like Alex, Bernard was a bit surprised to hear June was in the studio. Unless she was recording, she rarely went in the studio. Even when Alex was working at home with other well-known artists, she hardly ever sat in on their recording sessions. The studio belonged to Alex. Bernard asked, "What's she doing?"

"I have no idea."

Unbeknownst to Alex and Bernard, June wasn't alone in the studio, as Mrs. Freda suggested. Torrence Clarke, one of the hottest young producers and recording engineers in the business, was in the studio with her. After meeting Torrence at a local talent showcase three years ago, Alex took the then seventeen-year-old from Detroit's Eastside under his wing. He debuted professionally the next year when Alex allowed him to produce two songs on June's third CD. Both songs were huge hits.

While Alex slept, June had called Torrence around five-thirty that morning and asked him to come over. "I wouldn't call and bother you this time of morning if it wasn't urgent," she told him. "I'm working on a song and I need your help. Can you come to the house?" Torrence's money-green Jag pulled into the driveway a few minutes after sunrise. They had been locked in the studio ever since.

He was working the huge audio mixing board while June was in the recording booth, preparing to do a take, when Alex and Bernard walked in the studio. June glanced at Alex and Bernard through the big glass window separating the control room and the recording booth. Unfazed by their presence, June adjusted the headphones over her ears then closed her eyes as Torrence cued the music.

"The years have healed the pain." Her achingly beautiful voice wafted through the studio. "We've learned to love again. Until that moment in time, when again we feel the rhythm, we hear the rhyme. It slowly starts to beat. Then those chapters of our lives start to repeat."

Bernard sat down next to Torrence, awestruck by the power of the lyrics. "Did you write this?"

"No. She did."

"What?" Bernard turned to Alex. "This is good."

Alex nodded, trying his best to disguise the indifference in his body language.

"Our eyes tell stories, of how we used to be," June continued singing. "Memories locked inside, never to be free."

June finished the song as Alex and Bernard looked on. She'd been around Alex long enough to read his body language, despite his stoic stare. He liked the song, but that didn't mean she was ready to face him. He was sitting in a corner when she walked out of the recording booth. The go-ahead-and-say-it look on his face told her that he'd figured out what inspired her to write this. She tried not to look at him, focusing her attention toward Bernard instead. "What do you think, B?" she asked.

"It's beautiful," he responded. "So, I see you've been moon-lighting as a songwriter?"

"Actually, Alex has been teaching me over the years. I just never sat down and tried it myself." She looked at Alex, trying to get a silent nod of corroboration. He looked away.

"Well, you're off to a hell of a start." Bernard was oblivious to the tension between Alex and June, too enthralled with what he'd just heard.

"It took me there when I first heard it this morning," Torrence added.

"Speaking of this morning." Bernard remembered why he had driven out to Grosse Pointe. "Why did you cancel your fitting? We're leaving for L.A. tonight."

June began to fidget, playing with her hands, trying to find some-thing to give her courage, despite her growing desire to hide. All morning, June had deliberated and mapped out what she would say and how she would bring the subject up. Instead of beating around the bush, she came right out and said, "I'm not going."

"Wait a minute." Bernard looked at June, trying to regard what she'd announced. He blinked a few times before he gathered his thoughts. "Now say that again."

"I'm not going."

"You're not going where?" Bernard asked for clarification.

"To L.A.," she calmly answered. "It doesn't matter if I'm there to sing the song or not. The winner has already been chosen." She turned to Torrence and asked, "Can I hear what we have so far?"

Torrence, feeling quite uneasy and privy to a moment he felt he should not be a part of, looked at Alex and Bernard for directions. Alex offered no assistance, sitting in his space with a faraway look in his eyes.

"Well, Alex?" Bernard asked.

"What do you want me to do?" Alex calmly asked. "This doesn't concern me."

"Man, what the hell is going on here? It doesn't concern you? You wrote and produced the damn song. If it wins, you're the one who'll walk up there and accept an Oscar! That doesn't concern you?"

Alex was unruffled. "It would concern me," he said. "If this wasn't just the tip of the iceberg." He calmly stood and walked out of the studio.

Bernard turned to June. "I don't know what's going on with you and Alex, and I'm going to stay out of it. But, I'm your manager, Junie, and you're supposed to talk to me before you go making decisions like this!"

"I'm sorry."

"Sorry?"

Torrence interrupted by saying, "I'll wait outside."

"No!" June stopped him. "I want to hear the song."

Torrence sat down again. He adjusted a few dials and then turned a knob and the recording began. "Yesterday's songs, some live forever. Their rhythm and their rhyme, still playing melodies in our minds."

"It'll sound a lot better when we add a few background vocal tracks," June said.

"I don't know," Torrence disagreed. "I don't think this song needs much background vocals."

Bernard stepped between June and Torrence, taking a decidedly calmer approach in speaking to his star client. "All right, Junie, you say you're not going. May I ask why?"

"Because I have something else I need to do."

"Something like what?"

"This CD."

"What CD?"

"I'm recording a new CD. This is the first song."

Bernard scratched his head. "Does Alex know anything about this?"

"No."

"And when were you going to tell him? And tell me?"

"I don't know. One day."

Bernard was speechless.

June began to hum in tune with the song. "You're right, Torrence. Let's keep the background vocals to a minimum."

Alex had not misjudged the size of the iceberg. Not only was June determined to record the CD, she insisted on writing and producing every song on it. She had coproduced two songs written by Alex on her three previous CDs, but it was always Alex who wrote, produced and charted out the direction of her music. This time, she said she didn't want his help. Her explanation was the project was personal and it was paramount that she wrote and recorded the CD now.

June's peculiar behavior didn't end there. She had been shuttered in the studio for nearly thirty-one hours when she called and told Bernard she was pulling out of the film, *For His Love*. It was the Tuesday Alex, Trevor and Bernard returned from the Academy Awards ceremony. She told him she couldn't do the film because her new *Pages* CD demanded all of her time.

Bernard and the rest of June's handlers, including Cynthia Duckett, the head of Duckett's PR, Inc., were already working over-time. The rumor mill was already circulating stories about cracks in June and Alex's picture-perfect relationship. First came the headline, "Alex and June, No Longer," after Alex attended the Oscars ceremony without June. Against Bernard and Cynthia's advice, he excluded her during his acceptance speech. Next was the headline, "June Quits Show Biz," pasted in bold letters across the top of more than one national tabloid after the news of her quitting the film began to swirl. The most hurtful story was the one that blared, "June Ready to Leave Alex for Old Lover."

Even Alex started believing the rumors after June backed out on their Easter trip to Hampton Springs. Trevor had been ready since last Thanksgiving's visit to get back to his grandmother's so he could ride the horse Kathryn bought him the previous Christmas. A promise was a promise, he angrily reminded his parents during breakfast. Breakfast was the only time they could count on seeing June outside the studio.

"We did promise," Alex told June later that morning. He stood in a corner of the studio watching June compose music for a new song on the electronic keyboard. "We can't simply break our promise to him," he said.

"I can't go," she answered, not bothering to look back at Alex. "I don't have time."

"So what do you want me to tell him?"

"I don't know. When's the next holiday? Mother's Day. Tell him we'll go for Mother's Day."

"We both promised him we would go this weekend."

"Well, I can't!"

Before he knew he was saying it, Alex replied sharply, "Fine! Then I'll take him! You don't have to go!" Alex didn't know where that statement came from, as the thought of going to Hampton Springs without her was never on his list of things he wanted to do. It wasn't that he didn't like Hampton Springs. Everybody in the town went out of their way to be nice and courteous to him. After all, he was with June. But he always felt they looked at him as her consolation prize instead of the man she really loved. He had never been to Hampton Springs without her, but a promise was a promise.

Alex marched out the studio, up the stairs and into Trevor's room, where Trevor was lying in bed staring up at the ceiling.

"Pack your bags." Alex tried to hide the contempt he was feeling. "Our plane's leaving in two hours."

Trevor wiped the stagnated tears from his eyes and sat up in bed. "Is Ma going?"

Alex walked over to the bed and sat down. "No. She can't because she's busy working."

"But she promised!"

"I know. But remember, she promised before she knew about her new CD. We both know that she wouldn't miss a trip to Hampton Springs unless something very important came up."

Trevor felt better knowing that his dad wasn't too upset because his mother wasn't going. "So who's going? Just me and you?"

"What's wrong with just me and you going?"

"Nothing," Trevor answered.

"You ashamed of your old man or something?"

"Come on, Dad." Trevor laughed. "Chill."

Alex and Trevor left on a Friday afternoon flight to Tallahassee and returned to Detroit Tuesday night. It was nearly one a.m. when they arrived home. Alex toted an exhausted Trevor up the stairs to his bedroom. Trevor passed out on the bed before his head hit the pillow. Alex put Trevor's pajamas on him, pulling the blanket over him. He turned the light off on his way out of the room.

Alex expected June to be asleep, but she wasn't in bed. The bed had not been slept in since he left. Anger consumed him as he imagined what she had been doing all weekend.

He saw no traces of Torrence in the studio, finding June alone instead. She looked like she was lost in her thoughts, but Alex's anger took over.

"So, is this where you were all weekend when your son was trying to call you?" Alex marched in the control room. June was still scribbling on the sheet. He noticed the title of the song at the top of the page, and it only served to infuriate him further.

"You're back," June looked up, acknowledging his presence.

"What do you think you're doing?"

"I'm working on a new song."

"It's two in the morning," he told her. "You can finish it tomorrow."

"I have to finish it now," she replied and began humming the chorus to the song as she played along on the keyboard.

"Because I love you," she sang. "And my love is true. I love you. No one else will do. Because without you, I cannot see. Who would I love and who would I be?"

Alex could take no more. He grabbed the keyboard and slammed it against the wall. "You would still be June Thomas without him!

You're who you are now because I was there for you! Not him! And I'm here now, Junie! Right here!"

"This isn't about you, Alex, so why are you acting so damn stupid?"

"Why isn't it about me? I'm here, Junie! Do you see me?"

June wasn't blind and she wasn't trying to ignore Alex, but her mind and eyes were on the three pages of sheet music to "Because I Love You" on the floor next to his foot.

"Oh, and for your information," he offered as advice, "this song sounds like shit!"

June dove on the floor and grabbed one of the pages, but Alex quickly snatched it from her hand and put his foot on the other two pages.

"Give it here!" June tried to snatch the page out of Alex's hand. "It's not yours."

"I want to hear you say, I love you, Alex," he implored her.

"Give it to me, you son-of-a-bitch!" Her eyes were wild as she tried her best to get the page out of his hand.

"Tell me you love me and not him," he demanded.

June charged into Alex, grabbed him around the waist then pushed him into the mixing board. Alex fell on the floor, hitting his knee against the chair. She fell on top of him, her only concern being the precious item in his grasp.

"It's mine!" June fought, scratching Alex's hands and ripping his shirt to get the page out of his hand. Alex pushed her off him and grabbed the other two pages off the floor and hurried to his feet.

"Does he mean that much to you?" he asked her. "Does he?"

"No, he doesn't," June tearfully responded. "I love you, Alex. I've told you that a hundred times. Now please give it to me."

"Do you love me as much as you love him?"

"Please, Alex, don't do this."

"I need to know now, Junie. Do you love me as much as you love him?"

June turned away. She always knew that one day he was going to ask this question and she wouldn't be able to answer it. At least not truthfully.

"Do you?"

She didn't want to hurt him any more than he was already hurting, but she couldn't tell him another lie. Too many lies had already been told. The answer to his question was abject silence.

Alex balled the pages up and threw them on the floor before he turned and limped toward the door. He had finally allowed himself to ask the question that had crossed his mind daily for the past ten years. He desperately wanted to know whom she loved more, but he'd been too afraid of the answer. He turned around and watched as she gathered the pages from the floor, straightened them out, and put them in their proper order. She didn't seem to notice the hurt in his eyes as she ironed the wrinkles out of the pages with her fingers. "Because I love you," he whispered to her, backed away and out of the room.

"Because I Love You" was the only song she wrote that she didn't include on the CD.

"Everybody take thirty. Better yet, go ahead and take an hour for lunch," Alex told the crew working on the video to the CD's title track, "The Pages We Forget."

Everyone made their way toward the door that led to the lounge, where a catered lunch of hoagies and various types of salads was set up.

Leatrice, the video's art director, was standing behind Alex. She walked onto the set after the stage area was clear.

"Leatrice, can I talk to Junie alone?" Alex asked.

"Sure, but give me a minute to check on my girl."

June and Leatrice sat on the bed. They became close friends seven years ago when Alex hired Leatrice as the art director for the first music video from June's second CD. June and Alex liked her work so much they brought her on as art director for their movie projects and for all of June's music videos. Leatrice also created June's signature fashion style—elegant, yet daring designs in eye-catching colors. Her unique look was often imitated.

They were best friends from the start because Leatrice was a good listener. Leatrice felt that beneath the enchanting voice and the glamorous image, there lived a woman who believed her life was ruined. She had listened and heard the words that June didn't always speak. When June was finally able to talk about the morning Keith left her standing on his parents' front porch, she told Leatrice how she hoped Keith would tell her why he ran away. And she told her how Keith ran when he saw her. She even mentioned how her tears would not stop falling. When June had finished telling Leatrice all of this, Leatrice reached for her hand and smiled understandingly. She didn't say anything. Still, June believed that somehow Leatrice had also heard the words, "Please don't," echo down the staircase, even though she kept that part of the story to herself.

"Are you all right?" Leatrice asked.

June wiped the tears from her eyes and tried to speak. She was too choked up to respond, so she forced a half-smile.

"Everything's going to be fine," Leatrice promised. "As soon as you're done shooting this video, we can take care of that other matter. So, don't give up."

Meanwhile, it was Alex who wanted to give up. Each day he was more distressed and fed up, but the thought of not having her in his life was even more unbearable. There was so much he loved about her. Her unquenchable passion. Her beauty. Her amazing voice. He loved her smile and the softness of her lips. The heart-shaped birthmark on the back of her right thigh. And her sense of humor before she started recording *The Pages We Forget*. He even loved her frailty at that very moment.

"What can I do to help?" he asked from the director's chair.

"I'll talk to you later," June told Leatrice.

"Are you sure you're okay?"

"I will be," June answered.

"Be strong," Leatrice encouraged as she walked off set.

"What can I do to make this easier for you?" Alex asked from the darkness as soon as he heard the door close behind Leatrice. June could barely see his face from where she sat on the bed, but she knew he was having as difficult a time with the video as she was. He was furious when he first learned that her concept for the video was to recreate the night she made love to Keith. Whether it was jealousy or the insane need to be there with her, he insisted on directing the video. June objected. Bernard warned. And Leatrice pleaded. But all to no avail.

Now, he wished he had listened.

"Talk to me, Junie!"

"I'm sorry I put you through all this." She pulled the comforter tighter around her. Her apology sounded sincere, so he softened his tone. He was willing to do anything to find a way to be closer to her when he felt she needed him most.

"Junie, I'd do anything for you. I'd find a way to walk across the sun if that's what you needed me to do. There's nothing I wouldn't do for you, Junie." He stared into her tear-filled eyes. "It doesn't matter what it is. Whenever you need me, I'll be there. Always."

"I know, Alex. I know."

"Then why won't you talk to me?"

"I can't. At least not now."

"Why not now?"

"I just can't," she cried. "Please, Alex. Believe me, if I could tell you now, I would."

"What am I up against, Junie?" Alex begged. "What is it about him?" He wanted to run to her, take her in his arms, hold her and make her world right, but he needed to know the answer to his question first. "What did he do to you or give you or say to you that I haven't?"

"This isn't about him, Alex!"

"Stop lying!" Alex marched on the set. "Don't try to tell me this isn't about him. He's the reason you did this album. And he's the reason we're standing in this room now."

June stood and tried to walk away, but Alex grabbed her by the arm. "Let go of me," she snapped.

"Not until you tell me what's going on."

"You're hurting me, Alex."

"I want to know and I want to know now! Sit down!"

June reluctantly sat down on the bed.

"I'm sorry about grabbing you. I'm sorry about a lot of things right now," Alex said and walked over to the window. "But I know you, Junie. And I know that something's not right. You're not yourself, baby. If it's me, I mean, if you want me to leave, all you have to do is tell me. It'll probably kill me, but I'll go if that's what you really want. But if you want me to stay, Junie, you've got to trust me enough to talk to me and tell me what's happening with us."

"Alex, you already know what I want," she said. "I'm not with you because I have to be. I'm here because I love you."

"Do you?" Alex turned and stared out the window as the last drops of water dissipated from the glass pane.

June walked over to the window and stood behind him. "I know this is hard for you, but it's hard for me, too." She put her hand on his shoulder. With her other hand, she reached for his hand. He stepped away from her.

"Why?" he asked. "I need to know why."

"Baby, I wanted this album to be about me. Just me," she explained. "It's about who I was before I spent the night in this room. I wasn't afraid of letting my heart feel how it feels to really love someone and to have someone love you back. I believed in miracles back then. I could do anything. If I dreamed it, then I could do it. This is about needing to find that person again while I still can."

"But without me?" he asked.

June reached out to him again. This time he didn't move, but he kept his hands out of her reach. She placed one of her hands on his shoulder and the other on his chest. She looked in his eyes and saw his unquestionable love for her. She saw the nights he sat up until morning watching over her so she could sleep without the nightmares after a stalker took a shot at her during a concert in St. Louis. She read the words, "I love you," that he wrote on Post-It notes and placed around the house, in her traveling bags and on the stage before every concert. He loved her and she knew it.

"Never without you," she answered and kissed him softly.

"Never?" he asked.

"Never."

"There's Gotta Be
A Reason"

(lyrics and arrangement by June)

I can't believe what I'm feeling.
I'm feeling like I've been your fool.
All taking and no giving,
you didn't love me by the rules.
But no matter what I'm feeling,
you're still the perfect man for me.
So, I'm gonna keep on trying.
I need you so desperately.

CHORUS:
There's gotta be a reason;
a reason you don't love me.
I know there's gotta be a reason;
there's just gotta be.

We shared a heated passion.
Your sweet embrace kept my fire burning.
I'm guessing that's the reason,
that for your love, my heart keeps on yearning.
You told me you loved me.
But your actions say it was a lie.
I never was a beggar,
so please don't make me lose my pride.

CHORUS

(MUSICAL BRIDGE)

There's nobody out there,
who's gonna love you like I do.
And you'll never find someone
who's more right for you.

CHORUS
(repeat to fade)

Chapter 4

Six weeks and two days.

That's all it took to write and record June's new CD, and she insisted her label release the CD within a month of its completion. The executives at Antmar Entertainment were shocked by her demand. Some even felt it was an impossible task without any marketing campaigns in place or advanced publicity, except for the blaring tabloid headlines prompted by her absence from the Academy Awards ceremony. But, June was used to getting what she wanted from the company, and this request would be no exception.

Her plan was simple. She would write and record the CD, shoot a video for the title track, then cross her fingers and hope and pray that Keith heard the CD or saw the music video for the title song. There would be no concerts, touring, guest appearances, or magazine and television interviews.

Of course, this plan met with a lot of opposition.

Bernard was the first barrier.

"It's not going to happen like that, Junie," he said as they sat at her kitchen counter the morning after she recorded "A Song Still Unsung," the last of the CD's fourteen songs. "You're going to have to bend some."

"Why?" she asked. She set her glass of apple juice on the counter. "What's that you and Alex always preaching? Oh yeah. Remember,

Junie, no matter how big you get, it's always about the music."
She placed a sarcastic tone in the words that were told to her. "If
it's always about the music, why can't I simply record the album
and let that be enough?"

"You already know why," Bernard replied. He stopped jotting
notes on the yellow pad and laid the pen on the counter. "When
I said that, I was talking about composing and singing, because
regardless of how personal recording this CD was for you, releasing
it is business."

"Well, I'm tired of the business. I've recorded the album, and
I've shot a music video to go with it. That's going to have to be
enough," she snapped. "I'm done! Through! I can't do this anymore, Bernard. I can't!"

"Why?"

June hesitated. She knew she could trust Bernard with her secret.
He wouldn't tell Alex, but he would find a way to talk her into
telling him. She met Bernard, who was Alex's roommate and best
friend, shortly after she met Alex. Since the beginning, Bernard
had managed hers and Alex's careers. He was their third partner
in White Flowers Entertainment. He was also Trevor's godfather,
and next to Leatrice, June's most trusted confidant.

"Junie, if you can give me one good reason, or any reason, for
rushing this CD, then at least I'll have something to go on this
afternoon when I tell the label what you're requesting."

"Tell them that Torrence will have the master ready for them in
a week and I want the CD on the market exactly one month from
today. That's what you tell them. If that isn't good enough, then
the hell with them."

Bernard walked around the counter and sat next to June. "All
right," he said. "Let's forget about the label for a minute. This isn't

about them now. It's about you and me and me being able to do my job, which is to take care of you and your career. Junie, I can't do that job if you don't talk to me and at least let me know what's going on."

"Sounds like you've been talking to Alex," she said.

"Yeah, we talked."

"Well, I'll tell you, like I told him. This is one of those times when you're going to have to trust me to know what I'm doing."

"Fine. You can start by telling me what you're doing."

June looked away, but she could still feel Bernard's discerning stare. He was waiting for an answer.

"I'm listening." He pressed on, no longer willing to blindly acquiesce to her request. "You said trust you, and I've trusted you. I had my doubts at first about this CD, but I stood behind you because singing is what you were born to do. Nobody does it better. That was trusting you. But what comes after singing and recording is my game, and like you, nobody does it better. I trusted you to do what you do, now you need to trust me to do what I do. You can start by letting me know what your plan is."

Bernard wasn't as physically striking as Alex. He was thinner and shorter. And, he was going bald and gray. What Bernard lacked in physical prowess, he more than made up for in confidence, business savvy, and sharp-as-a-whip wit. He was always dressed in blue, gray or dark pinstriped suits by his favorite designers, Ron and Ron Delice. His regal demeanor was adornment enough. He was a commanding presence, so it took a great deal for June to say, "I'm doing it my way, B. Nobody else's but mine."

"Okay." Bernard gathered his notes and put them in his leather briefcase. "We'll do it your way." Bernard's face was stoic. He was there at the beginning. It was Bernard, even more so than Alex, who was responsible for her success. Alex wrote the songs and produced the music, but he was the one who sold her to America and the world. Her career had been a paint-by-numbers blueprint that he drafted. "I better get going. I have to meet Alex over at Dreamland in an hour. We're hoping they'll postpone production on *For His Love* until July, which will give you a little time to take care of whatever it is you're doing. But, I don't know how much longer we can keep Zoe attached to the project."

"I'll give her a call," June said.

"Whatever." He started toward the door, shaking his head while trying to figure out what was going on with his friend.

"B," June called. He stopped but didn't turn around. "Thanks for understanding."

"Junie, I'll be honest with you." He slowly turned to face her. He didn't bother to disguise the perplexed look on his face, and his body language suggested that he didn't much care. "I don't understand, and I won't pretend to. I don't know why all of a sudden you needed to record this CD. Or why you said to hell with one of the most important nights of your life. Or why you're breaking contractual agreements that could end your career. And I damn sure don't understand why you're willing to risk what you have with Alex for..." Bernard stammered.

"For Keith?" She stood and stared at Bernard. "Is that what you wanted to say? How many times am I going to have to tell you, this isn't about Keith?"

Bernard walked over to the counter. "Listen, Junie. If this CD isn't about Keith, why is every song on it about missing an old lover? And why would you put your prom picture with Keith on the cover? I won't even go into the video."

"That doesn't mean it's about Keith. I know you don't believe me, but this album is supposed to be about me and that time in my life."

"Keith was your life then. I don't get it, Junie. I don't know what you're trying to do, but I can tell you this. It's not worth it. I want to know something. Have you forgotten what Keith did to you? Do I need to remind you? You thought your life was over."

"That was then," she replied. "Bernard, I can't sit here and tell you that Keith doesn't mean anything to me now, because he does. It's been seven years since I've seen him, but every time I look at my son, I see him. So he's been here with me every day. He's never been completely gone." She paused. "But I love Alex, and I'm happy with Alex."

"Junie, I don't doubt you love Alex. As a matter of fact, I know you love him. And you may not think it, but I understand how hard it's been for you. But, what I don't get is why you're still longing for Keith. Why can't you put him behind you?"

"Behind me?"

"Yes, behind you," Bernard answered. "Ten years behind you."

June sat and watched Bernard walk out of the kitchen. She heard him say good-bye to Mrs. Freda. No longer hearing Bernard's voice, she heard Mrs. Freda coming.

"Junie, what would you like for lunch?" Mrs. Freda asked.

"I'm not really hungry," June answered. "Mrs. Freda, I don't want to be disturbed today, so I'm not taking any calls, unless it's Trevor or Leatrice."

"Your mother called this morning while you were in the studio, and she was really upset. She told me to tell you her exact words which were, 'If I don't hear from you today, I will see you in the morning!'"

June took a sip of juice. Her mother would make good on her

threat, there were no two ways about it. "I'll make sure I call her. By the way, did Alex say what time he would be in?"

"No. He seemed a little distracted this morning. He didn't say much. He took Trevor to school and said that Willie was going to pick Trevor up."

June started out of the kitchen.

"June," Mrs. Freda called. "Why don't you get some sleep? You look exhausted."

"I am."

June took a shower, put on one of Alex's big T-shirts, and climbed in bed. She'd been up nineteen hours, but she was still restless. She tossed and turned for twenty minutes before she gave up on the notion of sleeping. She got up and went to the studio. Her mind was on the straw pocketbook that her mother brought her from the Bahamas several years ago. She'd looked for it earlier, which was why she missed breakfast. It was an ordinary straw clutch pocketbook with a red straw handle and red and yellow embroi-dered flowers. Its contents were what was important. She kept the pocketbook in a hatbox on a closet shelf, but she had taken it out of the box when she started recording her new CD. Every letter Keith had written her throughout their courtship was in the pocketbook. Even though they lived next door to each other, they frequently wrote and mailed letters to each other. The old letters and the stories they told were part of the inspiration for most of the songs on the CD. She would always take out the letters, put them in chronological order, and read each one.

Junie, I just wanted to say thanks for covering for me the other day when I missed baseball practice, he wrote in one of the letters. *Coach*

Rickards was really upset and going to suspend me for a game, but when you told him you were sick and that I was with you because your mother was out of town, he excused me.

She remembered almost every word of every letter, and she recited one letter after another as she tore the studio up looking for the pocketbook.

I'm sorry I stood you up the other night, but Coach Rickards wanted me to go with him to see Wakulla High play Madison High, another letter began. *I would have called and told you, but I didn't know until the last minute and we were already running late. Junie, Coach really thinks that I have what it takes to make it as a major league pitcher one day. He says that I have something special.*

"You are special," June said to herself as she looked behind a stack of small boxes in a corner of the studio. She paced back and forth around the room, trying to retrace her steps. She was getting more and more worried about the missing letters, which, along with Trevor, was all she had to keep Keith a real flesh and blood man and not a canonized lover.

When she read the letters, she saw a person who could be engaging and open one minute and the very next minute retreat to a distant and impenetrable place inside of himself. Moments of extreme happiness and optimism were often followed by reclusiveness and detachment. He never offered an explanation for his roller coaster mood swings and the depression he hid from everyone. By the beginning of their senior year, he had grown obsessively attached to her. He was at her side when she woke up before sunrise to dance in the morning light; with her during every break between classes; after baseball practice; and in the evening after he managed to make it through another day. Sometimes, she'd fall asleep with him sitting on the floor at the foot of her bed writing letters to her, and awake to find him there asleep, wrapped in a blanket that her mother had thrown across him during the night.

I don't know how to say this, Junie, so forgive me if it doesn't come out right, he wrote in the last letter. *I have to say this and I wish I could say it directly to you, but I can't. Junie, if I never get the chance to say this again, please remember, I love you.*

That was all he wrote.

Two days later, on prom night, he whispered those same words in her ear as they posed for the photo that now graced the cover of her new CD. The next morning, two hours after he walked out of her life without saying good-bye, the letter arrived in the mail.

"Junie, if I never get the chance to say this again, please remember," she recited as she walked in the recording booth to search for the pocketbook. "I love you," she finished.

Even though she'd memorized each of the letters word for word, she couldn't recall if those were his exact words.

"It's got to be here somewhere." Her search became more frantic. "I left it here this morning," she told herself, stopping momentarily to think where else it could be. "I don't remember, but maybe I took it upstairs."

As June raced up the stairs, she tried to remember the exact wording of his last letter.

"Junie, if I never get the chance to say this again, please remember, I love you," she recited. "If I never get the chance. If I never get the chance. If I never get the chance." June stopped midway up the stairs. It had been more than ten years since Keith had written the letter. Ten years and a thousand readings, and she had never questioned his choice of words. "If I never."

"He knew he was going to leave!"

She felt lightheaded, so she hurried to her bedroom.

"He knew," she cried. Sharp pains began to race through her body. "Aawww!" she screamed and fell to the floor. "Please, no. Not now." she balled up in a fetal position. "Lord, help me. Please. Aaawww!" She screamed.

"Ma!" The door flung open and Trevor ran into the room. He stopped in his tracks when he saw his mother on the floor.

"Trevor?"

He rushed over to June and kneeled beside her. "Ma, what's wrong?"

June saw the tears already forming in his eyes and heard the fear in his voice. She had to say something to calm him down before Mrs. Freda heard him and came running into the room. She could force Trevor to keep quiet, but Mrs. Freda would tell Alex, even if it meant putting her job on the line.

"I'm all right," she said and reached for his hand. "I ate something I shouldn't have," she told him.

"I'm going to get Mrs. Freda." Trevor started for the door, but June grabbed his arm.

"No, Trevor! Stay here, with me."

"But you need help!"

"No, I'm all right. I just need you to help me up."

Trevor put one of June's arms around his neck and put his arm around her lower back and tried to lift her up. She was too heavy.

"Hold on, baby. Let me grab the edge of the bed. That way I can help pull myself up." She reached for the bedpost. "You ready?"

Trevor nodded.

"Together now."

June pulled herself up on the bed and tried to regain her composure as Trevor stood in front of her, staring into her eyes, trying to see for himself if she was still hurting.

"Trevor, I need you to make me a promise."

"Why?" He remembered what his dad had said about people wanting you to make promises: Always question their motives.

"I need you to promise me that you will keep this between the two of us," she said.

"Why can't we tell Dad?"

"Because we can't," she answered. "It was just something I ate. Daddy doesn't have to know about every little thing. You know how busy he is. Why worry him about some bad tuna?"

"That's what it was?"

"Yeah. It was a tuna sandwich."

"Then I better tell Mrs. Freda."

"I made it myself. And I already threw it out. So let's not bother Mrs. Freda either. She's busy, too. Okay?"

Trevor's eyes mirrored the confusion and doubt he felt.

"See. I'm feeling better already." She tried to assure him by standing without holding on to the bedpost.

Reluctantly, he smiled.

"So you promise?"

"I promise."

"Thank you." She kissed him on the forehead. "Now, I need to get a glass of water."

"I'll get it for you," he said. "You just sit here until I come back."

When Trevor walked out the room, June picked up the phone and dialed Leatrice's cell phone number. "Come on. Answer."

"Hi, this is Leatrice," she answered.

"It's me. Where are you?"

"Downtown. I'm just leaving the office. Is everything okay? You sound a little shaky."

"Trevor just caught me."

"Caught you? Doing what?"

"I was having a bad cramp."

"How bad was it?"

June hesitated.

"How bad of a cramp, Junie?"

"I was on the floor."

"On the floor? Get dressed! I'm on my way to your house and you're going to see Dr. Wylie, even if I have to drag you to his office."

"Leatrice."

"Get dressed! I'm on my way." Leatrice pressed the end call button before June could say another word.

June looked up as Trevor was walking in the room.

"Here's your water, Ma." He handed her the glass and she put the phone on the hook.

"Thank you, baby." June drank the water and tried to appear relaxed.

"Who was that on the phone?"

"Leatrice."

Thirty-two minutes later, Leatrice pulled into June's driveway. Trevor was lying on the floor in the family room playing "World Cup Soccer" on the Xbox 360 when Leatrice marched into the room. "Trevor, where's your mother?"

"Upstairs resting," he answered.

Leatrice headed for the stairway.

"Auntie Lea," Trevor called. He paused the game. "She needs to rest because she's not feeling good. She ate some bad tuna."

"All right," Leatrice said. "I'll only be a minute."

"She's already asleep," Trevor advised her. "You can wait down here until she wakes up."

"I need to see her now, so you go on and play."

"She needs her rest!" Trevor stood and insisted.

"Who do you think you're talking to?" Leatrice turned to meet Trevor. "Boy, I will—"

"Hello, Leatrice." June stood at the top of the stairway. "Looks like I got here just in time." She grinned.

"Yeah, just in time to see me whip his lil ass. I always said you didn't need bodyguards because you have," she nodded at Trevor, who stood at the bottom of the stairway, "Mighty Mouse."

"You can leave my boy alone," June said. "He's only looking out for his mother."

"That's right," Trevor seconded.

"Okay, Trevor," June stopped him. "That's enough. I can handle it from here."

"I was playing with Auntie Lea, Ma. Chill."

"You're gonna be the one chilling the next time you raise your voice at me," Leatrice said and then turned to June. "And you, how come you're not dressed?"

"Can I talk to you in the room?" June started toward the bedroom.

"There's nothing to talk about," Leatrice said. "Slip something on and let's go."

"Auntie Lea, where's she going?" Trevor asked.

Leatrice wasn't prepared for Trevor's question, so she stared straight ahead at June. She didn't want to look at Trevor because there was no way she could lie to him while looking him in the face.

"Are you ready to tell him?" June asked and turned and walked toward the bedroom.

"Tell me what?"

"Nothing, Trevor," Leatrice answered and choked back the tears.

"We were going shopping, but since she has a stomachache, we'll go tomorrow." She followed June into the bedroom.

June was sitting on the bed staring somberly at the doorway when Leatrice walked into the room and closed the door behind her.

"Did you tell him?"

Leatrice didn't answer. She stood there shaking her head and coming undone. It was only a matter of seconds before the dam broke.

"Why are you doing this?" Leatrice marched over to the bed and stood directly in front of June. "How do you think I feel knowing what I know? Do you think it's easy for me? Do you? I can't do this anymore, Junie! I can't stand here and watch you commit suicide because that's what you're doing!"

June reached for Leatrice's hand, but Leatrice stepped back and said, "No! Either you get dressed and come with me to Dr. Wylie's or I'm calling Alex."

"Leatrice, listen."

"No! I'm tired of listening. It's been nearly seven weeks since we learned the results of the biopsy, and what have you done about it? Nothing! Junie, I know you're scared. I'm scared. But we've got to do something and we've got to do it now. It's not going to simply go away."

"I know, Leatrice. But I had to do the CD first!"

"Well, the CD's done. What are you waiting for now?"

June looked away.

"Junie, I know what you're hoping for. I know and I sympathize. But even if Keith hears the CD and shows up on your doorstep the next day, is that going to cure you?"

"Don't be ridiculous!"

"I'm not the one who's being ridiculous." Leatrice huffed, "That word best describes the reason you're putting your life on the line. Junie, I love you like a sister. Maybe even more. And all I want is what's best for you. That's why I'm begging you to come with me to Dr. Wylie's office. He'll tell you what I've been telling you all along. We can beat this, but you've got to start the treatment now." Leatrice put her hand on June's shoulder. "Please, talk to him. That's all I'm asking. Please. If not for yourself, do it for Trevor."

June hesitated for a moment before tearfully replying, "Next week. Call and set me an appointment for next week. I'll be ready then."

"Thank you." Leatrice cried, showing her relief. "Thank you."

Trevor, on the other hand, felt the burden of secrecy pressing down on him. He sat quietly through dinner, which was unusual. It had been over three weeks since he and both of his parents had eaten dinner together. He was supposed to be ecstatic, giggling and talking nonstop, but he wasn't. That's how Alex knew something was bothering him. Alex was silent while they ate. He figured that whatever was troubling Trevor had something to do with his mother. And there was no way Trevor would betray June's trust with her sitting beside him. He would have to approach Trevor about it when June wasn't around.

Later that night, as he tucked Trevor in, Alex asked, "So what was your day like?"

"It was all right," Trevor answered. "I talked to Gramps."

"She called?"

"No. Ma called her."

"What did Gramps have to say?"

"She didn't talk that much to me, but she was yelling at Ma on the phone. I think she's still mad with Ma for not coming home for Easter and for not hardly calling her."

"Well, you and I are going to stay out of this one. Junie made her bed hard, so she's got to sleep in it." Alex pulled the cover up around Trevor's chest. "By the way, is that what was bothering you during dinner?"

"Wasn't nothing bothering me."

"Are you sure? You looked a little worried."

"Me, worry? Come on, Dad." Trevor sat up and began popping his fingers and singing, "Don't worry. Be happy. Don't worry. Be happy now."

Alex wasn't amused. "Trevor, this isn't a joke. I know you think you're helping your mother by keeping quiet about whatever it is, but you're not. If something is wrong, I need to know about it, so I can help her. So we both can help her."

"I don't know anything," Trevor claimed.

"Would you tell me if you did?"

Trevor wanted to look away, but he knew if he did, Alex would take it as a sign he was hiding something. "Yes, sir," he answered. Under his breath, he asked God to forgive him.

"All right." Alex kissed Trevor on the forehead and then turned off the lamp beside the bed. "See you in the morning, sport."

"Night, Dad."

"Night."

June was in the shower when Alex walked in their dimly lit bedroom. He had time to do what he needed to do. He walked in his closet, kneeled down and reached far behind a row of more than twenty designer suits, and pulled out a gray duffle bag. He reached inside the bag and pulled out a stack of old envelopes. He looked through them and singled out an envelope. He walked out onto the balcony and removed a one-page letter from the envelope. He held the page at an angle so the moonlight and the bedroom light shone on the handwritten letter.

I don't know how to say this, Junie, so forgive me if it doesn't come out right, he read from the letter. *I have to say this and I wish I could say it directly to you, but I can't. Junie, if I never get the chance to say this again, please remember, I love you.*

Alex felt uneasy about what he was doing. These were her private letters and, if he was honest with himself, it was a betrayal of trust to even have them in his possession. He kept telling himself that he should not be reading them. When he walked into the studio to get her for breakfast and saw the pocketbook and letters, he initially turned and walked away. But he thought about all the questions he'd wanted to ask June about Keith, but couldn't bring himself to do it. He thought the letters might hold the answers to some of those questions. It was his chance to learn more about this man whom she still loved, even though she hadn't seen him in seven years. That was enough to convince Alex to take the pocketbook and letters.

He took the letters with him to the office and spent the morning reading them. Whether it was insane jealousy or the beguiling joy of self-inflicted pain, he could not put the letters down or give them back. What was it about Keith's words that touched her so? Was it his particular choice of words? The phrasing? Or was there something else? He planned to read and keep reading until he found out.

Alex caught his reflection in the glass door and saw a troubled man staring back at him. For years he had tried to hide his insecurity. He had done a good job of it until June's out-of-nowhere decision to record *The Pages We Forget,* which to him, was as sure a sign as any that her heart still belonged to Keith. Even so, he couldn't simply let her walk out of his life. They shared too much. Her life was his life and he wasn't about to let a night she spent in another man's arms ten years ago take that from him.

Reading the letters charged him up, but it was Bernard who lit the fuse. They were on their way back to the office from a meeting when Bernard turned to him and said, "Man, you're losing."

"How's that?" Alex asked. "Didn't I talk the studio into postponing film production for almost two months?"

"Damn the studio, damn the record company, damn everybody. Right now, Junie is the only person that counts. Period. And, man, if you don't get it together, you're going to lose her. And to whom? An idiot. A man stupid enough to walk away and leave her."

"B, don't get me wrong, but I really don't want to hear this."

"All right," Bernard said. He stopped for a red light at East Jefferson. That's when he asked, "What are you going to do when she leaves?" The fuse was lit.

Alex put the letter back in the envelope and walked inside. He could hear the shower and smell the raspberry-scented bath gel she loved so much. He imagined how she looked as the lather covered her breasts and trickled downward to her navel. He put the letter in the duffle bag with the others as he began undressing. He took off the Nike T-shirt and his sweatpants.

He hesitated before going into the bathroom. *What do you plan to do when she leaves?* he recalled Bernard asking. What would he do? He turned the doorknob and then opened the door and walked inside.

"Alex, is that you?" June asked from the shower. "Alex?"

He stepped out of his fitted boxer briefs and opened the shower door.

"Alex, what are you doing?"

He placed his index finger over her lips and closed the shower door behind him. "Ssshhhh." He moved to kiss her softly on the lips.

In his eyes she saw a man who felt forgotten. The man standing in front of her, touching her, saved her once. But now his eyes were showing a side of him that she had never seen. Defeat. Loss. She could see everything he was feeling by looking into his eyes.

"I'm sorry," she said. "I'm so sorry."

"It's not your fault, baby."

And there it was again. The thing she loved most about him. After all these years, he was still able to forgive her for not being completely satisfied with his unconditional love.

"I really do love you, Alex." The tears flowed freely as her emotions came to bear.

"I know." He gently wiped the water off of her face and the tears streaming from her eyes. He kissed her trembling lips. "I'm here, Junie. Right here, baby." He kissed her again, first on the lips, moving to that extremely sensitive spot on her neck right below her right earlobe. Then, he moved down to her tender breasts.

Her knees buckled. "I love you, Alex," she professed. She opened her arms, her heart and her mind and took him inside of her. "I love you."

"I Know You From Somewhere"

(lyrics and arrangement by June)

It's been too long
since I've seen your smile.
Way too long
since I looked into your eyes.
But now I see
someone staring back at me,
who has your smile
and that sparkle in your eyes.
Could it be,
finally,
the one I gave my heart to?
Is it really you?

CHORUS:
I know you;
you know I know you.
I don't mean to stand here staring,
but I know you from somewhere.
I know it's you;
boy you know I know you.
Because in your eyes I see him there.
I know you from somewhere.

If you're just a dream,
please don't wake me.

Right here is where I want to be,
loving you eternally.
But like an old memory,
your face haunts me
and takes me back to that day
when you turned and walked away.
So please tell me,
is it you I see?
The one who said his love was true?
Is it really you?

CHORUS

So please tell me,
is it you I see?
The one who said his love was true?
Is it really you?

Chapter 5

"It's been too long since I've seen your smile," June sang as she descended the winding stairway to open her *Pages* concert. The executives at her label insisted on the Showtime Network exclusive concert, which was broadcast live from Detroit's Fox Theatre. The concert was a part of the rush marketing of her new CD. Initially, June refused, but Alex and Bernard managed to talk her into it. Same as they talked her into interviews and cover layouts with *Rolling Stone, Entertainment Weekly, Cosmopolitan, Ebony* and *Essence* magazines. "Way too long," June's voice purred. "Since I looked into your eyes."

June stopped halfway down the stairs and teased the audience. "Is it you I see?" she asked and stared into one of the cameras as it zoomed in for a close-up. "Is it you?"

"It's me, June!" a young man near the stage yelled. "I'm right here, baby!"

"Did you find the fountain of youth or what?" she asked, shaking her head. "You were older than sixteen the last time I saw you."

"Age ain't nothing but a number!" the man yelled.

She winked, joking with him. "Will somebody tell this cute young fellow in the front that he's what we older girls call jailbait?"

She turned to the audience and shouted, "I love you, Detroit!"

Applause erupted throughout the venue.

June smiled and blew kisses at the crowd. The locals had taken her into their hearts as though she were one of their own home-grown divas. Detroit was Alex's home and the birthplace of the Motown sound that he recreated so well for some of June's biggest hits. She came here with Alex right after Bernard, also a Detroit native, negotiated her recording contract with Antmar Entertainment. She was one of the first artists on the year-old label based in the Motor City. She blossomed and became a star. Now, everything was about to change.

Leatrice tried to talk her out of it before the concert, but June was determined to go on as planned. Leatrice felt somewhat responsible because she was the one who pressured June into seeing Dr. Wylie again. She even made the Tuesday morning appointment. Leatrice figured that if Dr. Wylie had not been so truthful and direct, June would not have made this decision. And it was her insistence that prompted June to get a second and then third opinion. Both yielded the same diagnosis: the cancer was spreading rapidly and treating it would be more difficult.

While Leatrice was helping June get dressed, she made a last-ditch effort to persuade June to rethink her decision. She zipped the burnt velvet Donna Karan gown, the first of three gowns June would wear during the concert. She adjusted the bodice and then walked around to face June.

"If I have to beg, I'm begging. Please give yourself a little more time to think about this."

"More time?" June scoffed. "Leatrice, this is all I've thought about during the past three months," June said, taking a seat at the vanity. "Besides, time is something I don't have a lot of."

"Stop saying that."

June stared in the mirror. "Will you look at me? My hair is ugly. This gown is too big, except for around the stomach, and that's because I'm bloated. I look a mess."

"You've lost some weight, but you're still beautiful."

"You're just saying that because it's your job to make me look like somebody."

"And it's a job you make easy," Leatrice responded. "Now stop complaining about nothing and listen to me. You're about to make one of the biggest decisions of your life. You shouldn't do that alone when you've got people who love you, myself included. If you were doing this because you were starting chemotherapy to-morrow, I would be behind you one-hundred percent. But that's not why you're doing it. You're still hoping for something that's not going to happen."

"My mind's made up!"

"Fine. Then do it. All I want you to do is tell Alex before you go out on that stage and tell the world."

"I can't."

"You can but you won't."

"Haven't I put him through enough already?"

"Well, how do you think he's going to feel when you're done tonight? Will he be all smiles? What do you think, Junie? Will he be happy for you?"

"No, he won't. But if I tried to talk to him now, he would auto-matically assume this was about Keith."

"Not if you told him the truth."

June stood and took a final look in the mirror. Although she complained about the way she looked, she was pleased with what she saw: a flawless, glowing complexion, perfect cheekbones, arched brows and big, brown, starving eyes. She was beautiful. Ravishing.

"If you told him the truth about the cancer, I promise you he'd understand."

"But can he fix it for me like he fixes everything else in my life?"

"I don't know, but at least—"

"But nothing!" June cut her off. She walked toward the door, intent on getting to the stage. "Alex isn't God. He can't simply wave his hand over my head and make everything okay."

"No, he isn't God. But he can still help you through this. He deserves to know, Junie. So does your mother. How can you do this to them? And to Trevor. What about Trevor?"

"This isn't about Trevor!"

"How come it's not about him? You're his mother and you're trying to die." Leatrice covered her mouth because she didn't mean to say what she had. She cut loose with the statement, letting it flow like the tears flooding her face. "I'm sorry." Her voice trailed, trying to find her volume again. "I didn't mean that."

June was out the door. She had heard enough. And besides, there was an audience of 5,000 adoring fans and legions of television viewers anxiously waiting to see and hear her perform the collection of songs that *Rolling Stone* called, "A classic for sure. One of music's finest songbirds at her soaring best. Brilliantly conceived. Stylishly and heartbreakingly delivered."

"Mesmerizing. You will never forget *The Pages We Forget*," proclaimed a *USA Today* review.

"Astonishing from the first note to the last," *Vibe* magazine's reviewer wrote. "A masterpiece."

Still, despite the critical raves and the CD's chart-topping debut, June walked down the spiral staircase to the center of the stage holding firmly to her plan. As the cameras and lights hovered around her, she strolled to the front of the stage and inconspicuously searched the mass of faces for someone she knew wasn't in the audience.

"But now I see, someone staring back at me," she sang. "Who has your smile, and that sparkle in your eyes."

Not far from the stage, sat a well-dressed black man with straight, black hair just like Keith's. Their complexions were about the same, but their faces were different. Keith's face was rounder, fuller. This guy's was long and narrow. And he didn't have those hard-to-look-into eyes like Keith. Keith's smile was timid, while the man's smile was one of befuddlement, especially when he realized June was looking at him. She smiled.

"Could it be, finally, the one I gave my heart to?" her voice wafted through the theater. "Is it really you?"

Ironically, on one of the rare days when she hadn't been forced to replay one of her memories of Keith, she thought she saw him. It was four years ago, during a concert in Orlando. She was half-way through a song when she looked into the audience and there he was. He was standing a few rows from the stage. She stood paralyzed, unable to sing or talk when their eyes met. Before she could gather her senses, the face in the crowd disappeared. June continued searching the crowd, but he was nowhere to be found. She never said anything about seeing Keith's face in the crowd to anyone, not even to Leatrice.

"I know you…You know I know you," she sang. "I don't mean to stand here staring, but I know you from somewhere. I know it's you. Boy, you know I know you. Because in your eyes I see him there. I know you from somewhere."

Alex and Trevor were sitting front and center. Dressed in matching pinstriped Armani suits, they were poised and ready for the television cameras to zoom in for the first of the obligatory close-ups. Trevor knew the routine as well as Alex: Sit up straight and look totally mesmerized, which didn't take any acting. June's four-octave powerhouse voice made sure of that.

Kathryn sat next to Trevor and Lucy Kaye sat next to Kathryn.

June, having conceived her plan beforehand, asked them to come up for the concert. They caught the train in Tallahassee Thursday and arrived in Detroit thirty-one hours later, on the morning of the concert.

Alex wasn't thrilled about Lucy Kaye visiting, but he stayed quiet. He didn't dislike her—he considered her a family member—but he knew June was on a quest to find Keith and Lucy Kaye was Keith's mother. Alex also felt Lucy Kaye had the ability to blow the lid off the secret that he, June, Kathryn, and Bernard had hidden from the rest of the world since the day Trevor was born. Alex never forgot the look on Lucy Kaye's face when she came to the hospital with Kathryn and first saw Trevor. It was a look of recognition, like she saw her son in him. She never said anything, but whenever Trevor was around, she couldn't keep her eyes off of him. When Trevor was six and they were vacationing in Hampton Springs, Alex overheard Lucy Kaye and Trevor talking on Kathryn's porch. Alex stood in the front doorway, slightly out of their view.

"You wanna know why you're one of my favorite people in the whole wide world, Trevor?" she asked as they swung back and forth on the porch swing. "Because you remind me so much of my son, Keith. You have hair like him. Eyes like him too."

"I wanna see him," Trevor said. "Is he home?"

"No," she answered. "He doesn't live at home anymore."

"Where does he live?"

From the doorway, Alex could see the tears forming in Lucy Kaye's eyes as she pondered how to answer Trevor's question.

"He lives in a place far, far from here," she answered and ran her fingers through Trevor's hair. "Trevor, can I ask you for a favor?"

"Yes, ma'am."

"May I put my arms around you?"

"To remind you of your son?"

"Yes, to remind me of my son."

Trevor smiled and threw his arms around her. She pulled him close and held on tight. Too many years had passed since she had hugged her son or looked into his sad eyes. Too many days of wondering why he kept running as she begged him to return.

Alex pushed the screen door open and walked out on the porch. He looked over at Lucy Kaye holding his son. His face was placid, but it was tearing him up inside to see Trevor in the arms of his real father's mother.

"Thank you, Trevor," Lucy Kaye said and wiped the tears from her eyes. "Forgive me for getting all teary-eyed."

"He understands," Alex intervened.

Even now, as June captivated the audience, Lucy Kaye was more interested in playing eye games with Trevor, who courteously played along with her.

"So please tell me, is it you I see?" June's lyrics pleaded. "The one who said his love was true? Is it really you?" Her voice faded into silence.

The audience responded with a standing ovation.

"Thank you," she said over the applause. "You are too kind." She turned and smiled at Alex. He looked so happy, clapping and shouting louder than anyone in the theater, with the possible exception of Trevor. She hated herself for what she was about to do to him, but she was doing what she thought was best.

"I love you," he signed to her.

"I love you back," she replied.

The crowd settled as the orchestra began playing soft background music.

"I would like to first thank all of you here at Detroit's Fox Theatre for coming and all of you watching on television, thanks for tuning in," June told the audience. "I must say that I'm more surprised than anyone by your overwhelming response to my new CD, *The Pages We Forget.*"

Cheers filled the theater.

"This album was a very personal project for me, and it really means a lot to me to know that you've embraced it as much as you have my other work. Thank you." She walked to the other side of the stage. "It was a difficult project for my family and me. But not that difficult," she sarcastically emphasized. "I know some of you read and believed the tabloid stories about all of the alleged, and I do mean alleged, fighting between my man and me while I was recording this album. Okay, I'll admit it. We had a few arguments, but trust me, it wasn't for the reasons the tabloids implied. I love my man and he loves me. Right, baby?"

"You know I love you!" Alex yelled, knowing this would be one of the television close-ups.

"I guess you heard that." June looked into the camera and smiled as the audience cheered at his response. "My baby loves me, and I love me some him," June teased and continued her scripted banter with the audience. "But seriously, this album was a way for me to look back at the young girl from Hampton Springs, the one my mother and everybody else back home called Junie. This is Junie's album. On my previous albums, what you heard was a collaboration of a whole lot of Alex and me. Let's hear it for my baby, Detroit!"

Trevor jumped up and led the audience in clapping.

"Give it up, Detroit!" June stirred the crowd. "Give it up!" She waved her arms to motion for Alex to stand.

Alex stood and waved at the cheering audience.

"As you probably already know, that handsome young man standing beside Alex is our son, Trevor," June continued. "And that's my beautiful mother, Mrs. Kathryn Thomas, sitting next to Trevor, and sitting next to Ma is a woman I've known and loved all my life, Mrs. Lucy Kaye Adams." June smiled at Lucy Kaye. "Mrs. Adams was my first music teacher, but, believe it or not, she's never been to one of my concerts. Can you believe that? My first music teacher has never been to one of my concerts. But, that's water under the bridge because I have her here now. Thanks for coming, Mrs. Adams."

Lucy Kaye nodded her head and smiled at June and then turned and winked at Trevor, who reached across his grandmother and shook Lucy Kaye's hand.

"Now where was I?" June asked as she walked across the stage. "Okay, as I was saying, my previous work was a collaborative effort between me, Alex and all the other songwriters and producers I've worked with during the past ten years. We recorded some really nice songs together, but this time I wanted you to hear Junie Ann Thomas. With the help of my boy, Torrence. Hold up a second. Torrence stand up."

Torrence, sitting next to Alex, blushed. Alex nudged him up. He stood and bashfully waved to the cheering crowd.

"People, you are looking at a musical genius." June blew a kiss at Torrence. "Give it up for him, Detroit! The boy is bad." The crowd, including Alex and Trevor, came to its feet. "I couldn't have done it without you, Torrence. Thank you! Thank you! Thank you!"

June walked to the center of the stage as the applause died down. The stairway had been replaced with the screened backdrop of a starry night. The orchestra began playing, "If You Were Here."

"When I'm with you," June's falsetto hummed, "there's no place I'd rather be. For you fulfill my every need, though you're only,

only in my dream." She was at her best singing dreamy ballads. "You've made my life so happy, and I'll always want you near. But what would I say, if you were really here?"

This song was one of the album's standouts. It was also Alex's favorite, even though it cut deeper than the others.

"You let me touch the sun, hold the moon in my hands," she sang.

Alex felt this song should have been about him. It was his love that lifted her and gave her the strength to stand on her own. He was the wind that helped her to soar high enough to touch the sun. To grasp the moon.

"And when I fail to be my best, you always understand."

He didn't run away. He stayed and made excuse after excuse for her inability to love him and only him, which should have been proof enough that he understood.

"I've never felt this way, because you've never let me down."

Never, he thought.

"When you hold me in your arms, you turn my world around."

Alex wished he could stand up and leave, at least until this song was over, but walking out would be admitting he was still unsure of his place in her life. There was no question about her place in his life. She was the axis that his world revolved around. But her world was one he shared with a man he'd never met. A man who was always present despite the fact that he lived nearly a thousand miles away in an old, but remodeled, gray-colored cracker farm-house surrounded by a small orange grove in the small North Central Florida town, Micanopy.

June didn't know it. No one knew. But back in April, when he was in Florida for Easter, Alex hired an investigator from Tallahassee to locate Keith. While June was preparing for the concert, Alex lied about a family crisis involving someone named Aunt Patricia, who lived in Kansas City. But, instead of going to Kansas City, he flew into Jacksonville, Florida and drove the ninety or so miles to Micanopy. As he drove through the small town of about 600 residents, he marveled at how much the town reminded him of Hampton Springs. The quaint village of antique and curio shops, bed and breakfast inns, wooden sidewalks, and moss-covered oaks could easily be mistaken for Hampton Springs, which was about 120 miles northwest of Micanopy.

Alex stopped at Vera's Coffee Shop on the corner of Cholokka Boulevard and Ocala Street. He went inside and asked the counter waitress, a wiry, young redhead, for directions.

"What do you want with Keith?" she asked as she poured Alex a cup of coffee.

"I'm an old friend."

"Well, why don't you just call him and ask him for directions? There's a phone at the end of the counter."

"Well, actually, I'm a friend of a friend."

"So, he doesn't know you?"

"No, he doesn't."

"Well, what do you want with him?"

"I just want to talk to him."

"Listen, Mister, I don't know what you want with Keith, but he doesn't really like being bothered. He doesn't come around that much anyway, but ever since June Thomas' new CD came out with his photo on the cover, he's been a real hermit. Last week, two reporters came through trying to find him, but no one would tell them where he lived."

"Why were they looking for him?"

"They wanted to talk to him about going to the prom with June Thomas."

"Why?"

"Do you know who June Thomas is?"

"Yes, but I still don't understand why it's such a big deal about who she went to the prom with."

"Well, first of all, the CD's full of nothing but romantic songs about her first love. That's enough to make anybody curious about who he is. And then she put their prom picture in a shattered picture frame on the cover. What do you think that says? To me, that says she's still in love with him."

"Who cares?" Alex asked and took a sip of coffee.

"Evidently you do. You came this far to see him." She paused and walked to the other end of the counter. She poured an elderly gentleman, the only other customer in the cafe, another cup of coffee.

"I heard he was a writer." Alex inquired, trying to get the waitress to open up a little more.

"He writes," she answered and walked back to where Alex sat. "I want you to be honest with me. What brought you all this way looking for him if the June Thomas connection isn't that big a deal with you?"

Alex was hesitant about telling the waitress the real reason he was in Micanopy looking for a man that he'd never seen or spoken to, but he'd come a long way to see this man and he wasn't going back until he saw him.

"What's your name?" Alex asked the young lady.

"Angeline," she answered. "And yours?"

"Alex."

"Well, Alex, are you going to tell me why you're really here?"

"Keith's an old friend of the woman I love."

Angeline sat down and stared at Alex. She cocked her head to the side, trying to measure her next question. "And who's this lucky lady?"

"Her name's June."

"June? June Thomas? Oh, wait a minute. You're Alex, what's his name?"

"That's me."

"Now that I know you're June Thomas' boyfriend, I'm really curious about why you're looking for Keith."

Alex insisted on changing the subject. "How well do you know Keith?"

"I've known him for years. My folks have run this cafe for nearly twenty years, and I can remember him stopping in on occasions when I was a little girl. Everybody in town thought he was kind of strange at first. I mean, don't take this the wrong way, but you don't see too many black folks living off to themselves like that. He still drops in for a bite every now and again. That's about the only time I see him."

"Has he ever mentioned her to you?"

"I can't say that he has."

"Are you sure?"

"If he had told me that he used to date June Thomas, I would remember it. That's the reason no one would tell those reporters where he lived. If after all this time he's been living here, and he's never mentioned her to anyone, he must not want to be bothered about it. I don't think he even knows about the CD. I don't know how true it is, but they say he lives out there without a TV or anything. If you really want to know what I think, I think you should get in your car and go on back where you're from. Leave well enough alone, if you get my drift. There's no need to go out there bothering him."

"I'm not here to bother him. I only want to see him."

"Why?"

"Listen, Angeline, will you please tell me where I can find him?"

"I've already told you more than I should have." Her demeanor changed in an instant as she walked in the kitchen. "Leave him alone."

Now, Alex wasn't sure whether or not he wanted to see Keith. He had lived with and loved June for ten years knowing all the time that her heart belonged to another man. A man he had only seen in pictures. Alex was conflicted because to finally see Keith in the flesh would humanize him and make him more than a haunting memory that he wished June could forget.

Out of nowhere, the answer to the question that Angeline refused to give came from the unlikeliest of sources.

"Go east on Cholokka about a mile and a half until you come to a dirt road called Philco Road," the man at the other end of the counter stated. "You should see an old wooden sign with Philco Road carved out on it."

"Thank you," Alex said. He didn't ask why the man decided to give the directions, nor did he want to waste time trying to find out. He placed a five-dollar bill on the counter and headed to the door. "Thank you so much."

"Can I ask you a question?" the old man asked as Alex pushed the door open to leave.

"What's that?"

"Does she still love him?"

Alex stared at the old man, who had turned completely around on the stool to face him, and then at Angeline, who walked out of the kitchen and stood in the doorway. They both anxiously awaited his response.

"She hasn't seen him in seven years," Alex hesitated before answering.

"That's not what I asked you," the old man said and put on his Florida Gators baseball cap. "I answered your question when you asked for directions, so I feel you owe me an answer."

"That's right," Angeline said. "It's not like we know you or June personally."

"Yes," Alex lowered his head, "she does."

The old man walked up to Alex and patted him on the shoulder. "I'm sorry to hear that. But listen, you don't have anything to worry about. Keith's what old-timers like me call a drop-out, somebody who doesn't want nothing or nobody in their world but them. For some reason, Micanopy attracts those types." He paid for his coffee and walked out the door.

Alex started out the door behind him.

"Good luck!" Angeline yelled.

"Thanks," he responded.

Alex got into the rented BMW, backed out and drove east along Cholokka Street. He read every road sign along the mile-and-a-half drive to the outskirts of downtown. "You're looking for Philco Road," he told himself as he slowed down to read the wooden sign nailed to a cypress tree. "Philco Road," he read. Alex stopped in the intersection of the two roads and stared down the narrow, unpaved, oak-shaded canopy road. The road ended at a fenced-in yard about a hundred yards away.

Alex turned onto Philco Road and drove slowly up the dirt road until it ended at the yard. He pulled up next to the picket fence and stared at the large wooden house with a screened-in porch that spanned the entire width of the house. It was painted the same bland gray as the mid-morning sky and the uneven picket fence.

Three wooden steps led to the screen door swinging back and forth in the gusting wind. His heart raced.

"Why am I nervous?" he asked himself. "I only want to see what he looks like. I don't want to talk to him or anything. Just see him."

Someone was coming toward the door. Alex saw the front door of the house open and then the silhouette of a man walk out on the porch. He leaned forward to get a better view as the man's hand reached for the screen door. Suddenly, without any conscious thought, Alex put the car in reverse and backed away right before Keith emerged from the house. As he drove away, he convinced himself that it was better to let Keith remain an unseen presence in their lives. He could deal with Keith being a memory but not a man.

Now, he couldn't keep his eyes off of Keith's mother as she watched Trevor. Now, he wished he had stayed another minute or so and saw the father of his son.

Trevor noticed his dad's vacuous stare. "Dad, are you okay?"

"Yeah, I'm fine." Alex forced a smile. He turned his attention to the stage.

"And I'd whisper in your ear," June sang softly. "I love you. If you were here. If you were here. If you were here."

The music faded and the light dimmed around June until darkness and silence enveloped the stage. A few scattered whistles pierced the silence.

"If you hear the words I'm saying and listen to my heart as I speak them, you will know that I really do love you," June spoke from the darkness. "And you will know that I am thankful for all the love and support you've given me through the years. You've been so good to me."

Alex felt it coming.

Bernard and Leatrice were watching from backstage. "What is she talking about?" Bernard looked at Leatrice, who was solemn and reserved. "That's not in the script."

"Just listen," Leatrice calmly answered.

"That's why it's so hard to say this," June said as a faint, circular spotlight slowly brightened and widened around her. "My mother always told me to follow my heart. And that's what I'm about to do. I'm following my heart."

Alex felt a lump in his throat. He turned to Kathryn for an explanation. She shrugged her shoulders. Although she and Lucy Kaye had spent the afternoon lounging around the house with June, she had no idea what her daughter was about to say.

"Tonight," June said and looked past Alex and her family at the other bewildered stares in the theater.

"Leatrice," Bernard shouted under his breath. "I want to know what's going on and I want to know now."

"I tried to talk her out of it," Leatrice tearfully replied. "But she wouldn't listen."

"You tried to talk her out of what?"

"Just listen."

"Tonight," June continued, "is a very special night for me because tonight is my swan song. It will be my final performance."

"Her what?" Bernard shouted to Leatrice.

"I tried," Leatrice answered and then walked away.

"Sit down, Trevor," Alex ordered his son, who sprang to his feet upon hearing his mother's announcement.

Like everybody else, Trevor couldn't believe what he was hearing. "But, Dad!"

"Please, Trevor," Alex pleaded. "Not now."

Kathryn reached for Trevor's hand and guided him back into

his seat. She was as surprised by June's announcement as everyone else. But she was even more surprised by the lack of a response from Alex. He sat calmly with his eyes fixated on June.

June could feel him staring at her and she knew if she didn't hold her head up and look at him now, she would never be able to face him. She walked to the front of the stage and stopped directly in front of him. She still had not looked into his eyes when the orchestra began to play "The Pages We Forget."

"Yesterday's songs," June closed her eyes and sang. "Some live forever. Their rhythm and their rhyme, still playing melodies in our minds. A story behind each, of a love we both promised to keep. So many, many years, of lonely nights filled with tears."

She had to look at him now.

"Our eyes tell stories, of how we used to be," she sang and then opened her eyes and gazed into his.

There were no stories in his eyes.

"Memories locked inside, never to be free," she sang.

No memories.

"And now after all this time, we pass like we've never met. Neither wanting to remember, the pages we forget."

She saw nothing. Nothing at all in his eyes.

"This Time"

(lyrics and arrangement by June)

My heart can't take no more of you.
You're tearing me down.
I wish you'd go—walk out my heart's door.
Don't come this way no more.

I gave you my heart, you gave it back.
I guess it wasn't enough.
That's why you're leaving, you're saying bye.
But this time, I'm not gonna cry.
'Cause my love is gone.
You were so wrong.
And it's time, I let you move on.

CHORUS:
This time, I hope I've seen the last of you.
This time, I'll accept that we're through.
My heart won't break, my eyes won't cry.
I'll be finally free of you.

This time, when you turn and walk away.
This time, I hope you're going to stay.
I won't let you break my heart this time.
No, not this time.

We can't keep going round and round.
Sooner or later, the bridge will fall down.

Still, I care about you—might can't live without you.
But this time, I'm finally through.

No longer will you darken my day.
There's a brighter tomorrow coming my way.
Still old memories, they linger on,
even though the clouds are gone.
And, it doesn't matter
who's wrong or right,
because I'm saying good-bye tonight.

CHORUS
(Repeat to fade)

Chapter 6

The Pioneer Day Festival would have to go on without her. Someone else would lead the gaslight antique car parade down Willow Street. Last year's festival director could fire the gun to start the bed race around Town Hall. Mayor Alexander wouldn't mind crowning one of the six local beauties vying for the title of Miss Pioneer Day. Although Kathryn had spent the past eight months working tirelessly to make this year's annual festival the best ever, she wasn't about to leave her daughter alone after June's unexpected announcement. Swarms of puzzled fans and unruly paparazzi descended on the Fox Theatre following the concert.

June's security team suggested that Kathryn, Trevor, and Lucy Kaye wait for June in the limo parked at the rear exit of the theater. Kathryn and Trevor vehemently refused to leave June's side, even after she asked them to wait for her in the car.

As soon as Willie, one of June's personal bodyguards, pushed the theater's back door open, the swarm attacked. June, holding her mother and son's hands, exited the theater behind Willie and Joe and four members of the theater's security staff.

"June! June! Why are you quitting?" a tall, slender, middle-aged photographer yelled over the crowd of screaming fans.

"Bernard is on his way out! He will answer all of your questions!" Willie yelled. "Now back up!"

"June! June! Look this way! Let me get a good shot!" a young man holding a camera high above the crowd yelled. "Help me out, June! I need the money!"

June pulled Trevor closer to her.

"Hey, man, can you tell us anything?" a young TV reporter yelled to Alex, who, with Leatrice, walked a step or two behind June and the others. "Talk to us, Alex!"

Alex didn't respond. He didn't feel he should have to. After all, he had no say in her decision to walk away from the life they'd built together. She didn't ask him what he thought or how he felt. She didn't even bother to tell him beforehand. He had to hear about it when she told the rest of the world. And even if he chose to respond to the reporter's question and take control like he normally did when things got this chaotic, what could he tell them? She's quitting to spend more time with her family? She's grown tired of performing and wants to try something different while she's still young enough to start over? Or maybe even, she simply wants to be left alone? He thought about all the things he could say to explain what had happened, but she made this decision without him, so she was going to have to deal with the avalanche of questions, rumors, and broken contracts that were sure to follow without him.

The wave of camera flashes was blinding, so June let go of her mother's hand and covered her eyes. Kathryn put her arm around June and clung to Willie with the other as they made their way to the waiting limo.

The theater's security personnel and a handful of police officers were already struggling to keep the near riotous crowd back. However, after two photographers jumped over the retention barricade, other photographers followed, starting a stampede.

"Get Trevor to the car!" June yelled to Joe. "Get Trevor!"

Joe and Willie pulled June, Trevor, and Kathryn in between them and then pushed their way toward the limo.

"Alex, what are you doing?" Leatrice yelled as she fought her way through the stampeding crowd. "Don't just stand there! Help her!"

Alex turned, looked at Leatrice, and then asked, "Why should I?"

"Alex, what—" Before she could finish her question, an over-zealous fan pushed her to the ground trying to get to June.

"You bastard!" Alex hit the man before he knew it. The lick did little to slow him down. The man shook it off and retaliated by charging into Alex, knocking him to the ground.

"Alex!" June screamed and snatched away from Joe. She fought her way back to where Alex and the man were scuffling. "Get off of him, you son-of-a-bitch!" June grabbed the man's hair. Leatrice already had her hands wrapped around the man's neck. "Let him go!" June yelled.

"Ma!" Trevor cried. Lucy Kaye, who was already in the limo, grabbed Trevor's arm and pulled him inside.

"Junie! Junie!" Kathryn tried to get away from Willie but couldn't.

"Mrs. Thomas, get in the car," Willie pleaded with her. "We'll get her."

"Willie, get my baby!" Kathryn yelled as Lucy Kaye pulled her inside the vehicle. "Get my baby!"

Willie knocked several people over as he bulldozed his way through the mayhem. By the time he reached June, Joe had already ended the fight with a short jab to the man's head.

"Get June and Leatrice to the car!" Joe shouted to Willie. "I'll get Alex!"

Willie covered June and Leatrice and Joe shielded Alex as they pressed toward the car.

"Ma!" Trevor yelled and pulled June into the car as soon as she was within arm's reach. "Ma, are you all right?"

"I'm okay." June fell back in the seat next to Trevor.

Willie helped Alex and Leatrice into the car and yelled for the driver to take off. The limo sped away. Joe pulled up in the Path-finder and Willie got in. The Pathfinder followed the limo as it made its way down Woodward Avenue, through downtown, and up East Jefferson Street.

No one said anything inside the limo as it headed for Grosse Pointe. Everyone except for Alex stared out at the city's skyline, the lights on Belle Isle, and anything else to distract them from each other. Alex's eyes targeted June. After several minutes, June found the courage to look at Alex, who sat directly in front of her. She turned away quickly to avoid his bemused gaze, but turned and looked back into his eyes. She'd never seen him look at her the way he was looking at her now. His eyes were fixated on her, but he was looking through her as though she wasn't there.

That scared her.

The car stopped for a traffic light at the intersection of East Jefferson and St. Jean. Kathryn broke the silence while the vehicle was idling. "Is everybody okay?"

"I'm all right," Leatrice answered.

"Trevor?"

"I'm okay, Gramps."

"Junie?"

"I'm fine, Ma."

"Alex?"

He answered by not answering.

Kathryn turned to Alex, who was seated next to her, and placed her hand on his clenched fist. He was still, but she could feel the hurt and the anger raging inside of him. "Everything's going to be all right," she told him, squeezing his hand to comfort him.

He didn't flinch. He barely moved, despite a slight trickle from his mouth.

"Oh God!" June yelled when she noticed Alex's busted lip. "Your mouth is bleeding." She hurried over to the seat beside him.

Leatrice turned on the backseat light to help June attend to Alex. June tried to wipe blood from the corner of his mouth with a handkerchief.

"Don't touch me!" He knocked her hand away. "Stay away from me."

"Alex, I think—" Kathryn tried speaking in calm tones to intervene in what she felt would become a highly emotional situation.

"I don't mean any disrespect, Mrs. Thomas, but please stay... No. Don't worry about it."

"Alex, I don't know what to say except I'm sorry," June said.

"You're always sorry!" he yelled. "Always!"

"What if I had told you, Alex?" June asked. "What would you have said?"

"I don't know what I would have said, but at least I would have had the chance to say *something*. You didn't give me a chance to say anything. Not one word. You didn't give a damn about how I was going to feel."

"Alex, please..." Kathryn tried to say something.

"I'm sorry, Mrs. Thomas, but for the last three or four months your daughter has walked around like nothing matters except what Junie wants. She keeps forgetting that this is our life. Not just her life. Ours!"

"Yes, it is our life," June retaliated and sat back in her seat. "But can't I decide some things by myself or do I have to ask you for permission every time I get ready to go to the bathroom?"

"You don't have to ask me anything anymore, Junie. I really don't care what you do. You can do anything you want and go anywhere you want from now on. So stop feeling sorry for me and just do it. Go find him if that's what you want!"

"Junie, what is he talking about?" Kathryn asked.

June didn't answer.

"It's your life, Junie. Nobody's but yours. So, why don't you tell your mother what's really happening?"

"I don't know what you're talking about, Alex."

"Don't cop out now, Junie," Alex pushed forward. "This is what you want, isn't it?"

"Alex, June, can't this wait until you get home?" Leatrice tried to ease the tension. "Please."

"No, this can't wait," Alex answered. "I want Junie to tell everyone what this new album's really all about. Or rather, *who* it's about."

Lucy Kaye looked at June. She had seen the CD's cover, and she'd listened to the fourteen songs about lost love, broken promises and wishful thinking. And although she felt *The Pages We Forget* was June's best album, the songs were nothing more than songs to her, another album to frame and place on the wall beside June's other three albums. Without trying, she made herself ignore the obvious.

"Junie?" Lucy Kaye waited for an answer.

Alex forced the issue. "Mrs. Adams is asking you a question, Junie."

"Please don't do this, Alex," June begged.

"Why not? You've let me live a lie for the past ten years. Ten years, and all the time it's been your life. Not ours. Isn't that what you said, Junie?"

"Alex, I know you're upset, but please think about what you're saying," Kathryn urged.

"Why?" Alex asked. "Give me one good reason why we shouldn't throw away all the lies and let the chips fall where they may. Just one!"

"Dad."

Alex looked at Trevor, whom he had not been able to see. Somehow he had missed Trevor, forgot he was there. While trying to emotionally detach himself from June, he had overlooked his main reason for staying with her during the turmoil. His son.

"Please don't be mad at her," Trevor pleaded with Alex.

Alex choked back the tears as he stared into Trevor's eyes. "All right," he said and unsuccessfully tried to force a smile. "I'll let it go for my boy." He turned to June. "But I want you to know that I'm tired, Junie. Tired and fed up."

No more words were spoken, but it was too late. Too much had been said, too much revealed. More than enough to make Lucy Kaye finally ask the question that had lingered in her mind since the day Kathryn called and told her that June was pregnant.

As soon as they arrived at the house, Lucy Kaye followed June into her bedroom. "Is Trevor my grandson?"

June wasn't caught off-guard by Lucy Kaye's question. She fully expected her to ask it after the remarks Alex made in the limo, but knowing she was going to ask didn't make answering any easier. Although she had rehearsed countless times how she would one day tell Keith and his mother the truth about Trevor, she wasn't prepared for the actual moment.

"Is Keith Trevor's father?"

June sat on the edge of the bed and looked up at Lucy Kaye, who stood near the door. For ten years, Lucy Kaye had allowed her to keep this secret. Surely, she knew all along that Trevor was Keith's son. They had the same deep brown eyes, straight black hair, and caramel complexion. Their smiles were identical, too.

Lucy Kaye closed the door and walked over to the bed and sat next to June. Neither said a word but they both knew the other was thinking about that April morning ten years ago when Keith walked out of both their lives. They sat together in his bedroom for most of the day silently contemplating what happened. Neither said much. Every now and then one or the other would break their silent vigil and say something about the weather or their absence from the afternoon choir rehearsal. They only spoke when they felt it necessary to acknowledge the other's presence or to keep from crying.

"I need to know, Junie."

June wasn't quite ready to answer. She was worried that the truth might be like her tears that morning seven years ago when Keith refused to speak to her. If she finally spoke the truth about Trevor's father to someone, would she be able to stop there? Or would answering Lucy Kaye's question today mean admitting the truth about that night tomorrow?

"I need to know the truth, Junie." Lucy Kaye's eyes pleaded with June. "I've only seen my son once during the last ten years and that was when he came home for his father's funeral seven years ago. I don't know why he ran away. I didn't know then and I don't know now. You're a mother, Junie. Try to imagine Trevor walking out your front door and never coming back. Not because someone's holding a gun to his head, but because he chooses not to come back."

"I'm sorry, Mrs. Adams," June sobbed. "I still don't know why he ran away. I don't know what I did to him."

"I'm not blaming you, Junie. Lord knows I'm not blaming you.

All I'm asking for is the truth about your son. I've always believed and I always will believe that—"

"Keith is Trevor's father." June finished for her, giving both a sense of closure. Before she realized it, something unexpected happened. She didn't know what it was, but she knew something had to have happened because everything was different now. The earth didn't tremble and the sky didn't fall, but the world had definitely changed. June could feel it. The truth had not crippled her. It felt good, better than good, to finally look into Lucy Kaye's plaintive eyes and say, "Yes, he's your grandson."

"My grandson?"

"Keith's son."

Trevor was unusually quiet as Kathryn helped him get ready for bed. It was easy to see that he was troubled by everything that had gone on. His mother had surprised everyone when she announced she was through doing what he felt she was born to do. He heard his dad say that about her during a television interview, and after going home and listening to her CDs later that day, he agreed. The argument between his parents on the way home did nothing to help matters. He heard what was bothering his father the most. His dad stated he was living a lie.

"Grandma, if you know something important and don't tell, is it a lie?" Trevor asked as she got ready to walk out the room.

"Well, let me think," Kathryn replied and sat on the edge of the bed.

"Is it?"

"Give Grandma a minute. This is a tough one."

Trevor sat up in bed and eagerly awaited his grandmother's response. "So, is it?"

"No. No, it's not a lie," Kathryn answered and scooted closer to Trevor. "If a person knows something that might help someone and doesn't say anything, that person wouldn't necessarily be telling a lie. I mean, why would the person not want to help someone?"

"What if the person promised he wouldn't say anything?"

"Well, that's different because a promise is a promise."

That wasn't the answer Trevor was looking for, and Kathryn could tell by the discouraged look on his face.

"I guess you're right," he said.

"But you won't be breaking your promise if you told me who asked you not to say anything," Kathryn said.

"I won't?"

"No, you won't," Kathryn answered. "As long as you don't tell what she asked you not to tell."

"Please don't tell her I told you, Gramps."

"I promise," Kathryn vowed, even though she already knew he was talking about June.

"Ma made me promise."

"When was this?"

"A few weeks ago," he answered. "Right after Dad and I came to Hampton Springs for Easter. Ma has been acting real strange since then, Gramps."

"Your mom looks a little thin," Kathryn said. "Has she been eating right or has she been acting sickly?"

Trevor hesitated before saying, "Sometimes."

"That's enough. You promised," Kathryn said and pulled the cover over him. "Don't worry. Grandma's here now, and everything's going to be fine. Okay?"

"Okay."

"Now, it's way past your bedtime. I'll talk to you in the morning." Kathryn kissed Trevor on the forehead. "Good night."

"Good night," Trevor said and rolled over. He felt better now. If anyone could straighten things out, it was his grandmother.

Kathryn overheard Alex, Bernard and Leatrice talking downstairs.

"She's scheduled to start filming *For His Love* in two weeks," Bernard said. "Does this mean she's backing out on the film?"

"I don't know," Alex answered. He turned the glass of brandy up and emptied it. "You'll have to ask her."

"Well, my phone's already ringing off the hook, and I have absolutely no idea what to say since I don't know what the hell she's doing. Somebody needs to talk to me. Leatrice, what's going on?"

Leatrice's hesitation in answering caught Kathryn's attention. Kathryn closed Trevor's door and walked over to the stairway so she could better hear the conversation.

"Well, Leatrice? I mean, she did tell you ahead of time what she was planning to do," Bernard said. "Did she say anything else?"

"No," she answered. "She didn't say anything."

"Did she tell you why she was quitting?"

"No."

Alex walked over to the window and stared out into the night. There wasn't much to see. A fog bank had crept from the lake across the estate and the only things visible were the lights along the driveway and the one on the dock. He thought about how much June liked the fog and the countless nights they spent sitting out on the dock in the midst of it. They were barely able to see each other, which meant there was a lot of touching and spontaneous lovemaking.

"I need you to talk to her tonight, Alex," Bernard said.

Alex couldn't hear him. Not now. The dock. The fog. The darkness. It had taken him back to the last time they made love under the misty cover. He recalled the chill in the air.

"Alex!" Bernard called.

"I'm sorry. What were you saying?" Alex turned to Bernard.

"I need you here with me, man." Bernard walked up to Alex and whispered, "I know what you're going through. Believe me, I do. But right now I need your help and I need you to be completely focused on what's happening."

"Alex," Kathryn called as she descended the stairway. "Can I speak with you for a moment?"

"Can it wait, Mrs. Thomas?" he asked.

"No," she replied and started toward the parlor. "This will only take a minute."

"Excuse me. I'll be right back," Alex told Bernard and Leatrice. He stopped at the bar and refilled his glass with brandy before following Kathryn into the parlor.

"Close the door behind you," she said. She walked over to the couch and sat down. Alex closed the door and turned to Kathryn. "Have a seat."

"I thought you said this would only take a minute."

"Sit down."

Alex walked over to Joy and sat on the stool. He turned and faced the piano.

"Look at me, Alex."

Alex hesitated before turning around. "I'm as lost as you are, Mrs. Thomas," he looked up at her, not knowing what to say. "There's nothing I can tell you. You'll have to talk to Junie."

"I plan to," Kathryn said. "But I wanted to talk to you first."

"Why?"

"First of all, why did you pretend to wholeheartedly support this album when you were in Florida for Easter?"

Alex shrugged his shoulders.

"It's okay. We're past that now. I'm more concerned about what Junie's hiding. I think she's hiding something from everyone."

"In case you haven't noticed, she isn't hiding it anymore," Alex said and took a sip of brandy. "She's told the whole world how much she still loves the guy."

"This isn't about Keith," Kathryn replied. "This is something far more serious."

"What are you talking about?"

"I don't know what it is, but I know my daughter. And I feel it every time I look at her and every time I talk to her. I feel it, Alex. Something's not right."

"Listen, Mrs. Thomas. I made excuse after excuse for Junie, like you're doing now. But I'm through doing that. If it's Keith she wants, I'll let her have him."

"Trust me, Alex. This isn't about Keith."

"Well, what else could it be? Why else would she turn her back on who she is? She loves her life. So why would she just walk away?"

"I don't know," Kathryn answered. "But I plan to stay here until I find out."

"That's fine," Alex said. "I hope you have better luck getting her to talk to you than I've had."

"I'll get her to talk."

"I hope so. Now, if you're done, I need to help Bernard straighten this whole mess out."

"That's all I wanted."

"Well, I'll talk to you in the morning," Alex walked out of the parlor, prepared to tackle the debacle at hand.

He, Bernard, and an out-of-it Leatrice spent the next two hours on a conference call with Cynthia. They discussed the few options they had for dealing with the impending broken contracts and bad publicity. It was late when they finished, so, Alex suggested they spend the night. Leatrice took the empty upstairs bedroom and Bernard slept in the guest cottage.

The lights were on in Alex and June's bedroom. June wasn't in the room, but there was a packed overnight bag and an envelope on the bed. Alex picked up the envelope. His name was written on the front and it was in June's handwriting. She was the only person he knew who couldn't write a single word without using both the cursive and print styles of writing. And it was her stationery.

Alex exhaled, realizing the possible meaning of the words on the pages in his hands. It was time to face the truth, look it in the face and accept the fact that the woman he loved was leaving him. He didn't know how he was going to handle her leaving. She wasn't his wife, but he had made plans to spend the rest of his life with her. They were supposed to grow old together, become grandparents, retire in Florida and learn to play golf. They were supposed to grow closer over the years. So close that people would say they looked like one another. All those dreams were fading away now and there was nothing he could do about it.

He rubbed the envelope's seal. Slowly, he picked at the seal. The gold parchment paper didn't budge. He placed his index finger underneath the corner of the seal. His finger stiffened. He willed his finger up, and a corner of the envelope ripped. "No," he suddenly said as though he was talking to her. "I want to hear it from you."

The light was on in the bathroom. "June!" There was no answer. He knocked on the bathroom door. Still, no answer. He put his ear to the door. Still, nothing. He turned the doorknob. It was stuck. He thought the worst. "June!" He ran into the door, and the door flung open. She wasn't there. "Stupid ass," he scolded himself. "You know her better than that. June, killing herself? Not if she was the last person on Earth."

He walked out the bathroom and immediately noticed the balcony door was unlocked. He was prepared to make her tell him what was inside the envelope, but now, he had to psyche himself up all over. During the fourteen steps between the bathroom and the balcony, his heart changed his mind. He was going to fight for her. He wasn't going to simply let her walk out of his life. Keith did it to her, but he was not about to let her do it to him.

He opened the balcony door intent on telling her, "You're not going anywhere."

She wasn't there.

Alex was starting to worry. Could she have already left and forgotten the overnight bag? Where would she go? He felt weak, leaning against the door to keep his legs from buckling. That's when he noticed the light on the dock was out. He remembered the light being on when he looked out earlier. "Either the bulb has blown or…"

He was right. June had turned the light out on the dock. This spot was hers. Every morning, she could be found standing here gazing out at the lake as she waited for the sun to rise. It was the lake that sold June on the idea of spending millions of dollars to build a home this far away from Hampton Springs. The lake afforded her the tranquility and privacy she longed for after spending her first three years in Detroit living in an upscale, high-rise apartment.

After the success of her first album and the top-of-the-charts debut of her second album, they decided it was time to move. She wanted a private place where she could lose her growing celebrity and she found it here.

With the light out and in the fog, a person could get lost sitting on the dock. That's exactly what June wanted. She wanted the world around her to be different for a while. If she could close her eyes and listen to the wind waltz across the lake and feel the mist caress her face, she could pretend she was lost. Lost in a place far from the questions everyone was bound to ask. Farther away from the answers and the man walking toward her.

"I brought you a jacket." Alex stopped a few feet away from the bench that June was sitting on and tossed the jacket to her. "I think we're going to get some rain tonight."

June was glad he couldn't see her or the tears she wiped away. "Thank you."

"Junie, I found this envelope on the bed with my name on it. Is there something you want to tell me?"

She hesitated before answering. She had to make a choice. She could tell him she wrote the letter because she had to go back and right what went wrong that night with Keith. Or, she could tell him she wrote the letter but her mind had changed and she had decided to forget that chapter of her life.

"You wrote it, Junie. Will you tell me what it says? I didn't bother to read it, because I wanted to hear it from you."

June could only see Alex's frame from where she sat, but she felt his heart breaking. So was hers.

"Talk to me, Junie. You're going or you're staying. Make up your mind." Alex took a step toward her. "I've gone along with you since the day we met. I stood by you and I loved you, even though I knew that deep down inside you still loved him. I went along, Junie, but you crossed the line. You went too far this time."

"Alex?"

"Staying or leaving, Junie?"

"I'm trying to talk to you."

"Staying or leaving?"

"Listen to me!" June shouted.

Alex didn't have to see her to figure out she was hurting as much as he was.

"I wrote the letter. And it says that I have to leave, that I have to find him and ask him why." She was drowning in her tears. "But that's not how I feel now. I know this is hard for you to understand. I don't understand why I thought I needed to find him. I thought I needed to know. I figured if he told me why he left that I could get him out of my life for good and out of my heart. But I guess that's not what's meant to be. My life now is meant to be. My life is here with you."

"Junie, I don't know what else to do."

"I'm sorry, Alex," she cried. "It wasn't supposed to happen this way."

Alex couldn't believe what he was about to say, but he had to say it. "Junie," he said. "I love you and I don't know how I'm going to live without you if you don't return. But, I have to let you go back to him."

"What?" June couldn't believe her ears. "What are you saying?"

"I know you love me, Junie. I've always known. But, I've fought so hard against you these past few months and I've said some terrible things. And, it dawned on me that I was scared. I was afraid of losing you to him. Right now, I'm scared to death, but I realize that I'll never be happy until I'm the only man you love. And that won't happen until you make peace with him."

"I can't and I won't do that to you, Alex," she said. "You don't really want me to go."

"I'm asking you to go." He heard her footsteps coming toward him. He couldn't see her face, but he felt their eyes connecting. "I need you to go, Junie."

The footsteps stopped directly in front of him.

"If I go, I'll have to take Trevor."

"I know."

"That means I'll have to tell him the truth."

"I know." His heart broke again. "Will you tell him that I love him and that he'll always be my son and I'll always be his dad?"

"I think you should tell him that."

"That wouldn't be a good idea." Alex wiped his eyes. "Take Trevor and go before I regret what I'm asking you to do. I'll straighten everything out with your mother and the others in the morning."

"How will I find him?"

"He lives in Florida," Alex answered. "In Micanopy. It's a small town near Gainesville."

"How do you know?"

"I know. Here are the directions to his house. And these are the letters you were looking for." He handed her the pocketbook and a sheet of paper with directions to Keith's house once she got to Micanopy.

"Where did you find them?"

"I took them."

"I don't know what to say." June threw her arms around Alex.

He pushed her away. "I don't need to be holding you right now, Junie. Not right now."

June stared at the silhouette in front of her. She felt his pain. "I'm sorry, Alex."

"You don't have anything to be sorry for," he said. "You've given me a lot, and now it's time for me to give something back."

"Alex?"

"Go now, Junie! Now," he begged.

The realization hit her like a ton of bricks. June discovered that walking away from him was the hardest thing she had ever had to do. She didn't know if it was her feet or her heart holding her there, but she couldn't move. "I love you." She cried and threw her arms around him. "I love you so much."

He wanted to push her away, but she loved him and he couldn't deny it. And, he loved her. So, he took her in his arms and held her close. After a few more moments of indulging in her essence, he gathered his courage to whisper, "Good-bye."

"Never," she replied. "Never good-bye."

"I'm Missing You"

(lyrics and arrangement by June)

I don't feel like celebrating.
I don't feel like conversating.
Don't feel like masquerading.
I'm letting time pass me by.

Don't know why my heart's still breaking.
Don't know why my song is fading.
Don't know much of nothing.
There's only one thing that I know.

CHORUS:
I'm missing you,
and the love we used to share.
You said whenever I reached for you,
you would always be there.
But tonight you're gone,
and I'm here all alone.
I'm missing you,
and I don't know what to do.

I don't feel like wondering what's next.
But I don't feel like letting go yet.
Don't feel like I'll ever forget,
that day you walked away.

Don't know why you turned and left me.
Don't know why your tears still haunt me.

Don't know much of nothing.
There's just one thing that I know.

CHORUS

Don't know when we'll meet again.
Don't know if you'll love me then.
Don't know how much longer I can,
go on without you here.

CHORUS
(repeat to fade)

Chapter 7

W*hat am I doing here? Where am I going? Wake up, Junie. Wake up. I'm up. I'm up. But if I'm not sleep, what the hell am I doing here? My God, what am I doing? Stop crying. Stop crying. I can't let Trevor see me crying. Stop crying, damn it! Just try not to think about it. Try, Junie! Okay, I won't think about it. I won't think about it. I'll just drive to the airport. Catch a flight to Gainesville. Rent a car and drive out to Micanopy. Lord, help me. What am I doing?*

"Ma? Where are we going?" Trevor sat up in the passenger seat of June's Mercedes as they cruised along the freeway.

Stop crying girl and answer him.

"We're going to Florida," June responded.

"What for? Gramps is here."

"We're not going home. We're going to Micanopy."

"Micanopy? Where's that? And, what for?"

"I'll tell you later. Right now, I need to focus on the road. It's been so long since I actually drove to the airport that I've almost forgotten how to get there."

There. That should hold him for a minute. I don't know what I'm going to tell him. When he asks again, and he will, why we're going to Florida, what will I say? Lord, give me strength. I just need to think. Give me a minute. No. Wait. Did that sign say airport, next exit? I better slow down. Let's see. How in the hell am I supposed to drive and read all these signs?

"Does Dad know we're gone?"

"Dad?"

"Does he know we're gone?"

"Do you think I would up and leave without telling Alex where we're going?"

"Then how come I didn't see him when we left?"

"Because he was really, really tired. He told me to tell you bye and that he'll see you when we get back."

"When are we coming back?"

"In a couple of days."

A couple of days. What do I hope to accomplish? What if Keith won't talk to me? I can't tell him about Trevor. Not until I know the truth about why he left. I don't want him feeling sorry for me.

"Why didn't Auntie Lea come with us? She always goes with us."

Trevor, why can't you just hush and ride?

"Earth to Ma!"

"What did you say?"

Trevor leaned toward June. "What's wrong, Ma?"

"Nothing's wrong." June glanced at Trevor. "What makes you think something's wrong? Haven't we gone on trips by ourselves before?"

"You're acting scared, Ma."

"Scared? Scared of what?"

"I don't know, but you're acting like you're scared of something."

"Well, I'm not."

It had been a long time since June traveled anywhere without at least part of her entourage of Alex, Bernard, Leatrice, Willie and Joe. And, it had been years since she'd had to ask for directions at an airport or stand at a ticket counter. She was a little intimidated by all the pointing arrows and the constantly changing departure and arrival monitors. There were people whose job it was to handle these tasks for her. Someone made all the arrangements in advance, picked up the tickets, ushered her into the terminals and onto the planes. Someone was always there. But not this time. She was on her own.

Although she was casually dressed in jeans and a pullover sweater, the handful of people entering and exiting Detroit Metropolitan Airport still recognized her. Most were a little shocked to see June Thomas standing in the ticket line. The young man working at the ticket counter was speechless. Standing behind her was an elderly white woman trying to whisper in her husband's hearing aid while pointing at June. The four people standing in line behind them, including Trevor, were all privy to the conversation.

"She's a singer," the woman said. "The one we saw on television last night?"

"That's her?" he asked and turned his good ear to his wife.

"You can't tell?"

"Well, now that you told me who she is, I can tell. She looks a lot different in person."

"They all do," she said. And after seeing Trevor staring at her, she spoke to him, "Hi."

Trevor frowned.

June was talking to the ticket agent and didn't hear the conversation between the couple, but she turned around in time to see Trevor's disapproving stare. June turned to the couple.

The woman smiled. "I was just saying hello to your son."

"His name is Trevor."

"Hi, Trevor," the woman said. "My name's Elizabeth, but all my friends call me Liz."

He didn't respond.

"He's a little upset with me for dragging him out of bed this early." June tried to make some sort of excuse to assuage his display of rudeness. "He's not a morning person."

"Neither is my husband, Charlie. Last night I asked him to stay up with me to watch your concert. He didn't want to at first. He kept complaining about how he had to get up early this morning. But after you started singing, I couldn't pull him away from the television."

"I think you're an amazing singer." The woman's husband smiled. "I can't remember the last time I heard a voice as beautiful as yours."

"Now, Charlie, stop embarrassing yourself," Liz said, poking him. She nudged June and whispered, "He never compliments any-one. For him to say something like that, he must really, really like you." She joked, "I bet if you weren't already married, he'd try to run off and leave me for you."

"She's not married," Trevor snapped.

"Really? I thought you were married to that Alex guy," Liz re-called. "I guess you two look so good together that you should be married."

"He's asked her to marry him three times, but she said no." Trevor's filter was completely off now, slinging dirt like the couple were entertainment reporters.

"Trevor!"

"I forgot, Ma." Trevor's surprising contempt shined brighter than a diamond under a noonday sun. He turned to Liz, leaning in like he wanted her to keep a secret. "She doesn't like for me to talk about our personal life."

"And you shouldn't," Liz replied, "especially not to strangers."

June was aware that Trevor was angry with her for making him go on a trip to a place he'd never heard of while his grandmother was in Grosse Pointe. And on top of that, she wouldn't let him say good-bye to his dad, his grandmother or Lucy Kaye. She might not have thought her plan to its fruition, compensating for the x-factor in the form of her son's irritation at the sudden change of schedule without an explanation.

"Excuse me, Miss Thomas." The ticket agent tried to find an opportunity to interrupt and get June's attention. "To avoid a five-hour layover in Atlanta, you may want to fly into Jacksonville instead of Gainesville. Gainesville is only an hour's drive from Jacksonville. But if you fly directly into Gainesville from Atlanta, you're going to have that long layover."

"I'll fly into Jacksonville."

"Are you from Florida?" the woman behind her asked.

"I grew up in North Florida."

"Where?"

"A small town called Hampton Springs."

"Is that near Tallahassee?"

"Yes, it's about forty miles from Tallahassee."

"Here are your tickets." The young man handed June two tickets. "Your flight departs at five forty-five. You'll be boarding at Gate A-12. Thank you for flying American Airlines."

"Thank you for all your help," June told the young man. She turned to the woman behind her and said, "It's been nice talking to you."

"Same here," she replied. "Have a safe trip."

June smiled and started toward Gate A-12, with Trevor lagging behind her. She was glad it was early and the few passengers arriving and departing were stumbling about, half-asleep. If it was the middle of the day, her presence after last night's concert would cause pure chaos at the airport. That's what happened when she came home following the attempt on her life in St. Louis seven years ago. A legion of local fans turned out at the airport to show their love and support for her. Things turned nasty when the paparazzi showed up. Her fans blamed the shooting on the paparazzi's exploitive fascination with her personal life. "June Suffering from Anorexia," "Man Leaves Wife and Children for June," and "June Cancels Shows, Too Wasted To Go On," were all front-page headlines in the tabloids when she burst on the scene. There was nothing to substantiate any of the stories because June and Alex had built a fortress around their personal lives in the beginning.

However, the obsessed fan who tried to shoot her in St. Louis, a 32-year-old mechanic from a small town in Indiana, believed what he read in the tabloids. He saw the beautiful woman he loved and whose pictures were plastered all over his bedroom wall, turning into a tramp. When he was captured he said he tried to kill her because she was living the life of a sinner. He said the industry's trappings had taken control of her life, and she needed to be stopped before it was too late. He almost succeeded with a 38-caliber revolver. A 29-year-old security guard died from a shot to the chest after he ran onstage and tried to shield June.

After the St. Louis shooting, Bernard showed her how to use the paparazzi to her advantage. She soon became a media darling, which helped boost her celebrity.

Trevor sat next to June and glanced at her. He turned sideways in the chair, with his back to her, and stared out at the runway. He wanted to pout. But what was the point? She was still daydreaming and wouldn't notice.

Am I doing the right thing? Maybe Leatrice was right. Is finding him going to cure me? It won't. But I can't live any longer without knowing. I have to know. And after I know, I can take care of the cancer. If he knew about it beforehand, he might feel sorry for me. Then I may never know the real truth.

"American Airlines Flight 842 to Atlanta is now boarding at Gate A-12," a voice announced over the airport intercom. It was time to go, but June didn't gather her things and hurry toward the plane. Instead, she sat staring at the other passengers as they boarded.

"Are we going or not?" Trevor asked.

Trevor's saying something.

"Ma! Are we going or not?"

"Yes," she answered. "We better get going."

Trevor wanted the seat by the window. June didn't mind, even though she knew he asked for the window seat to be spiteful. She always sat next to the window and he was aware of it. But since she'd forced him to go on this trip, she felt the least she could do was go along with his rebellious antics.

"Buckle up," she told him.

"I already did," he said and looked out the window.

"Sun's about to come up," June said.

"So?"

"It should be a beautiful sunrise."

"And...?"

Trevor did not share his mother's enthusiasm for sunrises. In fact, he hated mornings. He never understood why every morning she went out to the dock and waited for the sun to rise. She tried to explain to him why she did it, but her explanation made no sense.

"You get to watch the world wake up," she told him on one of the mornings she dragged him out of bed to join her.

"And?"

"If you listen closely you can hear God."

"Yeah, right."

"Well, I've been doing this since I was a little girl," she continued.

"Why?"

"I just told you why," she answered. "To watch the world wake up and to listen to God."

"I don't wanna watch the world wake up. I wanna go back to sleep," he said and started back toward the house.

"No," she yelled in a whispered voice to keep from disturbing the silence. "Look at this."

"I don't see anything."

"Then listen! Listen closely, and I swear you'll be able to hear God speak. Don't you want to hear God?"

"Not really," he said and continued toward the house.

She forced Trevor to get up with her the next three mornings, but he never saw or heard the phenomenon that made her crave sunrises.

"Miss Thomas." One of the flight attendants started up a conversation after the plane was in flight. "I was at your concert last night and I just want to say good luck in whatever it is you choose to do next."

"Thank you."

"If you or Trevor need anything, let me know. My name's Tammy."

"We will."

Trevor did his best to ignore June. Every time she looked his way, he looked the other way. When she tried to say something to him, he sang to himself.

"Trevor."

"How many ways can a man get rich?" he rapped a verse of the hit song by Southern Spice. "How many ways can you lay in a ditch? I wanna know."

"Trevor, I wish you wouldn't," June shook her head and said.

"How many ways can I rock your world?" he rapped. "How many ways?"

"Trevor!"

He had succeeded in making her angry.

"When I'm talking, Trevor, you better listen."

"Why?"

"Because I said so!"

Trevor was satisfied now that she was feeling like he was feeling. He pushed her and she fell for it.

"I don't know what's gotten into you…" A sharp pain ripped through her abdomen. "Aaagh," she moaned and grabbed her stomach.

Trevor pretended not to notice by staring out the window.

"Aaagghh."

He turned to her slowly, now noticing her screams were genuine. Her face was clenched tight. "Ma?"

"Trevor, there's a bottle of pills in my bag. Get them for me."

Trevor unbuckled his seatbelt and grabbed his mother's pocketbook. "Hold on, Ma." He searched the bag, which June had filled with the few things she needed for the trip: a purse for the $793 she scraped up before leaving, the bottle of pain medicine Dr. Wylie prescribed, and the letters from Keith. "Is this it?"

"Yes." She bent over in agony. "Open it and give me two." The pain was becoming unbearable.

"Are you all right, Miss Thomas?" Tammy asked.

"She needs some water," Trevor answered.

Tammy's haste in getting the water made several of the other passengers seated near June and Trevor stand to see what was going on.

"Is she all right?" asked a middle-aged man with silver hair seated behind Trevor.

"Yes," Trevor answered. He opened the bottle and poured two of the pills in his hand. "She just forgot to take her medicine." He handed the pills to June.

"Something's going on up there," another passenger in the rear of the plane yelled, alarming the others in that section.

"It's June Thomas! She's sick," a passenger seated closer to June yelled back.

"Will everyone please return to your seats," one of the flight attendants announced over the intercom. "I need for everyone to return to their seats."

The passengers settled back into their seats but that didn't stop them from hanging over the sides and staring down the aisle to see the comings and goings of the flight attendants. They began to relay second-by-second accounts to the passengers who couldn't see.

"Here you are," Tammy said and handed Trevor a cup of water.

June put the pills in her mouth and Trevor held the cup while she sipped the water.

"Thank you," she told Tammy and closed her eyes. She frowned as another pain tore through her abdomen.

"Are you sure you're going to be okay?" Tammy asked.

"I'll be fine in a minute," she answered. "It's something I ate."

Trevor didn't buy her something-I-ate explanation this time.

"Ma, I think we should go back home since you're sick," he told June. "We can go wherever it is another day."

"We have to go today."

"But you're sick."

"I'm not sick, Trevor," she said. Her eyes misted over. "I'm not."

Trevor sensed that something was seriously wrong, and promise or no promise he was calling his dad and his grandmother as soon as the plane landed. Until then, he had to find a way to help her.

"Look, Ma," he exclaimed. "Look out the window at the sunrise." Trevor knew that if anything could help her deal with the pain, it was watching the sun's ascension in the distant horizon.

June opened her eyes slowly and peered out the window as the first rays of sunlight shimmered like pearls on the billowy clouds below.

"It's beautiful," she said. "So beautiful."

Trevor agreed. "Listen, Ma. Can you hear God?"

June listened closely to hear the familiar silence of the morning. Surely, this close to Heaven, she could hear God's soothing voice. But instead of hearing God's voice, she heard Dr. Wylie's advice three days ago.

"We can't wait any longer, June," he said. "You need to start chemotherapy today."

"I understand your concern, Dr. Wylie, but there's something I have to take care of first."

"I don't think you heard me clearly." Dr. Wylie stood and walked around the desk. He leaned against the desk facing June and Leatrice. "June, I don't mean to sound harsh, but there seems to be no other way to get through to you. If we don't start treating this now, you could die."

"I just need a few more days."

"You don't have a few more days. If you don't start today, you might not be here much longer to take care of anything."

"Dr. Wylie," Leatrice intervened, "would it help if we went ahead and set a date to begin the chemotherapy?"

"If it's within the next day or so," he answered.

"Today's Thursday. She has a concert Saturday, so let's say Monday." Leatrice looked at June. "Is Monday okay?"

"Monday's fine if she promises to start then."

June nodded.

The clock was ticking faster now, and June knew that if she was ever going to find out the truth about that night ten years ago, she had to find Keith while she was still able.

"Is she okay?" the man seated behind Trevor asked.

"She's feeling better," Trevor answered.

"I'm glad to hear that. She had me pretty scared for a minute. Excuse my manners, I'm Will Phillips."

"My name's Trevor."

Will leaned further over the seat. He saw that June's eyes were closed. She appeared to be sleeping.

"Trevor, are you sure your mom's all right? I mean, she said she was retiring last night."

"She's okay. It's just something she ate."

"Did she tell you why she was retiring?"

"No."

"Well, she looks like she's feeling better."

"I hope so."

"If you don't mind me asking, Trevor," he leaned even closer and whispered. "Where are you and your mother going?"

"To Florida," he answered.

"Where in Florida?"

"I done forgot the name of the place."

"It wouldn't be Hampton Springs because you would remember that since that's where your grandmother lives, right?"

"How do you know where my grandmother lives?" Trevor turned around and asked.

"I've been a big fan of your mother's for years, and I read a lot."

"Oh." Trevor sat back down.

"Trevor, you don't look too enthused about this trip. Why's that?"

"Because Ma's not feeling well."

"I thought it was just something she ate."

"It was."

"Does she get sick like this a lot?"

"I shouldn't be talking with you," Trevor said after realizing the personal nature of Will's questions.

"Hey, I'm sorry. I didn't mean to get personal. I'm not trying to get in your mother's business. It's just that I really love her music, and I'm a little concerned about why she's giving it up."

"I think she'll start back singing when she's feeling better."

"I hope so," Will said. "Those pills you just gave her, are they helping any?"

"I think so."

"What are they?"

"Why don't you ask his mother," Tammy interrupted. "If she wants you to know, she'll tell you."

"Trevor?" June opened her eyes and saw Will leaning over the seat. "What's going on?"

"He was just asking me something," Trevor answered.

"He was asking very personal questions about you," Tammy told June. "Questions a reporter should be asking the source instead of her child."

"You're a reporter?" Trevor turned to face Will.

"Sit down, Trevor," June said, tugging at his shirt.

"Are you a reporter?" Trevor demanded.

"I'm a writer," Will answered.

"Are you writing about my mother?"

"Trevor, please sit down," June begged.

Trevor was never disobedient. He always did what he was told. Right now, he was downright defiant because he was trying to protect her. Willie and Joe weren't there and neither was his father, Bernard or Leatrice. He felt it was his job to look after June. His dad would expect it of him. "Are you?"

"If she'll talk to me, I am."

"No, I won't talk to you," June took over. "Now leave us alone."

Trevor continued staring angrily at Will.

"Go ahead and sit back down, Trevor," Tammy said. "He won't bother you anymore."

Trevor settled back in the seat but kept a watchful eye on Will.

"Thanks again," June said to Tammy.

"You're more than welcome."

The alarm on Trevor's watch began to beep.

"It's seven-thirty," he said. "Time to get up and start getting ready for Sunday school."

"And time for Momma to wake up and find out we're gone." June was talking to herself, but Trevor overheard her.

"Gramps doesn't know we're gone?"

"She does now."

"She what?" Kathryn almost dropped the coffee pot on the floor. "Please say that again, because I don't think I heard you right."

"She went to see Keith," Alex obliged. There was a calmness in his voice that caught her off-guard.

Kathryn wasn't as accommodating. "Oh, my God. What is she thinking?"

"She had to go."

"What are you talking about?"

"She needs to know, Mrs. Thomas."

"Know what?"

"Why he ran away."

Kathryn threw her hands up. "Junie! Junie! What are you doing? That was so many years ago."

"Ten years ago."

"So why is she still—"

"Because she needs to know."

Kathryn sat on a stool and tried to gather her senses. "She told me she didn't know where he lived."

"She didn't," Alex said, pouring a cup of coffee. "I told her where to find him."

"*You* told her?"

"I need for her to do this. It's the only way she's ever going to get him out of her system."

"But what if it backfires again and she ends up hurting even more?"

"Then I'll have to help her through it again." Alex sat down, facing Kathryn. "Mrs. Thomas, I love Junie. I love her more than I love myself. I've loved her since the day I first saw her. I've always known that one day she would have to go back to him and make things right. I prayed every day that when the time came for her to go back, that I would be strong enough to let her go. I didn't think I would be, but I was. I let her go. It was the hardest thing I've ever had to do, but I kept telling myself that she was never going to be mine until she made peace with him. She has to find a way to let him go because I can't keep sharing her with him."

"I understand that, but I don't think you know how strongly she feels about him. Her feelings for him were always too deep. It scares me how he makes her feel."

"So you know how I feel. I've loved June for more than ten years and regardless of what happens when she finds him, I'm going to keep loving her. I won't be able to stop loving her if she decides to stay with him. So, what am I supposed to do? Keep my fingers crossed and hope that he never takes the notion to walk back into her life? I can't keep living like that."

Lucy Kaye walked into the kitchen. "Good morning," she said.

"Good morning, Lucy," Kathryn answered.

"Good morning, Mrs. Adams." Alex offered her the stool beside him. "Here's a seat."

Lucy Kaye sat down and immediately noticed the nervous look on both of their faces. "Where's Junie?"

"She's gone," Alex answered.

"Gone?"

"To see your son."

"Keith?"

"And she took Trevor," Alex said.

"You didn't tell me she took Trevor!" Kathryn shouted.

"I was about to get to that."

"Is she planning on telling him?" Kathryn started to ask.

"Planning on telling me what?" Bernard jokingly asked when he walked into the kitchen with a newspaper in his hand.

"We're talking about Junie," Alex told him.

"I can't believe she's not up yet," Bernard said.

"She's up, but she's not here."

"Where is she?"

"She took a trip."

"What kind of trip?"

Alex shifted on the stool and then answered, "She went to see Keith."

"And you let her go?"

"She's a grown woman. Besides, I was the one who told her she should go."

"Have you lost your mind?"

"No, I haven't." Alex stood and turned to Bernard, who looked dumbfounded standing in the doorway. "She needed to do this."

"What she needs to do is get her behind back here and use the next two weeks to get herself together. She starts filming *For His Love* in two weeks."

"She's not doing the film," Alex informed him. "I've already asked Thandie to take over the role and she said she would."

"Sounds like you already knew she was planning to skip town," Bernard said.

"No, I didn't know."

"Well, do you know when she will be back?"

"I'm hoping real soon."

Bernard was getting more and more frustrated. "Who went with her?"

"Trevor."

"That's it? You mean to tell me, you let her leave here by herself after last night? What in the hell were you thinking?"

"She wanted to go by herself."

"Damn what she wanted!" He threw the newspaper on the counter. On the front page, there was a picture of June singing the last song of her concert.

"What a finale!" Bernard read the headline. "She's today's top story and the media is going to be behind her like crazy. There's no way you should have let her go."

"I see you don't know Junie that well," Kathryn said. She walked around the counter and put her arm around Lucy Kaye, who sat in tears over the latest twist of events.

"Where's Junie?" Leatrice said, walking into the kitchen. "Did she go?"

No one answered. No one had to.

"Hold on to me," Trevor told June as they exited the plane at Atlanta International Airport. He put June's bag on his shoulder, placing his arm around her waist and led her into the terminal.

Suddenly, a camera flashed in their faces. Will was taking pictures of them. He continued snapping as he barraged her with questions. "Are you really through, June?"

"Damn you!" June shouted.

"Get away from us!" Trevor yelled at Will, trying to shield June from the camera. "Get back!"

As soon as Tammy walked into the terminal she saw June and Trevor trying to dodge Will and his intrusive camera. She rushed over to where Will had them cornered.

"June! Trevor! Come with me!" Tammy pushed Will back and shouted, "Back up off them, you asshole!" She put her arm around Trevor and took June by the hand and led them to a nearby door marked: Employees Only.

"He can't follow you in here," she said and opened the door.

"I don't know how to thank you," June said.

"You don't have to. I really do think he's an asshole."

"So do I," Trevor agreed.

"Tammy, I hate to ask, but I need one more favor," June said as soon as the door closed behind them.

"Just name it."

"We have to catch a plane to Jacksonville that is boarding now. Can you help us get there without having to go back out there? I don't want him to follow us."

"Sure. Follow me."

Tammy contacted a security officer and told him about June's predicament. The officer and Tammy led June and Trevor through a maze of hallways that were off limits to the public. Trevor stuck his hand in his jacket pocket. He had his cell phone, but he couldn't call his dad without June finding out, and there wasn't enough time to slip off from her and call him. He would have to wait until they arrived in Jacksonville.

"Love Has Got To Be Real"

(lyrics and arrangement by June)

After so many nights
spent mending my broken heart,
I became too afraid
to make a new start.
But suddenly,
I don't know what I feel.
I'm feeling so alive,
your love has got to be real.

CHORUS:
Can you promise me,
that you will always be,
right here,
beside me?
Is forever
what our futures reveal?
This time baby,
love has got to be real.

I'd given up on love.
I was watching out for me.
Until you came back,
and set my heart free.
Now, I don't understand
all these emotions I feel.

But I'm feeling so alive,
your love has got to be real.

CHORUS

Now suddenly,
I don't know what I feel.
But I'm feeling so alive,
your love has got to be real.

CHORUS
(repeat to fade)

Chapter 8

I t isn't hard to spot a woman whose heart has been broken. Smile at her and she coerces a smile back. Listen to her. She speaks but her voice doesn't carry. Stop and look at her. She's searching for something, but she doesn't know what it is she seeks. Watch her eyes though, because they will tell her story.

"Excuse me?" A small woman, who looked twenty years younger than her silver hair and AARP cap suggested, rolled a small gray suitcase up to June at Jacksonville International Airport. "Can I help you find something?" she asked. Her smile was warm.

"I'm trying to find Enterprise Rent-a-Car," June answered.

"Well, you're going in the right direction," the woman said. "It's just up the terminal."

"Thank you," June said and coerced a smile.

"You're welcome," the woman replied and turned to walk off. She hesitated after two steps, then turned around and walked back to June. She looked over the rim of her glasses at June and smiled. "I don't know you, but I couldn't walk away without telling you that sometimes it takes the dark to bring out the light. My grandfather told me that a long time ago, back when I was a teenager. Back then, I didn't understand what he meant. Now, I'm an old lady flying up to Pittsburgh to see my first great-grandchild. If there's one thing that I've learned during this long life of mine, it's that sometimes you have to go through a lot of grief and sorrow before you find that piece of happiness you're looking for."

This wasn't the first time a stranger had approached June knowing what she had known since the morning Keith ran away: She was a woman whose heart had been irreparably broken. And, that she wasn't hard to spot.

"You're a beautiful woman, inside and out. I can tell. Love and happiness follow people like you," the woman said to June. "Remember that and everything will be fine."

June smiled and said, "I'll try to keep that in mind."

"Don't just try. Do it." The woman looked at Trevor and smiled. "Take care of your mother."

He smiled and nodded his head.

"It's been nice talking to you," the woman said and went on her way.

June wished she could be as confident about her own happiness, but she couldn't because she already knew from personal experience that some broken hearts never mend. She had found happiness again with Alex only to realize that his unconditional love couldn't erase the memory of Keith's touch that night or the tears in his eyes the next morning.

"I need to use the bathroom, Ma," Trevor said as soon as they moved down the terminal.

"Can you hold it for a minute?"

"No," he responded. "I have to go now. Please."

"Okay," June said and looked around for a restroom.

"There's one," Trevor yelled and darted off.

"Trevor!" June called behind him, but he pretended not to hear her and ran into the restroom.

Trevor didn't have to use the restroom. This was his way of getting away from June so he could call his daddy without her knowing. Trevor took the cell phone out of his jacket pocket and dialed Alex's phone number. He put the phone to his ear and waited for Alex to answer. He frowned and looked at the phone's display. He wasn't getting a signal. Trevor looked around the bathroom and saw that there was only one way out, which was the door he came through. He walked over to the door and opened the door slightly. He saw his mother standing with her back to the door. He eased the door open and slid past her.

June didn't see Trevor sneak out the bathroom because she was busy trying to distract attention away from her.

"People stop me all the time thinking I'm her," she told two teenage boys, who came over and asked for her autograph.

"That's because you look just like her," one of the boys said. "I mean just like her."

"Well, thanks for the compliment," she said and forced a smile. "That was a compliment, wasn't it?"

"Hell yeah!" He took another hard look at June and shook his head before walking away. He stopped, turned around and stared at her again. "Are you sure you're not her?"

"Last time I checked, I wasn't."

"All right." He turned to his friend, still in disbelief. "I think she's just messing with us."

"Word," the friend agreed as they walked away.

June looked at her watch and then at the bathroom door. Trevor had been in the restroom too long, nearly ten minutes. She opened the door and called out his name. "Trevor!" No one answered.

June looked inside. There was no one using the dozen or so urinals lining the wall. "Trevor," she called again. When he didn't answer, she walked on in. She opened the door of the nearest stall. He wasn't there. She was starting to get scared. "Trevor!" He wasn't in the next stall. Or the next.

The bathroom door opened and a young man walked in with a toddler in tow. "Excuse me. Is something wrong?" he asked when he saw June running down the line of stalls pushing every door open.

"My son's gone!" June was frantic. "I'm looking for my son!"

"What does he look like?"

June didn't have time to answer as she ran out the restroom.

"Trevor!" she yelled as she visually scanned the terminal. He was nowhere to be seen.

"Can I help you?" an airport security officer asked.

"My son is missing," June replied and then ran down the terminal with the officer hurrying behind her. "I've got to find my boy!"

"How old is he?"

"Nine," she answered. "Trevor!"

The officer radioed for assistance, rushing behind June. "What is he wearing?"

"A pair of black jeans and a black and white striped shirt," she answered. "And, and a jean jacket tied around his waist." By now, June was terrified and thinking the worst.

A female security officer joined in the search. "Where did you last see him?" she asked June.

"He went into the restroom back there."

"Did you see him come out?"

"No," June answered as tears filled her eyes. "That's why I went in the restroom to look for him."

"Don't worry, ma'am, we'll find him."

"Aaaaah!" June folded over, barely able to stand from the pain.

"Are you all right?" the female officer asked.

June tried to answer but couldn't.

"Let me help you sit down."

"Harry," she called for the other guard who had run ahead of them. "I need some help here!"

The officer's assistance came too late. June fell to the floor.

Harry ran over to June and his coworker and knelt beside June, now curled up on the floor. "Phyllis, radio med and tell them to get here on the double. And then get these people back. She needs some air."

Phyllis made the call and turned her attention to the crowd of onlookers gathering around. "That looks like June Thomas. Is that her?" a young woman asked Phyllis.

"I don't think so," Phyllis answered. "Now move back."

June wasn't worried about herself or the razor-sharp pains that had temporarily crippled her. Her son was missing and a thousand gory scenarios raced through her mind. Was he lost? Scared? Abducted?

"Oh God!" She begged Harry, "Please find my son."

"We have some people out looking for him now, and I'm sure they'll find him."

"Trevor!" June called. "Trevor!"

She heard his voice calling in the distance, "Ma!"

"Trevor," June cried.

"Ma!"

When Phyllis saw Trevor running toward them, she pushed her way through the crowd to meet him. "Let him through! Let him through!"

"Ma!" Trevor kneeled beside her. "You need your medicine!" He opened her pocketbook and took out the bottle of pills. "She needs something to drink," he told Harry.

"I'll get it," Phyllis said and rushed off to get a drink from the machine.

"It's going to be all right, Ma! I called Dad and he's coming to get us! He'll take you to the doctor when he gets here." Trevor fumbled with the bottle as he tried to open it. "Hold on, Ma! Dad's coming!"

"He can't. We have to go, Trevor."

"No, Ma. We need to wait for Dad!"

"Help me up, Trevor." June put her arm around his shoulders. "Help me, Trevor."

"But, Ma."

"We have to go now!"

Trevor put his arm around his mother, and with Harry's assistance, helped her to her feet.

"I think you should wait and at least let the nurse here check you out," Harry suggested to June.

"I don't have time. I have to go now."

Phyllis returned with a Pepsi in her hand. She handed it to June. Trevor gave her the two pills he'd been holding in his free hand. June thanked Phyllis for the drink as she took the pills. She reached for Trevor's hand as they walked toward the Enterprise counter, with Harry and Phyllis walking close beside them.

"Should I cancel the med call?" Phyllis asked Harry.

"Go ahead, but tell them to stay alert."

All June had to do was pick up the keys when she got to the counter. Tammy had called ahead and reserved a car for her. The Enterprise representative was anxiously awaiting June's arrival.

"Tammy said you wanted a mid-sized car." The woman opened her mouth wide, showing her toothy smile. "So, I reserved you a Grand Prix with GPS. I think they're the best-looking cars you can buy this year."

"So do I," Harry chimed in. "My wife just traded her car for a burgundy one."

"I bet that's nice," she remarked and turned to June. "Here are your keys. I had the car pulled up front for you."

"Thank you."

"You're more than welcome," she said and then extended an Enterprise pamphlet. "Before you go, can I get your autograph? That's the only way my boyfriend's going to believe me when I tell him I rented you a car today."

"What's your name?"

"Cynthia."

"Cynthia, thanks for the ride." June jotted down the memo in her signature style. "Your friend, June."

A minute later, June and Trevor were on their way to Micanopy. She had driven about fifteen miles west along Interstate 10 before either of them spoke a word.

"I have something to tell you," June finally uttered. She waited for him to respond. After he didn't, she continued. "I should have told you this a long time ago, but I didn't know how to back then. I'm still not sure, but I think it's time you know."

"We should have waited for Dad."

"We couldn't."

"Why not?" Trevor asked.

"Because."

"You're sick, Ma. I can tell. That's why we should have waited."

"Listen to me, Trevor. There's nothing seriously wrong with me. It's just that lately I've been having these really bad stomach cramps. I don't know why, but the doctor said it's nothing." June was having a hard time lying to Trevor because she knew that regardless of what she said he was going to believe what he already believed. "Why am I lying to you? You need to know the truth." June sighed.

If she was going to tell Trevor the truth about Keith, she needed to tell him the whole truth.

"Ma, why don't we wait for Dad?" Trevor wasn't sure he wanted to hear what she was about to say. He was only a child, but he understood, even at his young age, that sometimes the truth could be a horrible thing to face. Why else would his mother make him promise not to tell his dad or anyone else about the cramps and the pills? And he remembered what his dad said last night on the way home from the concert. Stop with the lies and face the truth. But no one listened to him. Not June. Not Kathryn. No one. Instead they hid behind the cloak of detachment and continued living with the lies. They had unknowingly let Trevor know they were afraid of the truth, which convinced him the truth was something to be feared. "You can tell me when Dad gets here."

"I have to tell you now," she said. "Before we get to Micanopy."

"Ma, I'm tired of listening."

"How can you be tired of listening when I haven't been saying that much?"

"My ears are tired." He covered his ears with his hands in a dramatic gesture. "My eardrums are hurting."

"Trevor, I know you don't want to hear what I'm about to say, but I have to tell you this."

"Can I listen to the radio?" Trevor didn't wait for an answer.

"I'm through with love," country singer Sandra Lloyd's voice burst from the speakers. "I'm through with hoping; I'm through with everything that I can't control."

"I'm walking out," Trevor sang along. "I'm letting it all go."

"I can't believe you know this song," June said.

"Why?"

"The last time I checked, you didn't like country music."

"I like Sandra Lloyd."

"Since when?"

"Since she got so fine," Trevor jokingly answered.

"So fine?"

"That's what Dad says."

"Oh, he does?"

"But he says she's nothing compared to you," Trevor said, trying to straighten his slip of the tongue.

"He better say that."

Trevor was glad he had momentarily diverted June away from the bullet she was about to fire. After watching his parents fight, make up and then fight again and again throughout the past few months, he'd found a way to hide or to at least dodge the verbal bullets they aimed at each other. He heard how they tangled and manipulated words to either hurt or pacify the other, and he saw their rueful faces when those words didn't match the feelings they harbored inside. They had let him see and hear too much for a boy his age.

"You run, Trevor," June said and glanced at him. "You run just like your father."

"Dad doesn't run," Trevor defended Alex.

"I'm not talking about Alex," June cut him off. "I'm talking about your real father."

Trevor pretended he didn't hear June. "I'm turning loose," he sang along with the radio, seemingly oblivious to his mother's confession. "The things I cannot hold."

"When I met Alex," June said, turning the radio off, "I was already pregnant with you." She looked at Trevor, who pretended not to hear her. The tears in his eyes betrayed the nonchalant look on his face. "Mrs. Adams has a son named Keith."

He already knew about Lucy Kaye's son, Keith. Trevor remembered the day Lucy Kaye told him he reminded her of Keith. She even asked to put her arms around him so she could remember how it felt to hold her son. "Now," Trevor told himself, "if her son is really my daddy, then that means."

He dismissed the thought. "I already have a daddy, and he's coming to get us. He's on his way now."

Tears filled June's eyes because she could feel the hurt her son was feeling. But, she had come too far to turn back.

"Baby, I know how much you want to go home, but we have to go to Micanopy first."

"Why?"

"So you can finally meet your father," June answered.

"Dad is my father," Trevor cried. "Dad is my father!"

The heartbreak in Trevor's eyes revealed the consumptive betrayal he was feeling. The confusion. Anger. And his horrific fear of any other truths she might be ready to tell him.

"I'm sorry, Trevor," June said and reached over to wipe the tears from his eyes. "But I had to tell you the truth." He pushed her hand away. "Please don't run," she begged. "Please don't run away from me now. Not now."

But he ran, just like his father had ten years earlier, when she unknowingly forced him to deal with a truth he couldn't live with. "Dad's coming for me." Trevor sobbed and retreated to a place where her words could not harm him. "He's coming."

Alex wasn't on his way to Micanopy like Trevor thought. He was sitting on the dock behind their house in Grosse Pointe watching the drizzling rain disappear into the lake. He'd dreaded this day since the first time he held June in his arms and felt the fullness and unfathomable depth of his love for her. From that moment, he knew he would not be able to live without her if she ever decided to go back to Keith. Alex never thought he would be able to let her go, but somehow he found the courage to set her free.

Then his son called.

"Dad! Dad! Ma's sick! You need to get here! Hurry up, Dad," Trevor yelled through the phone.

"Slow down, Trevor," Alex whispered and walked out of the den to keep Kathryn and Lucy Kaye from hearing the conversation. "Now what's going on?"

"Ma's sick, Dad! She's real sick!"

"What's wrong with her?"

"She's having real bad stomach cramps. She had them before we left, but she made me promise not to tell you!"

"Where is she now?"

"She's down the hall waiting for me."

"Does she know you're calling me?"

"No," Trevor answered. "Leave now, Dad!"

There was no doubt in Trevor's mind that Alex would be on the next plane out of Detroit because his dad came running whenever he called. This time, however, Alex said he was on his way, but he wasn't. After he hung up the phone, he walked out to the dock and waited for Kathryn and Lucy Kaye to pack for their trip home.

Alex felt numb after lying to Trevor, but he couldn't stop June. Not now. She'll see Keith, ask a few questions, shed a few tears and realize that his hold on her had nothing to do with loving him. Rather, it was a desperate need to know the truth. That's what he hoped. If he stopped her, she would never know why he ran away, which meant she would never be free of him. Knowing that she was sick worried him, but not enough to stop her.

"Alex," Kathryn said. "I brought you a jacket and an umbrella."

He didn't respond so Kathryn wrapped the jacket around his shoulders and held her umbrella over his head. "Are you sure you don't want me to stay?"

"I'll be fine," he answered. "Anyway, Junie might need you in Florida."

Kathryn remembered that Sunday morning seven years ago when Keith came home for his father's funeral. "I'm scared, Alex," she said. "What if he won't talk to her? And what if he runs away again? What's going to happen to my baby?"

Alex turned to Kathryn. "Mrs. Thomas, promise me you won't follow her and try to stop her. She needs to do this and I need you to let her."

"Something is wrong with my baby," Kathryn said. "A mother knows when something is wrong with her child. So, I'm not going to promise you I won't be going behind her. If I don't hear from her by tomorrow morning, I'm going to Micanopy. If you don't want me to do that, then the next time she calls, you better tell her to call me."

"That wasn't Junie on the phone."

"Then it was Trevor," Kathryn said. "Alex, I'm not blind. I saw the expression on your face when you answered the phone. I didn't say anything then because I didn't want to upset Lucy."

"If she calls, I'll tell her to call you," he said.

"All right," she replied. "I have to go now or I'll miss my flight. But, you make sure she calls me."

"I will."

The look in his eyes showed he needed reassurance that he had done the right thing by letting her go. Kathryn felt bad because all she had done was threaten him. "She'll be back," Kathryn said. "Soon. Real soon."

"Will she?"

"Junie loves you."

"Yeah, I know. She loves me, but right now, she's on her way to see the man she loves more."

June was minutes away from Keith's place. She had gotten off the interstate and driven through the towns of Starke, Waldo and Gainesville. Now, she was turning off Highway 441 onto Cholokka Boulevard in Micanopy. On another day, she would have spent the entire trip pointing out familiar sites as she dispensed interesting, and sometimes irrelevant tidbits about each of the towns they passed through. But today's trip had been quiet and somber, especially after she told Trevor about Keith.

As June drove through downtown, she was stunned by the similarities between Micanopy and Hampton Springs. Both towns had managed to retain the nostalgic atmosphere of an early 19th century small town. Large, moss-covered oaks lined the street and provided shade over the wooden sidewalks in front of the antique and curio shops. She slowed down to watch two mockingbirds chase a squirrel as it darted across the green park benches along the street's median. She looked down at the directions Alex had given her.

"Take Cholokka Boulevard west to Philco Road," she read aloud. She turned and looked at Trevor, who was also amazed at how much this town looked like Hampton Springs. "Are you okay?"

He didn't answer.

"I really am sorry."

Trevor, pretending not to hear her, let the window down and stared at a young couple browsing through a shelf of used books in front of O. Brisky Books.

"I thought you needed to know," June said.

Trevor was trying hard to forget everything his mother had said. She may have thought he needed to know that the man he called Dad wasn't his father, but it was actually a truth he could have lived without.

"We're just about there," June said. "According to your dad's directions, Philco Road should be about a mile up the road."

Trevor couldn't believe what he had just heard. He thought, *Dad knows about this? He knows that he's not my dad?* He was worried now. How could he face Alex? He wasn't sure what he would say to him or how to look at him now that he knew. He wished that he could pretend not to know this horrible truth like he pretended not to hear his mother.

"There's his house," she said and leaned forward to get a better look at the gray house at the end of the dirt road. She pulled up slowly beside the uneven picket fence surrounding the old, but well-kept, cracker farmhouse. She turned the car off. "We're here."

Trevor eyed the house suspiciously. He turned away quickly when he saw a man's figure walk out of the house and onto the screened-in porch. When June saw the man, she hurried out of the car.

After seven long years, there he was. All she could see was the silhouette of a man, but there was no mistaking it in her mind's eye. It was Keith. She felt him. She opened the gate and walked into the yard.

At first, he didn't recognize her as she walked up the pine straw covered walkway leading to the house. But once he did, he slammed the screen door shut and hurried back in the house.

June stopped walking. Once again, he'd run away. Shut her out. And, like that morning seven years ago, the tears started and wouldn't stop.

She cried out against the façade of the house, the memories flooding her conscious mind. "Why won't you talk to me?"

She had waited forever to hear his voice and to see his smile, and she'd prayed too many prayers to let it end this way. She wasn't going to let him keep running away, especially not after she had told her son the truth. She decided at that moment not to leave without knowing why he trashed all their dreams and vanished from her life. Ten years had not lessened her need to know the truth.

"What did I do to make you hate me so much?" June tried to pull the screen door open, but the lock wouldn't give. She banged on the door. "What are you so afraid of?" She kicked the door, despair giving way to anger. "Open the door and talk to me!"

Trevor was watching from the car. He had never seen his mother so desperate, never so helpless.

"Please, Keith," she begged. "I just want to talk to you. Please don't do this to me again."

Although Trevor was angry with his mother, he knew he had to help her. He opened the car door, got out and walked to the gate. Before opening the gate, he told himself that what he was about to do didn't mean he believed anything she had said about his dad. He was only trying to help her. He stepped up to the door next to his mother and knocked.

There was no reply.

June reached for Trevor's other hand, but he put his hand in his pocket. He wasn't letting her off the hook just like that.

He knocked again.

I'm doing this for Ma, Trevor reminded himself before he called out to Keith, "Dad!"

June couldn't believe her ears. Trevor hadn't run away like she thought. He really was listening. And now he was going against everything he believed in, including his loyalty to Alex.

"Dad," Trevor called again and then knocked on the door.

The inside door opened slowly and Keith stepped out on the porch. He stared at the little boy standing on the other side of the screen door and saw his reflection staring back at him.

"Did you call me Dad?" Keith asked.

"You'll Never Love Another Girl"

(lyrics and arrangement by June)

We started out as friends,
and we found a love we thought would never end.
With the rest of the world, we fell out of touch.
Until your heart told you, that you loved me too much.

Now you're running away.
You have your pride and it won't let you stay.
You didn't mean to fall so deep in love with me.
And you think that time, that time is gonna set you free.

CHORUS:

But you'll never love another girl like this.
You need my warm embrace and my tender kiss.
We had a special love that you're gonna miss.
You'll never love another girl like this.

Now you're trying to tell me that time will heal the pain.
And you're leaving me, all alone to face the falling rain.
I don't know what it is, just what you're hoping to find.
But no matter where it takes you, you will still be mine.

CHORUS
(Followed by BRIDGE)

You'll never love another girl.
You'll never love another girl like this.

You'll never love another girl.
I'll always be your only girl.

So go on and listen to what your heart says.
You have your pride and it won't let you stay.
But one day, you're going to change your mind,
when you start to miss the love you left behind.

CHORUS
(followed by fading bridge)

Chapter 9

Keith had seen this boy's face before.

It was on a Saturday morning a few years ago as he was waiting for Mrs. Carmichael, Micanopy's librarian, to copy some newspaper articles. He knew it was a Saturday morning because Saturday was the only day he went to the library, which shared the same two-story building as Towne Hall. Whenever he went to the library during the week, most of his time was spent dodging idle chit-chat with folks he hardly knew. He began making his weekly trips into town on Saturdays when he realized there were fewer people to contend with.

It was June's eyes that he saw first staring at him from beneath three other periodicals. He saw her eyes and her name glaring from the cover of the partially exposed magazine. He looked away quickly. It had been too many years, six to be exact, since he welcomed the warmth of her big brown eyes.

Here in this town, believed to be the second oldest settlement in Florida, he avoided the spellbinding light June's star cast. Before *The Pages We Forget* was released with his picture on the cover, he had heard very little about her in the secluded world he'd built for himself. He didn't have a television or radio in the house, so it was a rare occurrence for him to even hear one of her songs. Once, in an effort to escape the deafening silence of the farmhouse, he found the courage to turn on the radio in his car, serving as his initial introduction into her world. It was the title song from her second album, *Feel My Love*, and he knew it was June as soon as he heard the first few words of the song. "Baby, are you ready," she purred, "to feel my love?" That was all he heard, but it was already more than he could stand to hear of the haunting voice. Then he saw her on the television down at Vera's Coffee Shop a few weeks after he came back from his father's funeral.

"Chaos broke out last night after a gunman fired two shots at singer June Thomas during a sold-out concert in St. Louis," the TV anchor announced.

"Can you believe that?" the waitress asked Keith. "Some crazy ass guy tried to kill her."

"Kill who?"

"June Thomas."

"Junie!"

"He shot at her, but luckily he missed," Angeline said. "Two other people were shot, though."

Keith stood and moved closer to the television. He watched as June held onto Alex as a security team led them out the arena. With all the commotion going on around her, she should have been trembling in fear, he thought. But she wasn't. He could see that she felt safe in Alex's arms by looking in her eyes.

Those same eyes were begging him to look into them again. He reluctantly reached for the magazine. He pulled the magazine out from under the others and saw the young boy in the photo with June. The boy's strikingly familiar face scared him. He recognized the boy's eyes, his hair, and his smile, but he couldn't recall where he had seen the boy's face. Perhaps it was one of the faces he created in his short stories and in his unfinished novel, which he wrote under the pen name, Clyde Goodman. Or maybe, he reminded him of the seven-year-old boy, whose picture was framed in the small wooden letter "L" on the shelf above his desk.

He glanced down at the picture again, the bold caption scripted under it telling the rest of the story: *Having It All, Motherhood and Stardom.*

"Her son?" he mused.

"Here you are, Keith," Mrs. Carmichael said and handed him the copies. "I did the best I could on that old copier."

"I'm sure they're okay." He glanced through the small stack of pages. "They're fine."

"Good."

"Well, I better be going," Keith said and started toward the door. "Thanks for all your help."

"You're welcome," Mrs. Carmichael replied.

As he hurried across the parking lot, he could not escape the indelible image of the boy's face. "I know that face," he told himself as he opened the door of his faded blue Cutlass. "I've seen him somewhere before." He put the key in the ignition and started the car. "But where?" He checked for traffic in the rearview mirror. The boy's eyes stared at him from the mirror.

Four years later, that same boy was knocking at his door and calling him dad. Keith unlatched the screen door and held the door open for June and Trevor to come inside. He couldn't take his eyes off of Trevor, who stood steadfast on the steps, even after June nudged him forward. "Would you like to come inside?" Keith asked him.

"I'm all right," Trevor answered without bothering to look back at Keith.

"Are you sure?"

"I said I was all right," Trevor snapped.

"I think he's waiting for Alex," June said nervously.

"Alex?" Keith asked.

"Alex is my real dad," Trevor said, frowning at Keith.

"I know I'm not wanted here," June said. "But I had to come and introduce you to our son, Trevor."

"I'm not his son," Trevor retorted.

"Trevor?" Keith's mind flipped a switch. He remembered years ago, before he ran away from Hampton Springs, they had chosen the names Trevor or Camille for their first child.

"One day you and I will get married and we'll have a family," he promised her one morning as they waited for the sun to rise over Bacon Street.

"If our first child's a boy, we will name him Keith Adams Jr.," she whispered in his ear.

"No. Not that. Let's name him something else, like Trevor," Keith responded. "Trevor was my best friend's name before we moved here. Keith isn't a good name. I never liked it."

"And what if she's a girl?" she asked.

"Camille," he answered.

"Why Camille?"

"Because it sounds as beautiful as she's going to be," he responded and kissed her softly. "Especially if she looks anything like her mother."

June never forgot that morning. And when their eyes finally met, she knew that he had not forgotten the promise he made. "You said Keith wasn't a good name," June reminded him. "So I named him Trevor like you wanted me to."

"But is he really my son?"

"Yes," she answered.

"He's not my father," Trevor yelled and jumped down from the steps. "My dad's coming to get me," he cried and backed down the walkway. "You're not my dad."

Keith saw himself in Trevor. Every backwards step Trevor made toward the gate made him remember the morning he backed away from his own mother as she pleaded with him to stay. Like Trevor, he had been forced to face a truth he wasn't ready to live with.

He recalled hearing his mother yell for her husband, who was still asleep in their upstairs bedroom. "Reverend!" She turned to him and begged, "Please, Keith. Please come back inside and tell me what's wrong."

"I can't, Ma. I have to go," he cried and backed out of the yard carrying an overpacked suitcase in one hand and a backpack in the other. "Tell Dad good-bye for me and tell him I love him."

"No! Keith, please! Please tell me what I did wrong."

"Ma, you didn't do anything wrong." He tried to assure her as best he could. "I couldn't have asked for better parents."

"Then how can you just leave us? How can you walk away without telling us why you're leaving or where you're going?"

"Ma, I have to go now while I still can." He closed the gate behind him. "I love you."

"No!" Mrs. Adams screamed and charged through the gate. "I won't let you go!" She grabbed the suitcase and tried to pull it and him back into the yard. "You are not going! You're not leaving us!"

"Lucy? Keith?" Reverend Adams ran out of the house in his pajamas. "What's going on out here?"

Reverend Adams was the one person Keith didn't want to see. There was no way he could face his father. Not now. Not ever again. So he pulled away from his mother and ran.

"Keith, come back here! Keith!" His dad called for him, but he kept running until he vanished in the early morning fog that covered Bacon Street.

"No!" his mother's heart-wrenching scream followed him across distance and time.

Now, Keith stood and watched as his son ignored June's cries and ran away.

"Let me talk to him," Keith suggested to June, who had already taken off behind Trevor.

"No," she responded. "This is all my fault, so I have to straighten it out."

"Junie," he called.

She stopped in her tracks.

"Please, Junie."

She had not heard him speak her name since that night at Mildred's Bed and Breakfast more than ten years ago.

"Let me at least try."

She nodded for him to go ahead.

Trevor was in the car with the door locked. "You're not my daddy," Trevor yelled as Keith walked up to the car. "I just said that so you would talk to her."

"I know I'm not your daddy."

"Then leave me alone!" Trevor crawled over to the driver's seat. The keys were still in the ignition switch.

"Trevor, I just want to talk to you," Keith said.

Trevor started the car.

"Trevor!" June screamed. "Stop him, Keith! Stop him!"

Before Keith could move, Trevor shifted the gear into "Drive" and the car crashed into the picket fence.

"Open the door, Trevor," June demanded. But he didn't. Instead, he sat motionless, staring blankly ahead, gripping the steering wheel with both hands.

"Don't worry about the fence," Keith told him. "We just want you to open the door."

"Not until my dad gets here." Trevor turned and stared angrily at June. "You said I should always tell the truth. How come you're not?"

"I am telling the truth." June gazed into Trevor's tear-filled eyes. "I wouldn't lie about something like this."

"Well, you did," he replied. "You said Dad was my father. Now you're saying Keith is."

"Trevor, I think you should open the door and let your mother explain," Keith said.

"She won't tell the truth. She never tells the truth."

"I've never lied to you about anything other than this, and there was a reason I did what I did."

"You lied about your cramps and you made me lie."

June didn't know how to respond. She had asked him to lie about the day he walked into her room and saw her on the floor.

"Trevor, this isn't entirely your mother's fault," Keith admitted. "If you're going to be mad with someone, then that someone should be me."

June couldn't believe her ears. She knew there was nothing Keith could tell Trevor to make him believe what they were saying about his father. But this guilt-ridden plea to Trevor was exactly what she'd been waiting to hear him say. It was her life that he destroyed when he eased out of the room that morning.

"I didn't leave her with any choice, except for the one she made," Keith explained to Trevor. "I'm the one you should blame."

"If you're my dad, why did you leave us?"

June anxiously awaited his answer to the question that had dogged her since that morning.

"You didn't love us?" Trevor asked.

"I did love you," Keith revealed. "I loved you more than I've ever loved anyone."

June knew Keith wasn't talking about Trevor. He couldn't have been. This was his first time seeing Trevor, so he had to be talking about loving her. He said he loved her more than he'd ever loved anyone. She convinced herself that that was what he meant to say. He didn't say why he left, but at least now, she knew it wasn't because he didn't love her.

"Please unlock the door," June implored.

"I want to go home," Trevor cried. He paused before unlocking the door. As soon as he pressed the unlock button, June snatched the door open and pulled him into her arms. "Please," he appealed to his mother. "I want to see Dad."

"Tomorrow," she said. "We'll go home tomorrow." If not for Trevor, June could have spent the rest of her life there with Keith. But her son needed her to help him put his life back together, and he came first. "Tomorrow we'll go home to Dad."

Keith had said more about his leaving than he had said since the day he left Hampton Springs. However, after inviting them inside, he immediately retreated back into the safety of his solitary world. Once again, he felt uneasy in her presence. The sound of her voice unnerved him. Her stolen glances left him feeling naked. But the worst thing was being able to sense her pain. That scared him.

"Can I get either of you anything to eat or drink?" he asked and stepped away from the room's only lamp. He hoped that the pockets of darkness created by the room's high ceiling and inadequate lighting could hide him from her.

"I'm fine," June answered. "What about you, Trevor?"

He didn't respond and only stared out of the window. It was

nearing nine o'clock, but Trevor still hadn't given up on his dad. He still expected him to show up and take him and his mother home. He wasn't afraid of facing Alex anymore. He wasn't going to ask his dad if his mother was telling the truth. In his heart, Alex was still going to be his dad, so he decided it was best to forget everything his mother had told him.

"He's okay," June said.

Trevor didn't seem to notice the uneasiness between his mother and Keith. He found solace in the dismal night sky, as he peered out the four-paned windows. Even after everything that had happened during the day, June was still having a hard time believing she was sitting in Keith's living room. She strained to catch a glimpse of him as he stood in the corner. She surveyed the room, but there was little to see because the lamp was covered by a gray-painted shade that was too large. Even in the darkness, June could tell that this old board and batten house, with its weather-worn exterior and bare walls, was much like its owner: An empty shell of what it once was.

"So, how have you been?" June asked Keith in a barely audible whisper. Keith didn't respond, which made June squirm in her seat. She didn't know what else to say. All those things she thought, wrote and even dreamed of saying when she saw him, somehow seemed inadequate. She wished that it was brighter inside the room so she could see his eyes. If she looked into his eyes, she would know what she could or could not say. They would tell her exactly what he was feeling.

"I didn't mean to drop in on you like this, but I really needed to see you," she told him, waiting for his reaction. Crickets chirping, owls hooting and the shrill baying of coyotes weren't enough to drown out the silence that filled the room. "I know you didn't want to see me, but I had no choice. I needed to talk to you." She waited for him to say something. Anything. But he didn't. "Can I be upfront with you?"

"No," he quickly answered.

"Keith, don't you think it's time we talked? I mean, it's been ten years. I don't know what I did to make you hate me so much, but don't you think it's time we at least talk about it?"

He ran away from home and the people he loved to keep from having to answer questions like the ones she was asking. He couldn't answer them then, so why should she expect him to be able to answer them now? Surely, he would have confessed and told her why he could no longer live with himself after that night if it was that easy. He ran and he kept running until he found a place that would allow him to start over and forget that chapter of his life.

"Keith," she said, "I need you to—"

Keith was out the front door before June finished her statement. He'd heard all he cared to hear. He wanted to stay and listen, to be strong for Trevor, whose eyes watched attentively as he hurried past him, but after ten years of denying nearly everything about his life with her, he didn't want to remember those forgotten pages.

"Why?" he questioned the heavens. He lost his faith the day he ran away. "Why won't you leave me alone?" He gave up praying and the special conversations he thought he had with God that day. "I did what I had to do. Didn't I?" The answers he sought never came.

By the time Keith built up enough courage to go back inside, Trevor was asleep on the sofa. June tried to get him to sleep in one of the bedrooms, but he insisted on sleeping in the living room so he could hear when Alex came. Keith closed the door behind him and tiptoed across the wooden floor so he wouldn't wake Trevor. He stared at Trevor, who was curled up under the crochet blanket Mrs. Adams made for him last Christmas. "My son," he told himself. And then he heard her singing.

"Suddenly," June's voice wafted from the shower. "I don't know what I feel. I'm feeling so alive, your love has got to be real."

He was drawn down the dimly lit hallway toward the bathroom.

"Can you promise me," she crooned over the pitter-patter of the shower, "that you will always be, right here, beside me? Is forever…what our future reveals? This time, boy, love has got to be real."

He remembered losing himself in her melodies.

"I'd given up on love. I was watching out for me. Until you came back, and set my heart free."

He missed her even more now.

"Now I don't understand all these emotions I feel," she sang. "But I'm feeling so alive, love has got to be real."

He was entranced. Which was probably why he didn't hear her turn off the shower or notice the widening shaft of light when she pushed the door open. He was more startled than June was when she stepped out of the bathroom with a towel wrapped around her.

"I'm sorry," he said and turned his head to keep from looking at her. "I didn't mean to scare you."

"Actually, it's my fault," she countered. "I should have asked you if it was okay to use the shower."

"Go right ahead," he said and stole a glimpse of her. "I mean, it's all right."

June didn't try to hide her staring. This was the first time since she arrived that she'd been able to look at him up close, so she took her time and meticulously examined him. His caramel complexion had been bronzed by the Florida sun which, with his straight black hair, made him look like he was of Indian descent. His mustache was more tapered and his hair was cut shorter than it used to be. But other than that he looked like he did the last time she saw him.

Keith knew she was staring at him. He wanted to walk away, but he felt paralyzed.

"Are you okay?" she asked.

"Yes," he answered. "Just feels a little unusual having someone else in the house."

"Well, we'll be leaving tomorrow," she stated, moving to one side of the narrow hallway so she could get past him.

"I didn't mean it like that."

"I know."

As Keith slid past June, he mumbled, "That was a nice song you were singing."

"Thank you. It's from my new album."

"I heard." She stood close to him, so close he could feel the warmth of her body. "I heard you had a new album. Actually, a few photographers and reporters came here wanting to talk to me because they said my picture was on the cover."

"Our prom picture."

Keith tensed up again. She was too close. "I'll go so you can get dressed."

"Please don't," June said before she even realized what she was saying. He assented, but continued looking away. "Will you look at me?"

Keith shook his head no.

"Please."

"I can't."

"Why?"

"I don't know why." June warily reached for his hand. Shivers went through both of them when she touched him. He snatched his hand away. "Junie, I can't."

"Keith, I came here because I had to see you," she said and fought to hold back the tears. "Right now, it doesn't matter what happened, or why you left. I need to feel you again." She let the tears flow. "I need you to hold me."

The woman standing in front of him was the girl he used to love. And if there was one thing he remembered about her, it was her ability to deal with whatever the situation was and move on. She was the reason he stayed in Hampton Springs as long as he did. Had it not been for her, he wouldn't have been able to stay past his fifteenth birthday.

"Please," she begged. "I don't expect anything more. I only need you to hold me."

"Hold you? How do I?"

"The same way you used to," she responded.

Keith knew that something other than the need to see him brought her here. She needed something more. Something he wasn't sure he would be able to give her.

"I'm sorry, Junie, but I can't do this."

"Why?" she asked.

"Because things are different now. You're different and I'm different."

"Yes, we are different. We've both changed. Time has a way of doing that to people."

"We can't go back there, Junie."

"I know we can't go back, but that doesn't mean we have to forget who we were then." She tried to get him to look at her again, but to no avail. "I went on with my life after you left, but I never gave up on you. I never gave up and I never forgot how much I loved you and how much you loved me. I couldn't forget. So how could you? How?"

"I didn't, Junie," he confessed and slowly opened his arms. "I didn't forget." He took her in his arms and held her close to him. Years ago, his touch ruined her life. Now, it was saving her.

"You Just Don't Know"

(lyrics and arrangement by June)

I didn't know you were going away.
You didn't say you were going to stay.
I don't know what went wrong;
Or why your love is gone.

CHORUS:
You just don't know,
how I've been missing you,
how I've missed kissing
and loving you.

You just don't know,
how I miss holding you,
holding you next to me.
My heart is so empty.

Every day that passes,
I think of what we had.
Why did you have to go?
Tell me, I need to know.

Cause I'm holding back the tears,
from loving you all these years.
I need you here with me.
Come back, oh baby please.

CHORUS

I've tried to forget your touch,
how I loved you so very much.
It's time that I let you know,
that I've never let you go.

(MUSICAL BRIDGE)

Oh, you just don't know,
how much I'm missing you.
missing holding you;
kissing and loving you;
You just don't know.

Chapter 10

"**D**earest," Keith typed. "Yesterday, the life I'd been running from caught up with me. It found me barely existing, hiding in a world inhabited by only myself and the creatures of the surrounding hammock."

He stopped typing, closed his eyes and listened for the familiar sounds that signaled the morning's approach. The unusually chilly autumn wind roused the cypress and oak leaves and blew the screen door open and shut. Other than that, there were no other sounds to be heard, which meant he would have to wait a little longer to see her. He could see the window of the bedroom where June slept from the porch. The room was still dark, but he knew she would be up soon. Even though it had been more than ten years since the last time they watched the sun rise over Bacon Street, he knew she still thirsted for sunrises.

He adjusted the wick on the small kerosene lantern to dim its warm glow. He turned and stared at the words he'd typed on the manual typewriter that once belonged to his father. "Yesterday, the life that I'd been running from caught up with me," he read aloud. "It found me hiding, barely existing, in a world inhabited by only myself and the creatures of the surrounding hammock."

He returned the carriage to the left margin, tabbed over a few spaces and typed, "It stared me in the eyes and made me remember."

The gleam of the lantern bathed the corner of the porch where

Keith sat in a pale yellow light. It cast a shadow across the rest of the porch. And it was from a dark corner on the opposite side of the porch that June first saw him smile. It was when he typed and then read, "And then the little boy with the familiar face called me Dad."

She had not been able to sleep, so she eased out of bed and slipped onto the porch, where she hid in the shadows and watched him. She sat quietly remembering things about him and moments spent with him she'd somehow forgotten. Moments like, giving him his first shave after he refused to clip the stubble that covered his face. For two hours, she reminisced and watched as he searched for words to describe everything that had transpired since she walked back into his life.

This was the way he expressed whatever he was feeling. He rarely verbalized the angst, the sadness or even the occasional joy he felt. Instead, whenever he was troubled or on one of the rare days when he found something to smile about, he put it down on paper. He regularly wrote letters to himself. "Dearest," was the way the letters always started. He would go on to record moments from what most people would consider an insignificant life. "I sat outside on the steps and watched as the afternoon rains came and went," might be the only thing he wrote on a day when words were scarce or he deemed them unnecessary. Some days he would ramble on about whatever came to mind, whether it was about the playful antics of the redbirds outside his bedroom window each morning or his pensive efforts to reassure himself that he'd done the right thing by leaving all those years ago. And the letters would end, all of them, with "Missing You, Keith."

Keith stopped typing and looked up at the bedroom window. The room's still dark, he thought, but it won't be long.

June wrapped up in the tattered brown cardigan sweater Keith had given her to ward off the cold. She pinched herself again. The first time was to see if she was dreaming when he held her in his arms. This time it was to make sure she hadn't died and gone to Heaven. Nothing she'd experienced during her enviable life could match the majesty of the moment.

"He's waiting for me," she whispered. "Surely," she thought, "this must be Heaven."

Since arriving here, she had not worried about the malignant growth inside of her or even felt the almost insufferable pain ripping through her body. She unconsciously believed everything would be all right once she found him. That she could walk away from her fading life and start a new life with him, the life she was supposed to live anyway.

A mockingbird's song echoed in the quietude and the wind stilled to a faint breeze. In the distance, high above the mass of trees bordering both sides of the yard, morning neared.

Keith saw morning coming, which meant it wouldn't be long before the sunlight chased away the darkness. He stayed up most nights until sunrise working on his still untitled novel, and right before the sun peered over the horizon he would walk out to the road in front of his house, stand underneath the oaks and silently spend the dawning with her wherever she was.

He looked at his watch, turning his attention up toward the bedroom window. "She's going to miss it," he said to himself.

He heard her appear out of the darkness.

"Good morning," she said.

Keith turned around slightly startled and saw her standing in the doorway.

"I'm sorry." June felt slightly embarrassed. "I didn't mean to sneak up on you."

"I didn't see your bedroom light come on, so I figured you were still asleep."

"What are you writing?" June asked and then walked over to Keith and looked down at the words he'd typed.

"Nothing." He quickly rolled the sheet of paper out of the type-writer and placed it face down on the table.

"Personal, huh?" she asked.

"No, not really," he responded. He mulled over his initial response and changed his answer. "Well, sort of." Keith stood and motioned toward the screen door. "There's something I want you to see."

June followed him into the yard, up the straw-covered walkway, and out the gate. She looked a bit bewildered, trying to figure out what he wanted.

"Where are we going?" she asked as they started up Philco Road.

"Look around you, Junie. Just look."

Massive oak trees, one with a trunk almost four feet wide, lined both sides of the narrow dirt road. Their limbs met and crisscrossed over the road. Through the cluster of leaves, limbs and moss, June saw the first rays of sunlight searching for a pathway through the darkness.

"It's just like at home," Keith whispered.

June was mesmerized by the beautiful and familiar sight. Morning was almost upon them, and as she'd done thousands of times before, she closed her eyes and listened. A redbird chirped as it emerged from the shadows. A small branch fell in the brush. Among the serene sounds she indulged in, June heard a voice ask, "Why did you come here, Junie?"

She opened her eyes and looked at Keith, who stood directly in front of her, staring at her, waiting for her to respond.

"I know you, Junie," he said. "And I can tell when something's wrong."

June wished she could open up and tell him everything, but there was something she needed to know first. "Can I ask you something, Keith?"

"As long as it's not about that night," he answered.

"No," she said. "It isn't."

June saw the first ray of sunlight when it pierced the thick cover of foliage above them. It was followed by another, and several others, bending and turning until flashes of light and shades of darkness existed side by side.

Keith was shrouded in a pocket of light. He tried to move out of its way like he playfully did those mornings on Bacon Street, but the sunlight changed directions and followed him. He never understood this phenomenon, but she did.

"You're blessed," she told him one morning. "And it's not because your father's a preacher. God blessed you."

But he never felt blessed.

"What were you going to ask me?"

June pulled the sweater tighter around her and turned her back to him to avoid looking into his penetrating eyes. She had to keep him from seeing the tears forming in hers.

"Junie?" He touched her on the shoulder.

"Do you still love me?" she asked.

"What?"

"Do you still love me?"

"I don't know," he answered and backed away from her.

"How can you not know?"

"Because I try not to think about it," he mumbled.

"Then think about it!" She turned around to face him, frustration tinging the tone in her voice. "I need you to know!"

"I don't know, Junie. And besides, it doesn't matter," he tried to explain. "It shouldn't matter how I feel. Not now."

"But it does, Keith. It matters to me."

"Why, Junie? That was so long ago."

"Yes, it was a long time ago." She was nearly at the point to where she was ready for the dam to break. "Ten years ago. But, I never stopped loving you or believing in you because I couldn't. Now, please answer me."

He stared into her eyes and asked, "What's wrong, Junie?"

"Do you still love me?"

"Tell me what's wrong," he demanded.

"Not until you answer me! Do you still love me?"

Keith was ready to run. Run again. And there was nothing holding him. Nothing keeping him from running, except his feet. They had taken root in the dirt road and no matter how much he willed them to move, to carry him to a place where her words could not reach him, they would not let him go.

In the midst of his inner struggle, he remembered her lying in bed, balled up in the green comforter, half-smiling as she slept. And he was there beside her, staring blankly out the window of Mildred's Bed and Breakfast Inn at the drizzling rain. It was all coming back to him. Once again, he felt the stinging tears in his eyes as he quietly eased out of bed and fumbled in the dark for his clothes. He slipped on his underwear and then the sky-blue pants and white shirt. He picked up the patent leather shoes, stuffed the socks inside them, and tucked the tuxedo jacket underneath his arm. Finally, he turned and stared back at her for what he thought was sure to be the last time.

"Do you still love me?" June begged, but he could not hear her. Not where he was. He was in another time and place, and not even her melodic voice could reach him.

There were six steps between the bed and the door of the bedroom at Mildred's.

"Do you still love me?"

The first step was the hardest part of the journey.

"Answer me, Keith!"

But he made it. Somehow, he found the strength to take the first step…and the next…and the next…until he was at the door.

"You can't keep running away from me." June tried to grab for him, determined to get the answers she desperately needed. "I won't let you. Not this time. Aaaahhh!"

He couldn't hear her, but nothing prevented him from feeling her excruciating pain. He turned and looked back in time to see her collapse and fall to the ground.

"Junie!"

His eyes were wide open but he could not see.

Alex didn't see the bewildered stares and pointing fingers as he rushed into the lobby of the Cancer Center at Shands Hospital in Gainesville. He didn't see the sign directly in front of him.

"Can I help you?" a hoarse voice asked from behind him.

He turned around and saw a burly security guard.

"I'm trying to find the Cancer Center."

"You're in the Cancer Center," the guard pointed to the sign. "Patient information is right down the hallway."

Alex half-nodded and hurried off down the hallway.

"Cancer," he said to himself. Alex wasn't sure he had heard Leatrice right when she revealed June's secret a few hours earlier. He was in the parlor playing a song from June's new CD on the piano when the doorbell rang.

"I don't feel like celebrating," he sang softly and took a big gulp from the glass of brandy on the piano. "I don't feel like conversating. Don't feel like masquerading. I'm letting time pass me by."

The doorbell rang again. This time it was followed by a fist pounding on the door.

Alex stopped playing and looked at his watch. "Who in the hell could that be? It's two-thirty in the morning."

"Alex! Alex!"

"Hold on, Leatrice." He stumbled toward the door. "I'm coming."

Alex opened the door and started back toward the parlor without bothering to look at Leatrice or the crumpled sheet of paper in her hand.

"I need to talk to you," Leatrice said and closed the door behind her.

"I don't feel like talking!" Alex yelled from the parlor. He sat down at the piano, turning the glass of brandy up and emptying it.

"I should have told you this from the start," Leatrice said, walking into the parlor. "I never should have agreed to keep it a secret."

"If it's about Junie, I don't want to hear it," Alex said and turned his attention to the piano keys. He played the C sharp key and listened closely. "It's a little off-key. Needs tuning."

"Stop it!" Leatrice slammed the sheet of paper down on the piano in front of Alex. "Look!"

The headline blared from the sheet of paper, "What's Ailing June?" There was a picture of June wearily departing an airplane at Hartsfield-Jackson International Airport. It was obvious from the photo that June was in distress. Trevor was beside her, holding her up and guiding her through the crowd of onlookers.

"What's this?" Alex asked.

"I printed it off the internet," Leatrice answered. "It'll be all over the news tomorrow."

Alex stared at the photo for a few moments, waiting for his alcohol-influenced vision to clear. With the paper in hand, he walked over to the window and looked out at the fog-covered lake.

The light was still out on the dock. He wished he could go outside and lose himself in the darkness. He didn't know what Leatrice was about to tell him, but he wasn't ready to hear it. He wasn't ready to know. He closed his eyes tightly and wished he was somewhere else.

"Cancer," is all he heard Leatrice say.

"Cancer?"

"June has ovarian cancer." She sat on the piano stool, ready for the flurry of questions that Alex may have had. "I wanted to tell you, Alex, but she made me promise not to."

"Cancer? Junie? My Junie has cancer?"

"I begged her to tell you."

"How long, Leatrice?"

"Four, maybe five months," she answered. "She needs you, Alex. She really needs you."

Alex bolted for the door. Leatrice hurried behind him, but he was backing out of the driveway when she rushed out the door. Within the hour, he was on a plane to Florida. He wasn't sure what he was going to say to her or how he could help her once he got there, but he had to be there with her. Nothing else mattered.

Everything made sense to him now. He understood her sudden need to record her new CD, *The Pages We Forget*, quitting the entertainment business which she loved so dearly, and most of all, her insatiable appetence for Keith. Maybe, Alex thought, everything that went on during the past few months was a direct result of her illness.

"Lord," he silently pleaded as he peered out of the airplane's window. "I know I haven't been much of a praying man, but please hear me now. I don't know what I would do if I lost her. I can't lose her. So please, if you're listening Lord, help her. Help her."

Alex didn't hear the flight attendant announce the plane's descent or tell passengers to fasten their seatbelts because he was watching the sunlight variegate across the morning sky. He never shared June's lust for sunrises, but staring out at the luminous flecks of sunlight sprinkled across the billowing clouds below, made him feel closer to her. He believed deep down that they were sharing this moment together.

"Excuse me, sir," the flight attendant leaned over and said. "Can you please fasten your seatbelt? We're about to land."

Alex fastened his seatbelt without taking his eyes off the dawning outside the window.

"Thank you," she said and walked off.

The black Escalade that Leatrice called and reserved for Alex was parked outside of the airport terminal. Within minutes of the plane's landing, he was on his way to Micanopy. He was an hour away when his cell phone rang.

"Dad," a tearful voice cried out through the phone.

"Trevor?"

"Dad, where are you?"

"I'm on my way there. Where's your mother?"

"She's in the hospital, Dad."

"Do you know the name of the hospital?"

"It's in Gainesville," Trevor answered. "It's called Shands Hospital."

"Where are you?"

"In the waiting room at the hospital."

"Is anyone there with you?"

Trevor hesitated before answering, "Yes, sir."

"Who?"

"His name is Keith."

Alex took a deep breath before responding. "Trevor, stay with Keith. I'm on my way."

"Hurry, Dad," Trevor's voice cracked over the phone, nearly breaking Alex's heart. "Please hurry."

The forty or so miles to Gainesville passed in a blur.

"Can I help you, sir?" a stocky male nurse asked when Alex ran up to the nurses' station.

Before Alex could respond, a nurse who recognized him said, "Miss Thomas is in room 509. It's right around here."

Alex was already turning the corner before anyone could react.

"Room 509," he repeated in his head as he raced down the corridor. A middle-aged woman was pushing her ill husband in a wheelchair. Her husband, a mere frame of the man his broad shoulders and big hands suggested he once was, stared blankly at Alex. Chemotherapy and radiation therapy had left him with only a few strands of sandy brown hair on his bobbing head. He looked weak and tired. Their eyes met for a moment when they passed. It was long enough for Alex to be staggered by the air of hopelessness that surrounded the man. He saw what he and June were up against.

"Dad!" a voice yelled from behind him.

Alex turned and saw Trevor running toward him. He dismissed the feelings of dread that had momentarily crippled him and hurried to meet his son. Trevor leaped into his arms. A river of tears flowed from Trevor's eyes as he tried to tell Alex everything that had happened since he and his mother left Michigan. "And Ma said that Keith was my daddy."

"I know," Alex whispered in his ear. "I know."

"But Dad!"

"Not now, Trevor," Alex pleaded. "Please, not now."

Trevor regarded his dad's expression. Everything his mother told him was true, and he was discerning enough to know the depth of his dad's pain. So he reached for his dad's hand. Trevor led him toward the room.

Alex stalled as they approached the door. He desperately tried to hold back his tears. "I can't, Trevor."

"It's okay, Dad." Trevor put his arm around Alex, steadying him. He eased the door open, guiding him inside. "Ma's going to be all right. She said she was."

Alex didn't know what to expect when he walked into the room. He was slightly relieved when he saw June sleeping peacefully. He stopped at the door and stared at June. Before she left for Micanopy, he had not noticed anything different about her. But now that he knew about the cancer, she looked sickly to him. Her eyes sat back in their sockets. Her skin was pale and she looked thin, a lot thinner than usual.

"Why, Junie?" he asked as he walked up to the bed. He stared down at her and then he took her hand in his. "Why didn't you tell me? I could have helped you."

He loved her more than he loved himself, and seeing her like this, so frail and anemic, was tearing him up inside.

"Dad, don't cry," Trevor said and reached across the bed to hold their hands. "She's going to get well."

Alex looked up at Trevor and tried to smile. He looked down at June, nodding at his son's words. "You're right, everything's going to be fine. I promise."

Trevor was even more certain his mother was going to be okay. His dad said she would be. He smiled, then looked past Alex. Suddenly, his smile soured.

"What?" Alex asked. "What's wrong?"

And then a voice called from behind him, "Alex."

Alex turned around and saw a man standing in a corner of the room. The man looked strikingly like his son.

"Hi. I'm Keith."

"Somewhere In Your Heart"

(music and lyrics by June)

There are a million stars in the sky tonight,
and I'm wishing on them all.
Hoping they'll lead you back to me,
and you know just where I'll be.

And if memories cloud your path,
make you forget your way home.
My love can lead you through the dark,
if you kept me in your heart.

CHORUS:
I'm hoping you found a place,
somewhere in your heart
to keep our dreams
while we're apart.

I hope you saved a place,
somewhere in your heart
that belongs to me
when your new life started.

I thought I saw your face tonight,
and heard your voice in the wind.
I felt you reaching out to me;
That's what I made myself believe.

Sometimes dreams can make you lose your way,
when you're going it all alone.
But my love can carry you through the dark,
if you kept me in your heart.

CHORUS

So when your world is cold,
and your spirits broke,
take a moment to look inside.
And wherever you are,
I will be there,
if you saved a place in your heart.

CHORUS
(Repeat to fade)

Chapter 11

Kathryn wasn't sure why she clipped the article from the *Orlando Sentinel* and then folded it neatly and placed it in a shoebox labeled: "Things Kept." Inside the shoebox was a Ziploc bag containing a crumpled yellow rose taken from the blanket of flowers that covered her husband's coffin, all of June's grade school and high school report cards, and an autographed copy of June's first single, "Something Special." She was sitting at the table eating breakfast when she opened the morning paper and saw the blaring headline: "Doctors try cancer drug on humans."

'LOS ANGELES—*A potential treatment for cancer that kills tumors by starving them of their blood supply is being tested on humans by doctors at the University of California here, researchers reported Wednesday.*'

That was all she read of Mark Egan's story, but she felt the piece was worth keeping. She carefully clipped the article from the front page and the jump from page A-16 then put it in the box of kept things. She didn't think about it again until one Sunday morning months later as she and Lucy Kaye were walking to church. After a few minutes of silently debating why she thought the article was important enough to keep, she concluded it was because her husband had died of prostate cancer and she had been subconsciously remembering how her prayers for a cure went unanswered.

Kathryn sat in front of the television watching *The Wendy Williams Show* and fumbling with the phone in her lap. She was already on pins and needles waiting to hear from June, when Lucy Kaye snatched the screen door open and ran into the living room. "Junie's in the hospital!"

"The hospital?" Kathryn stood.

"Keith just called me."

"What happened? What did he say?"

Lucy Kaye hesitated before saying, "He said she has cancer and—"

Kathryn didn't wait for Lucy Kaye to finish telling her what Keith had said. She was already in her bedroom closet pulling out her box of "Things Kept."

"Keith said she collapsed this morning, but she's stable right now," Lucy Kaye walked into the room and said. "Alex just got there."

Kathryn didn't hear anything Lucy Kaye was saying because her mind was on the article.

"Kathryn, what are you looking for?"

She opened the box and there it was, underneath a yellow daisy-shaped Mother's Day card Trevor made a year ago.

"What's that?" Lucy Kaye asked when Kathryn took the article out of the box.

Kathryn grabbed her pocketbook off a hook in the closet and rushed by Lucy Kaye.

"I'm going with you!" Lucy Kaye yelled and hurried down the stairs behind Kathryn.

An hour and twenty-seven minutes was all it took for Kathryn to drive the 112 miles to Gainesville. Along the way, she explained to Lucy Kaye how she had seen the article in the newspaper one morning about thirteen years ago, then after reading only the first paragraph she deemed it worth keeping.

It was a little past noon when Kathryn weaved the silver Cadillac through the congested traffic and to the valet parking area. A handful of reporters and photographers were already planted across the street from the hospital's entrance. Pictures of June at the airport in Atlanta were all over the internet and in newspapers across the country, and her sickly appearance in the photos following her sudden retirement led to much speculations. Earlier that morning, Keith rushed into the emergency room, grabbed a wheelchair, and ran back to get June. Three hours later, as June was being transferred to the Cancer Center, calls from the media began flooding the hospital's phone system.

"Mrs. Thomas!" one of the reporters yelled when Kathryn got out of the car. "What can you tell us about your daughter's condition?"

Kathryn ignored the question, grabbed Lucy Kaye by the hand, and rushed inside.

"Room 509," Kathryn repeated as they hurried down the hallway.

"Can I help you?" a nurse asked Kathryn and Lucy Kaye.

"I'm looking for room 509," Kathryn responded.

"May I ask who you are?" the nurse questioned.

"I'm her mother."

The nurse looked suspiciously at Kathryn and Lucy Kaye.

"She's telling the truth," Lucy Kaye interjected. "She's Junie's mother and I'm her neighbor."

"Follow me." The nurse got up from her station. "She's right this way."

Kathryn and Lucy Kaye followed the nurse down the hallway.

"Excuse me, but I didn't get your name," Lucy Kaye commented to the nurse as they followed her down the hallway.

"Beverly," the nurse replied. "Beverly Flanders."

"Beverly's a pretty name." Lucy Kaye smiled. "My name's Lucy Kaye Adams. I'm Kathryn's—"

"Lucy, please!" Kathryn cut her off. "Not now."

Lucy Kaye apologized, even though the small talk with Beverly allowed her to distance herself from the anxiety and uncertainty Kathryn felt as they approached June's hospital room. She'd been down this road before. She was unwilling to believe that the article clutched between Kathryn's trembling fingers was going to make everything all right. Her friend's iteration of Psalm 23 as they walked toward the room was as futile an effort as the article.

As much as she wanted to shield her friend, Lucy Kaye could only help Kathryn understand the sobering truth that she was subjected to: that a mother's love, no matter how unconditional and strong, can't cure all their children's ailments. She understood that truth. Her son, who she had not seen in over seven years, walked out of her life without ever saying why. And all her love, all her prayers, could not bring him back.

When Keith returned home for his father's funeral, Kathryn's advice to Lucy Kaye was to demand that he stay home. "You're his mother," Kathryn told her. "Don't let him go back. Make him stay." But she couldn't. She saw the same hurt in his eyes that she had seen the morning he ran away.

At first she prayed for his return and she believed her prayers were heard by someone other than her. But after ten years of praying for his return, her prayers were more out of routine than actual appeals to God. Even still, when she turned the corner and saw Keith walk out of June's room, she stopped in her tracks, thanked God, and burst into tears.

Keith saw his mother about the same time she saw him. Unable to will his feet to move, he stared mutely at Lucy Kaye until her empty arms reached out for him.

"Keith," she called to him, waving her arms slightly, willing him to her. "Baby."

Until a few hours ago, he was content with the life he'd resigned himself to. He was despondent when he walked away from his mother, father, June, and everyone else who loved him because he could no longer live with the fear that they might find out the horrible secret he was living with.

So he ran. And ran.

"Please," Lucy Kaye begged.

"Ma." He rushed into her arms, the tears coming with the ferocity of a monsoon. "I'm sorry. I'm so sorry. I had to go. I had to, Ma."

"It doesn't matter." She pulled him closer. "You're here and nothing else matters."

Kathryn put her arms around Lucy Kaye and Keith, whispering in Lucy Kaye's ear, "Hold on to him, Lucy. This time, hold on and don't let go. Never let go of him."

Kathryn kissed Keith on the forehead then went to June's room.

Alex was sitting in a chair at the foot of June's bed when Kathryn eased the door open. She stopped in the doorway and stared disbelievingly at her daughter who was still asleep. Kathryn didn't notice Alex when he stood and walked over to her. She didn't feel him when he put his arms around her and waited for her to embrace him in the secure and maternal way she always did.

"I didn't know," he told her.

Kathryn didn't speak, but Alex took comfort in her recognition of his presence as she put her arms around him, held him for a brief moment, and patted him on the back.

"I have to check on Trevor." Alex broke from their embrace. "I asked a nurse to sit with him in the waiting room while I spoke with the doctors."

"And?"

"They're still running tests," Alex answered. "But it's not looking too good."

Kathryn felt lightheaded and her knees buckled, but Alex was there to keep her from falling.

"Are you okay?" Alex asked and helped her to a chair.

"I'm fine," Kathryn answered. "Now, go check on my grandson."

Alex turned and walked out of the room. He stared back at June as the door closed behind him. He didn't want to leave her, but he knew Kathryn needed this time with her daughter.

A few minutes passed before Kathryn moved toward June's bed. She stood there gazing at her peaked daughter, wondering how she could have been so blind. Although she felt something was wrong in June's life when she saw her two days ago, she didn't figure it was anything like this.

Kathryn took a step toward the bed and hesitated before going any closer. She was convinced that she held the answer to June's problems in her hand. Still, she could not force herself to go any closer because it was like reliving the morning her husband died.

"Go outside with Junie," she remembered him telling her that morning. "Go outside and watch the sunrise with our girl."

"No," she responded. "I'm not leaving you alone. I'm staying right here."

"Please," he begged.

"I said no."

He could barely lift his hand so he turned his hand palm-side-up and she placed her hand in his. It was in that moment that she told the only man she'd ever loved that it was okay for him to close his eyes and let go. Her heart broke but she had to release him. No matter how much he suffered he would not leave until she let him go.

"If it's time to go, then go." She kissed his forehead. "Please don't stay here suffering for us. We'll be all right."

She felt his body tremble and then their teary eyes met. Kathryn realized it would be the last time she lost herself in his now listless eyes. "I love you, Henry," she avowed. "I've always loved you and I always will."

He closed his eyes and passed away quietly, listening to the joyful laughter of his six-year-old daughter as she welcomed the sunrise underneath the tree canopy covering Bacon Street.

Now, twenty-three years later, Kathryn recalled details about that morning that she hadn't thought about since then. She remembered waking up and listening to her husband and daughter talking. She was surprised because June wasn't an early riser. But that morning, she was wide awake.

"I couldn't sleep last night, Daddy." June bent down and whispered to her dad as he lay in bed staring out the open window. "An angel kept talking to me in my sleep."

Henry tried to smile. "What did the angel say?"

"She said it was time for you to come home," June answered. "I told her you were already home."

Henry motioned for June to be quiet when Kathryn, pretending to be asleep, rolled over, continuing her pretense.

"Junie," Henry said softly. "Do you know where God lives?"

"In Heaven," she answered.

"Do you know who else lives there?"

"The angels."

"And who are the angels?" he asked.

"Good people who died," she replied.

"That's right, baby. When good people die, they go to Heaven to live with God and become angels." He finally managed a smile. "I'm going to let you in on a secret. The best time to talk to God or simply to hear Him and the angels speak is in the morning right as the sun begins to rise."

"Really?"

"If you go outside and listen real close, you'll hear Him. It might not be words you hear, but if you listen closely, Junie, you'll hear Him and the angels."

"Can I see Him, Daddy?"

"You might not see Him, but you'll feel His presence," Henry answered. "Why don't you go outside and see?"

June turned and ran toward the bedroom door.

"Junie," Henry called. "Daddy loves you and I always will. Don't you forget that."

"I won't," she said and started out the room. She turned around suddenly, walked back to the bed, then leaned over and kissed him. "I love you, too."

"You better hurry," he said, trying his best to hold back the tears. "Sounds like I hear Him."

"Don't go to sleep, Daddy." June turned and blew a kiss. "I'm coming right back."

"I won't," he answered.

When Kathryn heard the front door close behind June, she turned to Henry, who stared out the window. "Henry, what was Junie talking about?"

"She had been dreaming," he answered.

"About what?"

"Angels." He recalled the recent conversation with a smile. "An angel told her it was time for me to come home."

Kathryn was silent. Even though she'd heard the entire conversation between Henry and June, Henry had never said anything to her that might suggest he knew he was dying. When Lucy Kaye's husband, Reverend Adams, came by to pray for him, he gratefully declined. Whenever the doctors' prognosis wasn't what he wanted to hear, he cordially thanked them for their professional opinion.

He even refused hospitalization, saying he was needed at home. After months of silent denial, he had finally spoken about going home.

Kathryn walked into the bathroom and closed the door behind her.

"Kat," Henry called for her.

Kathryn opened the bathroom door and stared at her dying husband.

"Kat, why don't you go outside with Junie? I'll be here when you get back. I promise you. I'm not going anywhere."

"Is it time, Henry?"

"No," he answered. He tried to hide the hesitation in his tone, giving a weak smile as proof of his conviction. "I'm not leaving my girls."

Kathryn sat down beside him. She'd watched him suffer over the past eight months, and as much as the thought of living without him terrified her, she wanted him to know that it was okay for him to go on home. He was ready to go, but he didn't think she was ready. Giving up wasn't part of her nature. She was a woman who held on. Her faith never wavered, until the morning she whispered to her husband, "If it's time to go, then go."

Kathryn's life went on, but everyone around her knew she lost more than her husband that morning.

Kathryn stared at June as she began to stir. She hadn't considered what she was going to say when June woke up. One thing was certain: She wasn't going to tell June it was okay to let go like she had told Henry. She was going to fight harder this time. Even if June didn't have the strength or will to fight, Kathryn had enough fight in her for both of them. There was no way she was going to let her daughter die.

June knew someone was standing near the bed. She couldn't see who it was, but she could feel the person staring at her. Her vision was blurred, so she squinted to get a better view of the person. "Ma?"

"It's me, Junie," Kathryn said.

June had hidden her illness from everyone except Leatrice. She realized that telling Alex would be hard and telling Trevor would be even harder. But having to tell her mother she had cancer was next to impossible. She was only a child when her father died, but more than anyone else, she was aware how much her mother lost when he died.

"Ma, is that you?"

"Yes, baby." Kathryn wiped away the tears she had fought desperately to hold back. "I'm right here and everything's going to be all right."

"But, Ma…" June tried to talk, ready to confess everything she'd been hiding. "I'm sick."

"Yes," Kathryn agreed. "But I promise you that you will be okay. You're going to get better."

June became her mother's reason for living when Kathryn's life ended with her husband's twenty-three years ago. Now, June was lying in a hospital bed facing her own mortality. But this time, Kathryn wasn't giving up. And she wasn't going to let her daughter give up, at least not without a fight.

"I'm Remembering"

(lyrics and arrangement by June)

There was a time,
when you were mine.
And we had the world
in our hands.

Now, you've gone away,
and left me blue.
So down and out,
I don't know what to do.

CHORUS:

I'm remembering how it used to be.
I'm missing you, oh can't you see.
I'm not the same, without you here.
I'm remembering, you my dear.

You were my first,
my first love.
To you I gave my all,
but it was not enough.

You broke my heart,
still no one can take your place.
You left tracks of tears
across my face.

CHORUS

What will it take
to bring you back?
I'm on my knees
begging please.

It's been too long;
Boy, I miss what we had.
Since you've been gone,
I've been so sad.

CHORUS
(repeat to fade)

Chapter 12

"I love her as much as any man could love a woman. I mean, I don't know what I'd do without her. I tried to do what I thought was right by helping her find you, but the second she walked away from me, my whole world fell apart. I wasn't even sure how I would wake up the next morning without her beside me. I'm not telling you this because I want you to run away and ignore her again. That's not what I want, especially not now. But I hope you'll understand and consider how much she means to Trevor and to me."

Alex glanced over at Keith, who stared blankly ahead. "I guess the real reason I'm telling you this is because I'm lost and I don't know what to do or what to expect anymore. Now that she's found you, I feel like I'm losing her. I haven't felt this threatened or scared since the day your father passed and she flew home hoping to see you. I made her leave Trevor at home with me, as sort of a guarantee that she would be back. That's how much I love her. But sometimes that's not enough for her. And the truth is it's because of you. Please don't take that the wrong way. It's just that you still have a place in her heart, a place that no one else will ever be able to occupy. I don't know what happened between the two of you back then, but she hasn't been able to get past it."

"Neither have I," Keith mumbled without taking his eyes off of the road or Kathryn's car. As they crossed the bridge over the Suwannee River into Dixie County, he could see June in the backseat of Kathryn's car. "I asked to ride with you because I wanted to thank you."

"Thank me?" Alex asked.

"For being there for Junie after I—"

"After you left?"

Keith answered by nodding his head as he continued staring ahead.

"I know it's none of my business and I already know you don't want to talk about it, but I need to know what happened that night. Why did you leave?"

"What did Junie tell you?"

"She doesn't know," Alex answered. "But she needs to know why you left. That's why she came here looking for you."

The blank expression on Keith's face suggested he wasn't listening, but Alex wasn't buying it. Keith had taken in every word he said, there was no denying it. Alex had seen this look before. June wore it often, and he recognized the nonchalant expression as nothing more than a mask. A way of distancing herself from the torrent of repressed emotions surrounding that part of her life.

Keith wore the same mask.

"So, why won't you talk to her? Or to me if talking to her is too difficult? That night has haunted her for way too long. And it's time, man. You have to put her mind at ease."

Alex anxiously awaited a response from Keith, but none came. He was hoping Keith would finally answer the question that had plagued not only June's life, but his own life. What he didn't expect was for Keith to suddenly confess to him what he hadn't told his mother, father or anyone else. It was easy to see that this man, who reminded him of his son Trevor, was still running. Keith still couldn't look directly at his mother, Kathryn, or June. Whenever they spoke to him or came near him, he lowered his head and retreated to a place inside himself far from the life and people he abandoned.

As the two cars headed north on U.S. 19 through Cross City and then Perry toward Hampton Springs, Bernard and Leatrice led a horde of photographers in another direction along Interstate 75. It was Bernard's idea to wait until about four a.m. to pull the limousine around to the rear entrance of the hospital and have Leatrice impersonate June, saying goodbye to everyone before getting in the car. That was sure to catch the attention of the photographers and videographers who had camped out across the street from the hospital since June was admitted. Bernard's plan was to have Alex tail the limousine in his car, and when the paparazzi pursued them, Kathryn would pull around to the emergency room entrance and pick up June. After Kathryn, June, Lucy Kaye and Trevor were well on their way to Hampton Springs, Alex and Keith would double back and meet them in Newberry, a small town west of Gainesville.

During the four weeks June was hospitalized, Dr. Wylie flew in from Detroit to work with the specialists at the Cancer Center. Tests showed that the cancer was in Stage Four, the most advanced stage. Distant metastasis had occurred and invaded organs outside the peritoneal cavity including the liver. Combinations of chemotherapy drugs were administered, but the cancer was very resistant. Kathryn even contacted one of the specialists cited in the article she'd saved and pleaded with him to come to Gainesville to evaluate June's condition. After speaking with the doctors already caring for June, he flew to Gainesville to pacify Kathryn.

"The drug we formulated won't be of any help now," he informed Kathryn after he reviewed June's medical records and her most recent treatment results.

"Are you telling me there's nothing you can do to help my daughter?"

"The doctors here are doing everything possible," he assured Kathryn. "I'm sure that Dr. Wylie will agree."

Dr. Wylie, who was seated in a chair beside Kathryn, nodded his head yes.

"They're some of the most knowledgeable doctors and specialists in the country when it comes to cancer research," Dr. Canon told Kathryn. "She's in very good hands."

"Good hands? If she's in such good hands, how come she's not getting any better? I've sat here twenty-four hours a day for almost a month and I've watched doctor after doctor come in here and administer test after test. But, in case no one's noticed, all these tests are not making her better. My daughter is getting sicker. She has never been big, but she weighs less than a hundred pounds now. She's nothing but skin and bones. Her hair's all gone. And I'm starting to think she can't talk anymore because she hardly ever says a word. I'm losing my baby and I'm not going to just sit here and let that happen." Kathryn's anger and frustration rose to the surface. "I want something done now. I want her up and feeling better. I want her laughing and talking with that little boy who has been lying in that bed beside her for the last four weeks. I need you to help her. I don't care about any tests. I just want you to help my baby get well."

"I'll do all I can," he reassured her and politely excused himself.

The next day, June made another decision that would change all of their lives.

"What do you think you're doing?" Alex marched in June's room and asked. "Dr. Wylie said you refused to go through the chemotherapy today."

"I'm done," June expressed in a dead pan manner.

"Sounds like you've given up." He walked over to the bed. "Is that what you've done?"

"Sit up, baby," June told Trevor, who lay beside her pretending to watch television.

"I asked you a question, Junie."

June closed her eyes and turned away from Alex.

"You can look away if you want to, but you're not leaving here until you're okay! So, whatever it is you're cooking up in that head of yours, you can forget it."

"I want to go home."

"Junie, you're sick! You can't simply up and go home! What about your treatments? How are you supposed to get better if you don't finish the chemotherapy?"

"Please, Alex. I want to spend my birthday at home."

"I know you're going through a lot, Junie, but we can't go to Michigan right now."

"I'm not talking about Michigan. I want to go to Hampton Springs. Alex, I need to see Hampton Springs one more time before—"

"Junie." Alex cut her off. "Please don't."

"Then take me to Hampton Springs. I've already told Dr. Wylie that I'm leaving."

Alex walked over to the window and looked out. He shook his head no. "Junie, I can't." Alex turned around and noticed Keith sitting in a chair in the far corner of the room.

"If you won't take me, Keith says he will," June said.

"Oh, really?" Alex turned to Keith. "So, did you help her make this decision?"

"No," Keith answered. "I'm as much against it as you are, but I understand why she wants to go back."

Alex understood, too, and like Keith, he wanted to give her everything she needed like he always did. However, this time doing so would be like giving her permission to give up and die. "I'm sorry, but I can't," he said.

When Dr. Wylie informed Kathryn of June's decision, Kathryn stormed into June's room. "What are you trying to do? If it is kill yourself, I won't be part of it! I'm your mother and I'm not going to help you die! You're going to stay right here and let the doctors do everything they can to help you! And you're going to help them by fighting! Do you hear me, Junie? You are going to fight!"

"I'm going home, Ma."

"Over my dead body!"

"Ma, I'm twenty-nine years old, which means I don't have to get your permission. But, I do want you. No, I need you to—"

"You need me? For what? To help you die? If that's what you need, I'm sorry but my answer is no."

Leatrice, who had been sitting in the room with June, put her arms around Kathryn. She and Lucy Kaye led Kathryn out of the room, leaving Alex, Keith and Trevor with June. Only a few seconds passed, but it felt like minutes before anyone spoke.

"Junie, you never did answer Alex's question," Keith reminded her. "Have you given up?"

"No, I haven't."

"So, why are you leaving?"

"Why? You want to know why I'm leaving?" she fired back. "For the same reason you left!"

Stunned by June's harsh retaliation, Keith stood and walked out of the room without saying another word or glancing her way.

"So, you're going to do what Junie wants to do and ignore the doctors and all the people who love you?" Alex asked. He never expected her to say what she did or to be so blunt and selfish.

"It's my life!"

"Your life?" Alex questioned. "Oh, really? So what about our son? Or have you forgotten about him? Tell me something, Junie. Are you going to give up and fade out of his life forever, or are you going to fight to stay here with him? The Junie I used to know would fight for him. She would never stop fighting for him!"

Alex turned and looked at Trevor, who was standing next to the window staring out. "I love you, Trevor. Don't ever forget that. Your dad loves you more than anything else in this world. And I will always love you."

He walked out the door without bothering to look back at June.

Trevor stood with his head hung low. He didn't want to look at his mother, because he promised her he would be strong, that he wouldn't cry.

"Who's your favorite girl?" June tearfully asked.

"You are," he answered, still not looking up at her.

"And who's my favorite boy?"

"Me...I guess."

"You guess?"

Trevor tried his best to ignore her by focusing on a group of children playing in an enclosed playground behind the hospital. Under any other circumstances, he would have gladly joined them. Instead, he wondered how they could be so cheerful while someone they knew and loved was inside sick.

"You guess, Trevor?"

He heard her but he didn't know how to respond, so he continued his charade, which he justified by pointing to her own months of pretense. He began to wonder how different things would be if she had not chosen to keep this horrible truth to herself. Trevor wasn't sure what he was feeling now. It wasn't anger. He was certain of that. It wasn't sadness because he hadn't given up. He still believed his mother was going to be all right. She promised him she would and that was enough for him. This feeling was one he'd never felt before.

"Trevor, I'm talking to you."

"Why?" he yelled, still with his back to her.

June wasn't prepared for Trevor's question. Alex and Kathryn asked the same question, but she felt no special obligation to answer them. But her son was a different story. She couldn't let his life be ruined like her life had been by that same question: Why? She owed him an answer, but giving him one proved to be more difficult than she imagined. She could tell him the truth. Dr. Wylie told her the cancer was highly treatable when it was first diagnosed, but instead of following his treatment plans, she elected to wait until she found the answer to her question.

"Why?"

"I don't know, Trevor. You may not believe me, but I really don't know why. When I first found out, I didn't do anything because I was just praying it would go away. I made myself believe it would. At least for a while. When it didn't, I got scared, and I tried not to think about it. I was scared, Trevor."

Trevor turned around and stared into June's tear-filled eyes. "Well, why are you leaving? Why won't you stay and let the doctors help you?"

Although June fully understood the inevitable, she'd never verbalized it to anyone other than Dr. Wylie, and she couldn't now. So she answered, "You know why, Trevor."

"No, I don't."

"Yes, you do," she pushed him to answer the question for himself. "I know how hard this is for you."

"Just tell me, Ma!"

No mother should have to tell her child what she was about to say. She needed help because her lips and heart would not allow her to speak those words. Not to him. His eyes begged for the truth, which meant that she had to tell him. So, she closed her eyes and uttered a prayer for the strength to tell Trevor. "I'm dying."

"Dying?"

Trevor was smart for his age, a man in a boy's body, his daddy often joked. He was strong and centered. Still, he was only a child.

"But, you promised!" he screamed. "Ma, you promised!"

"Don't, baby." June reached out for him. "Please don't cry. Please."

Slowly, he found his way into her waiting arms.

The next day, against everyone's pleas, she checked out of the hospital.

Trevor was lying in the backseat with his head in June's lap as the two cars turned onto Highway 98 in Perry. *Another sixteen miles and we'll be in Hampton Springs*, June thought as she stared out the window at the once familiar sights along the highway. Several elderly and middle-aged women were busy setting up for a yard and bake sale at Stewart Memorial A.M.E. Church. On the other side of the street, an elderly black man with a full, washed-out gray beard and a headful of jet-black hair was opening up a neighborhood bar. He waved to the women across the street and yelled something that made all of the women laugh. One laughed so hard, she fell on a table filled with pies. Had it not been for the lady on the other side of the table, the bake sale would have been without pies. June smiled. She wished she could have heard what the man said. She wanted to laugh like the women were laughing. She could barely remember what her own laugh sounded like.

"Do I need to turn on the air conditioner?" Kathryn asked, glancing in the rearview mirror at June.

June shook her head no. She and Kathryn exchanged glances in the rearview mirror and then both turned away. The two had not spoken directly to each other since June decided to leave the hospital. There was so much June wanted to tell her mother, but she knew Kathryn wasn't going to listen to anything she had to say until she told her why she kept the cancer a secret and why she refused further treatment.

Kathryn, on the other hand, had nothing to say, even if June offered an explanation. She felt betrayed in the worst way. How could her daughter do this to her? How could she simply give up? There was nothing June could tell her to make her understand. Kathryn wasn't going to abandon her daughter, though. June was ill and Kathryn was going to take care of her like she always did. But that would be it. She decided June's betrayal, deception and unwillingness to fight were unforgivable.

"Kathryn," Lucy Kaye said. "Why don't you let me cook Junie's birthday dinner, so you can spend the day with her instead of in the kitchen?"

"That sounds nice, Lucy," Kathryn replied, looking in the rearview mirror, ensuring that Trevor was still asleep. "But I'm not sure Junie wants to waste any time with me."

"Kathryn, don't say that." Lucy Kaye nudged her. "I think time with her mother is what Junie needs more than anything else. When she said she wanted to go home, she meant here with you. Right, Junie?"

Kathryn looked in the rearview mirror at June, whose tear-filled eyes were staring back at her in the mirror.

"Tell her," Lucy Kaye urged June. "Tell your mother how much you need her."

"Stop it, Lucy!" Kathryn demanded and defiantly pushed back the tears that were starting to blur the road ahead of them. "Just leave it alone!"

For the next twenty minutes, everyone sat quietly staring ahead until the car approached a sign that read: *Hampton Springs: Next Left*. Kathryn slowed down and put on her left blinker. June shifted Trevor's head in her lap and looked back to see Alex turning behind them. Kathryn looked in the mirror again at June, and was slightly startled by her daughter's radiant glow. Gone were the tears that smothered the childish sparkle in her eyes. Now, all she could see was June's famous million-watt smile.

"Precious Memories." June read the mini-billboard that hung over the antique shop at the edge of downtown. The sign, a painted montage of four children and their father tiptoeing through a pasture of pink and yellow tulips, had become a town marker. The painting also graced the back covers of the local telephone book and the Chamber of Commerce's annual "Welcome to Hampton Springs" pamphlet. The historic hotel graced the front covers of both. June worked at the store one summer when she was fourteen. It was the summer after Mrs. Rosa Lee's stroke. Mrs. Rosa Lee was a widow and mother of four children. Two of her children, a boy and a girl, died when they were children. Her son drowned while trying to catch tadpoles in a rain pond behind their house during dog days when he was five, and her daughter died of meningitis at the age of seven. Her firstborn son was declared missing in action while serving a tour of duty in Vietnam. Mrs. Rosa Lee once said she was convinced he was dead because she felt him die after being shot twice in the chest and neck. The baby boy was the only one living but he might as well be dead. He was serving a life sentence for killing a store clerk during a botched robbery in Perry. Mr. Bishop, her deceased husband, was the one who collected antiques. Mrs. Rosa Lee opened the store on July 4, 1976, the day after Mr. Bishop died. She said that the paintings, the clocks, the tin washtub and scrub board, and all the other items he treasured, made her miss him more. The store was open every day of every year until April 1986 when she had the stroke. It was closed for two months while Mrs. Rosa Lee recovered. When she opened again, she asked June to work there part-time until she got back on her feet. The store started out on her front porch but had expanded until it was hard to tell where the store ended and where the three-bedroom living quarters began. Nearly everything in the house was for sale.

One day, Mrs. Rosa Lee was in the kitchen frying chicken in a black cast iron pan while June helped a customer who had driven from Perry to shop at the curio shops along Willow Street.

The lady rushed over to the stove when she saw the cast iron pan. "I haven't seen one of those since I was a child."

"What?" June asked.

"This skillet," she answered. "My grandmother used to fry the best chicken in one just like this when I was a girl."

"Hi, I'm Rosa Lee."

"I'm Neddie Daniels. Please tell me, where did you find this skillet?"

"My cousin bought it in Madison four or five years ago," Mrs. Rosa Lee answered.

"And I've been looking for one like it for just about that long."

"This one's for sale."

"Really?" June gasped along with the lady.

"If you can wait until I finish frying this chicken."

As soon as she was done, Mrs. Rosa Lee washed and dried the skillet, placed a twelve-dollar tag on it and handed it to Neddie, along with the set of silverware, which was twenty-five dollars. She even invited Neddie to have lunch with them.

The job lasted two months. The school year started and Kathryn wouldn't allow June to work, thinking it might affect her grades. June continued to drop by and help out when she could, and she never forgot the advice Mrs. Rosa Lee gave her a few days after Keith ran away.

"You're going to have a wonderful life, Junie," Mrs. Rosa Lee told her. "Don't think of this as the end of your life. Look at it as a new beginning. You've got a whole new life ahead of you. This time, remember not to get too attached to anything you can't carry in your pocket. If it's too big to fit in your pocket, it's gonna either walk off, get toted off, be so heavy that it holds you down, or die on you. That goes for your children, too, if you ever have any. Love them. Love them with all your heart. But don't forget, sometimes there's a penalty for loving too much. That's why you're hurting now. You're paying the penalty. But remember, the pain will pass. You will smile again, and you will love again."

Inez strolled leisurely on the sidewalk toward the beauty salon she owned. Kathryn switched the car's headlights on and off to get her attention. When Inez saw Kathryn's car, she immediately turned and stared at the back seat. Her eyes met June's.

"I love you, Junie," Inez signed and then blew a kiss to her.

June signed back, "I love you, too."

She and Inez were best friends growing up, and they were still very close. Whenever June came to town, she had to spend an afternoon in Inez's chair. Inez always closed the shop for June's visit so they could spend the day like they used to in June's bedroom or on her back porch. While Inez practiced and perfected all kinds of styles on June, June would sing. And although Inez was born deaf and couldn't hear a word of what June was singing, she could feel the emotions in June's voice.

"There's the bakery," June mumbled to herself. "And Jeannette's."

June immediately thought about the baby-blue prom gown her

mother bought her from Jeannette's a month before that April night all those years ago. They were about to drive over to Tallahassee to look for a gown, when Kathryn suggested they at least look at the selection Jeannette had ordered. When June saw the spaghetti-strapped gown, she knew it was the one.

June basted in the turn-of-the-century ambiance of downtown. The buildings still looked the same as they did when the first trading post was erected in 1891. Two years later, the hotel began to lure visitors from around the country to the area. The former trading post now housed the only real Dime Store in North Florida. Mildred's Bed and Breakfast Inn, Citizen's Bank, The Philmore Mansion, another bed and breakfast, Pearl's Soda Fountain, Kathryn's Bakery, Inez's, the Historical Society, Towne Hall, six antique and curio shops, a Christian bookstore, and Doc Weathers' medical office made up the rest of the three blocks of downtown. Moss-covered oaks and dogwoods lined the two-lane street. The lanes were separated by a greenway of shaded park benches, birdbaths and drinking fountains. But the sight she longed for most was a little further up Willow Street. June let the back window down and stared out at the historical marker ahead until she was close enough to read it. A picture of the old Hampton Springs Hotel and the words "Sight of the Historic Hampton Springs Hotel" were engraved in the varnished cypress.

"Trevor's not too hot back there, is he?" Kathryn asked.

"He's fine," June answered and leaned closer to the window. She took in a breath of the lightly sulfur-tinged air.

Kathryn made the right turn onto Bacon Street, and waved at Deputy Anderson, who was sitting in his patrol car. He smiled and waved at June. When Kathryn told Sheriff Walker that June was coming home, he closed the street off to everyone except residents. A wooden fence bordered both sides of the narrow road, which was wide enough for two cars to pass. Mt. Nebo Missionary Baptist Church and the church cemetery sat off the dirt road to the left. The railroad tracks that once brought guests from all over the country to the old hotel was on the right.

A little further ahead, after the tracks crossed the road and disappeared into the forest behind the church, the towering oaks constructed a half-mile-long corridor along Bacon Street. This was where John Bacon, the hotel's founder, built majestic Victorian-style houses for his family, business associates, and living quarters for his more prestigious Northern guests. The houses were now occupied by the descendants of the hotel's African-American servants, who resided in rundown and cramped quarters behind the hotel. They called the servant housing area, Brown Quarters. When Mr. Bacon died in 1956, a few years after the hotel burned down, he left the houses and 125 acres to each of the seven Black families who were still living in Brown Quarters. Those families, which included June's Uncle Ben and Keith's grandfather, used the 125 acres of land to build their dreams. It wasn't long before they became part of the town's elite. Although they were very much a part of Hampton Springs' financial, social and political landscape, they saw themselves as a separate community.

Mrs. Croft, June's fifth grade teacher, was trimming the azaleas that surrounded her neatly manicured yard. When the cars passed, Mrs. Croft stopped what she was doing and hurried toward the road waving. She had read the newspaper articles and saw stories on TV about June's failing health. One network premiered an hour-long special, "Her Final Song," which really upset Mrs. Croft. She'd spoken with Kathryn on the phone several times while June was hospitalized, so she realized that most of the reports were true, but it still angered her to read and see news stories that talked about June like she was already dead.

Mr. and Mrs. Whitehurst stood at the gate to their yard, anxiously waiting for Kathryn's car. They met Mrs. Croft in the road and they walked together behind the two cars. They were joined by Miss Blue Hen and her fourteen-year-old grandson, and by Coach Rickards. By the time Kathryn and Alex pulled into the driveway, nearly every member of the seven families who lived on the street was walking in the yard behind them.

Alex parked behind Kathryn. He was about to open the door when he glanced over at Keith, who seemed oblivious to everything that was going on.

"Are you okay?" he asked Keith.

Keith didn't answer.

"Hey, man, I know this has to be hard for you, but you can handle it." Alex opened the door and got out of the car. "Junie needs you. We all need you," he said before closing the door. He walked over to Kathryn's car and opened the door for June.

"Hold on a second," Alex told June. "Let me get the wheelchair out of the trunk."

"That's okay," she responded. "I can still walk."

"I didn't mean it like that."

"I know you didn't."

Mrs. Croft stared tearfully at June. "Oh, my baby," Mrs. Croft cried. Lucy Kaye got out the car and put her arms around Mrs. Croft. "I can't believe this, Lucy. I can't believe this is happening."

"I can't, either," Lucy Kaye said and led her toward the porch. "But try not to let Junie see you upset."

The others gathered around. Some watched through tear-filled eyes, while others wore pasted-on smiles to hide the terrible loss they felt. They all claimed June as their own, and each in their own way, struggled to deal with the now certain outcome.

Alex helped June get her feet out of the car and lifted her up.

Trevor got out behind her and put his arm around her waist. Alex put one of her arms around his shoulders and they both supported her as she walked to the porch, glancing back at Keith.

"Alex, how's Keith?" Lucy Kaye asked. "Why hasn't he gotten out of the car?"

"He's coming. Give him a minute." Trevor and June both turned back to look at Keith, but Alex reassured them. "Trust me. He'll be okay."

"I hope so," Lucy Kaye said. "Oh, how I wish his daddy was here. He'd be able to talk to him."

Kathryn, who sat almost as paralyzed as Keith, finally got out of the car and immediately stepped into Coach Rickard's strong, supportive embrace. "Jordan, tell me why this is happening," she whispered in her friend's ear. "I need to know why."

"I don't know, Kathryn, but I'd give anything to make things right again. Anything."

Coach Rickards and Mr. and Mrs. Whitehurst followed Kathryn into the house, while the others stayed on the porch with June, Alex and Trevor. June exhaled. She was finally home with the people who truly knew her and loved her. Everyone was here, caring for her and wishing her well. Everyone except for him.

"Keith." Mrs. Blue Hen tapped on the car window. "Are you going to get out?"

Keith turned and looked at the stately old lady, nicknamed Mrs. Blue Hen because she began coloring her hair a dark shade of royal blue forty years ago when she discovered her first strand of gray hair.

"Hi," he said nervously.

She opened the door and stepped back so he could get out. "Keith," Mrs. Blue Hen whispered. "You know Mrs. Blue Hen isn't going to let anything happen to you, so give me a chance. Give us a chance. Please." She reached for his hand, which he placed in hers and stepped out of the car. Her grandson walked up and she introduced him to Keith. "This is my grandson, Simon. I don't know if you remember him."

"I do, but he was a little bitty fellow when I last saw him."

"He's fifteen now."

"Fifteen?"

Keith was fifteen when his troubles started.

"He's a freshman in high school," Mrs. Blue Hen said. "He's already a starting pitcher on the varsity baseball team. Coach Rickards says if he keeps it up and works hard, he's got a real shot at going to the majors one day."

His troubles started here in this place he used to call home fifteen years ago.

"Keith was one of the best ballplayers in the state when he was in high school," she told Simon. "He could have gone to the majors, too."

"Why did you quit playing?" Simon asked.

The look on Keith's face revealed he didn't have an answer to Simon's question, so Mrs. Blue Hen answered for him. "He decided to be a writer instead. And he's a very good writer."

"Do you ever miss playing ball?" Simon asked. "I mean, do you still dream of playing major league ball?"

"Not really," Keith replied. "I guess my dreams changed."

"My only dream is to pitch for the Braves." Simon beamed as he boasted about his dream. "And nothing's going to change that."

"Then hold on to that dream, and don't let anybody take it from you," Keith said and started up the walkway. "Hold on, Simon," he whispered to himself. "Hold on."

"*Sorry*"

(lyrics and arrangement by June)

Baby lay down,
here next to me.
Forget your worries,
let your heart beat free.
I won't get too close;
or ask what's going on.
I'm not here to judge you,
or to say what went wrong.
But there is one thing
that I need you to do.
You don't have to explain your actions.
But I need to hear sorry come from you.

CHORUS:

So baby, baby, baby,
why can't you say,
say you're sorry?
Cause baby, baby, baby,
I need to hear you say,
say you're sorry.

Sometimes it takes the dark
to bring out the light,
and the words, I'm sorry,
to end the fight.
So lay your troubles down,
give them all to me.

My love can keep you,
if you just believe.
But there is one thing,
that I need you to do.
You don't have to explain your actions.
I just need to hear sorry come from you.

CHORUS
(Repeat to fade with background)

Sorry is what I need. (Background)

Chapter 13

Can I touch you?
Touch me?
Yes. Can I?
Why do you want to touch me?
Because.
I'm sorry, but I don't want to do—
Sshhhh.
Please don't. Please.

That was when the line was crossed. Trust became an aphrodisiac, precipitating a violation that would undo Keith's life and all of their lives. Footsteps in the middle of the night when everyone should be asleep decided their fate. A wavering voice whispered into unreceptive ears. A button pried loose. *Sshhhh.* Lips kissing parts they shouldn't. Keith was the first to topple. Soon, like dominos, the others followed.

Reverend Adams had the hardest time living after the breach. He blamed himself, even though he never knew the line existed, let alone was crossed. He punished himself by concocting all kinds of unfounded reasons for Keith's leaving, eventually placing the blame squarely on himself. He had moved his family back to Hampton Springs so he could pastor the church on the corner of Bacon Street after his father, the church's minister, passed. He put

Keith on a pedestal and was raising him to be the next minister of Mt. Nebo, which had been led by an Adams since it was founded in 1903.

He expected a lot from his son. Reverend Adams acquiesced after three years of obsessive soul-searching that maybe he had put too much pressure on Keith and that's why he ran away. During those years, all of his sermons were about the need for parents and everyone in the community to open their eyes and truly see their family members and friends. Nobody minded the repetitious sermons. Easter. Christmas. Mother's Day. Father's Day. Every Sunday. They understood and they sympathized because they understood that he saw himself as a failure. He spent every day pondering the unfathomable. Why did his son walk, no, run out of his life?

"Stop doing this to yourself," Lucy Kaye would respond whenever he came up with what he thought was the most obvious reason. The reason that had been staring him in the face all along and he had been too blind to see it.

"That has to be it," he would tell her. "Why else would he leave?"

"Why are you doing this to yourself?"

"Because I need to know!"

Lucy Kaye didn't have the answers and Keith didn't provide any when he wrote to them a year after his departure. No matter how many possible scenarios Reverend Adams invented, he never questioned Keith about them in the daily letters he wrote back. He thought Keith's occasional replies were a sign that he would be coming home soon, so he didn't want to trouble him. Months passed and he never came, which forced Reverend Adams to spend more and more time waiting and looking for answers in the wrong places.

He started suffering from insomnia. Every night, when he was sure Lucy Kaye was asleep, he would slip outside, get in his car and attempt to go after his son. But something inside him would not allow him to leave the yard. No matter how hard he tried to back out the yard, he couldn't. Knowing his son was in Micanopy, two hours away, became even more unbearable than not knowing his whereabouts. One night, out of desperation, he got down on his knees and begged Lucy Kaye to take him to Micanopy.

"Please." He completely broke down. "You have to take me. I have to see my boy."

"Reverend, you know I can't do that," she told him. "Remember what he said? He said he would run again if we went there."

"Then why did he write and tell us where he was?"

"He told us so we would know."

"No! That wasn't why! He wants us to come after him! I know my son! And that's what he wants us to do!"

"That's not what he said. He said he would run. Is that what you want? He's not here with us anymore, but at least we still have him." She sat up in bed and guided his head into her lap. Then she tried to caress away his pain. "I know how much it hurts, but we have to let this be enough for now. We have to keep holding on. Keep believing. Remember what you said right after he left? You told me to keep the faith. And that's what we have to do."

"What did I do, Lucy? What? I've spent my whole life preaching the gospel and trying to save lives. Trying to rescue lost souls. Now, look at me. I couldn't even save my own son. I couldn't stop him. I called him but he kept running. Why did he keep running, Lucy? Please tell me. You're his mother and if anybody knows, you know. So, why won't you tell me? Why?"

He died of a broken heart the following night, still believing that he would see his son again. The night he died his prayer was unusually brief. "Please let me see him just one more time," he pleaded. A moment was all he said he needed with him. "Just long enough to say I'm sorry."

After his prayer, he went to sleep, knowing full well he would not see another sunrise. Redemption came a little after midnight. Lucy Kaye was sitting up in bed quietly watching over him. She knew it wouldn't be long. He was lying beside her, but she could tell he was mostly somewhere else. In his mind he was staring at a wooden sign nailed to a cypress tree on Philco Road perhaps. Gliding above the dirt road toward a large wooden house, where a young man sat alone on the screened-in porch typing under the glow of a kerosene lantern.

He was looking into his son's eyes, whispering the words, "I'm sorry." And Keith was staring into the darkness of the cool January night and somehow seeing his father and hearing his apology. She watched as Reverend Adams took his last breath, imagining Keith reaching out to him. Holding him. Finally forgiving him. Her eyes filled with tears. How could she cry when he looked so relieved? So thankful?

Don't tell.
I can't.
That's good.
Is it?
It's what's best.
For who?

The shame hurt more than being touched. So tell? Tell who? Tell what? Even if there were words to describe the transgression, the consequences of speaking them would be insufferable. Telling would only turn his pain into theirs. And he was not going to let that happen. No one else should have to fall.

Still, June fell. But unlike Reverend Adams, she kept living, even though her life was ruined. She had to keep living for Trevor, who was sitting next to her, cautiously eyeing the two men across the table. One was his dad and the other was a man whose presence scared him, yet someone he was undeniably drawn to. He saw who he would become in Keith. He saw the physical features, like the straight black hair, the caramel complexion, and their dark, penetrating eyes. Alex saw them, too.

"You haven't eaten anything," Alex said. "What's up?"

"Nothing," Trevor answered. "I'm just not hungry."

"I can't believe that. You must be an impostor. My boy would never let all this good food go to waste."

"I'll put his plate in the microwave," said Kathryn, who was sitting at the head of her dining room table. "He can eat it later."

"I'm going riding," Trevor announced.

"No!" June's frail hand reached for him. His hand met hers. "You can't just skip out on my birthday dinner. I want you to eat dinner with me. Okay?"

Trevor nodded and began eating.

"Thank you," she said and smiled at him.

Everybody was here. Trevor. Her mother. Alex. Keith. Lucy Kaye. Leatrice. Bernard. Willie and Joe. These were the people she held most dear. There were others who dropped by, like Mrs. Rosa Lee, who brought a honey glazed ham. Mrs. Blue Hen and her grandson, Simon, brought a sour cream pound cake. Mrs. Croft baked two pumpkin pies. Inez brought flowers and balloons. And the Whitehursts came with a basket of fruit.

"Ma, can I go horseback riding after I'm done eating?"

"Maybe tomorrow," June answered. "When I can watch you."

"But I want to ride today!"

"Trevor, I really don't—"

"I'll watch him," Keith said. "If he doesn't mind." He wasn't sure why he offered to watch Trevor. The words simply came out.

Everyone stared at Trevor. Alex felt a lump in his throat as he waited on pins and needles for his son's response.

"Trevor, would you like for Keith to go riding with you?" This was the opportunity June had hoped for. She wanted Trevor and Keith to spend some time together so they could get to know each other.

Trevor saw his befriending Keith as betraying Alex. He glanced up at Alex, who had stopped chewing mid-bite. He turned and stared at Keith out the corner of his eye. "That's okay."

"Are you sure?" Keith asked. "It's been a while, but I used to be a pretty good rider."

"Thanks." He lowered his head. "I'll wait until tomorrow."

Alex said, "Tell you what, Trevor. All of a sudden, I feel like riding. So, why don't you, Keith, and I go get saddled up." He said it before he realized he was saying it.

"Can I, Ma?"

"Sure," she answered. "When you're done eating."

"I'm done!" Trevor kissed June on the cheek. "Last one to the stable is a sissy," he yelled and ran toward the back door.

"Put your jacket on!" June yelled to Trevor.

"It's not cold," Trevor hollered back.

"Trevor!" Kathryn intervened. "You heard your mother."

"All right, Gramps."

Keith gave Alex a grateful smile and a pat on the shoulder before rushing off behind Trevor.

"Alex, you're a good man," Lucy Kaye said.

"The best," June said and then reached across the table to cover his hand with hers. She stared into his eyes and allowed him to stare back into hers. "I don't know if I've told you this enough lately, but I love you."

This was the moment Alex had been waiting for. He had to ask her now. Fear and uncertainty stopped him while June was in the hospital. He'd planned on asking her the previous night, but when he walked into the room, she was sitting next to the window staring at Keith's bedroom window. He couldn't ask her then because he felt her heart and her mind were with the man next door. Now he was seeing what he'd been praying for. Love in her eyes. Love for him.

Bernard saw it coming and tried to warn everybody. "Get ready. Here it comes."

"What are you talking about?" Lucy Kaye asked.

"He's fixin' to do it!"

"Do what?" Kathryn looked to June for an answer.

"I don't know," June said.

"Here comes the…" Bernard sang. "Here comes the…"

"Stop before you ruin the surprise!" Leatrice shoved Bernard.

"I was only helping him out," he laughed. "Giving him a little push."

"Thanks, but I don't need any pushing." Alex leaned over and kissed June's hand. "I love this woman. I love her with everything I am, and that's why I'm asking her, actually I'm begging her." He turned his hand over and took hers in his. He stared into her eyes and touched the one place inside of her that she'd never allowed him to touch. "Junie, I don't know how many times I've asked you this, but here goes again. Will you marry me? Will you be my wife?"

"Yes."

Alex blinked. "What did you say?"

"I said, 'Yes.'"

He stared confoundedly at everyone who was sitting next to him. "What? Did she say?"

"She said she'd rather marry me." Bernard joked.

"Don't make me nut up in here." Alex turned to June. "You said yes?"

June smiled.

"Thank you." He excused himself from the table, still in disbelief, but grateful. "Thank you," he yelled back as he walked out of the back door. "Thank you."

"Why can't I find a man like that?" Leatrice asked.

"It's all in where you look," Bernard advised.

"Tell me about it." Leatrice winked at June before nodding slyly at Bernard.

"Well, Kathryn, looks like we have a wedding to plan," Lucy Kaye said. "I'm so happy for you, Junie." She kissed June on the forehead. "And I want you to be happy. You deserve to be."

The mini celebration was interrupted when the doorbell rang.

"I'll get it." Lucy Kaye walked into the living room and opened the door. "Come on in. We're having dinner now."

Coach Rickards walked into the dining room behind Lucy Kaye. Tall, handsome, and rather young-looking for a 62-year-old, he was the last of the Bacon Street boys. June's dad, Henry, Reverend Adams, and Coach grew up on Bacon Street, and it was a rare sighting when one was seen without the other two. After graduating from high school, they attended the historically Black university, Florida A & M University in Tallahassee, and all three married girls they met at the university. They each came back to Bacon Street; Henry and Coach right after they graduated, and Reverend Adams, a few years later. This was their home.

Coach and his wife, who was from Philadelphia, divorced amicably after three years. Everyone realized the reason for their divorce. She could not live in the wide open confines of such a small town and he could not live anywhere else. She went back to Philadelphia, but still vacationed in Hampton Springs two weeks every summer. Although they never remarried, they never fell out of love with each other.

Years later, after Henry and Reverend Adams died, Coach was the person the community leaned on most. Whatever the mishap, he was there to help fix it. A dead car battery. A leaking faucet. Raccoons during harvest. Those were the extent of their problems. Emotionally, they took care of each other. Financially, they were all well off. So Coach, like the Whitehursts, Mrs. Blue Hen, and the other families on Bacon Street, came with small tokens of appreciation and kind words to brighten June's day.

"These are for you." Coach gave June a large bouquet of yellow, pink and white tulips. The flowers perfectly complemented the pastel scarf tied around her head. "Happy birthday."

"Thank you, Coach. These are beautiful."

"But not nearly as beautiful as you."

"Sit down, Jordan," Kathryn said, "and have some dinner."

"I was waiting for you to invite me."

"Invite you?" Lucy Kaye went into the kitchen and then returned with a plate and silverware. "Nobody's ever had to invite you to a plate of food." She handed Coach the plate and utensils. "Everybody always cooks extra because we know you're coming."

"That's why I love you folks," he replied. He piled two large spoonfuls of collards on his plate and then a slice of ham, macaroni and cheese, potato salad and a piece of fried chicken.

"Where are my manners?" Kathryn remembered that she had

not introduced Coach to her guests. "Jordan, I want to introduce you to everyone."

"I already know everybody," Coach reminded her.

"Well, did you know Alex asked Junie to marry him?"

"Really? What did she say?"

"There she is," Kathryn said and continued concealing her excitement. "Ask her."

"Junie?"

"I said yes."

Coach Rickards walked over to June. "This is from your daddy and me." He kneeled beside her. Then he took her in his arms and held her. "He would be so happy. Yes, he would."

As Kathryn watched Coach Rickards hugging June, she imagined it was her husband, Henry, who was proudly holding his daughter. Kathryn smiled and listened intently as Henry turned to her and whispered, "Can you believe it? Our little girl is getting married."

Where have you been?

Why?

Because I've missed you.

Missed me?

Yes. I miss you when you're not here.

Don't touch me!

Why?

Because I said don't!

Why are you doing this to me?

Why am I doing this to you?

I thought—

You thought?

Shame turned to anger. Anger turned to depression. Depression turned to the need to run. Now, a lifetime later, he was back. And for the first time since he left, he let himself imagine what could have been. Growing old with the woman he loved. Being a dad and knowing the young boy who looked so much like him. Happiness. Fulfillment. Purpose. He longed for that life. But it was too late for wishful thinking because he ran. And he couldn't stop running.

"Trevor! Hold up!" Keith was having a hard time keeping up with Trevor, who seemed to be deliberately losing him on the trails around the old hotel grounds.

Trevor stopped and looked back at Keith, who appeared to be in a trancelike state as he marveled at the once familiar landscape. Trevor waited. After he saw Keith wasn't coming, he rode off.

Keith was trapped, held hostage by involuntarily memories of the long-gone days he and June spent getting lost in the ruins of this once famed resort. It was here, on the crumbling steps that led to the main entrance, that he first told her he loved her. It was the summer he turned fifteen.

Keith smiled. *Remembering doesn't hurt so badly after all*, he thought.

"Where's Trevor?" Alex rode up and asked.

Keith turned around. "I didn't hear you ride up."

"My bad."

"So, what were you saying?"

"I was just asking about Trevor."

"He rode on ahead," Keith said and grinned. "I think he was trying to leave me."

"I did it, man!" Alex blurted out. "I asked her to marry me."

"I'm assuming by the expression on your face that she said yes."

"Finally."

Keith looked past Alex and remembered how he had planned to bring June here and ask her to marry him. This was where he wanted to propose to her, because these grounds were special to them.

"Congratulations," Keith said and started down the trail that led to the old train depot.

"You know she doesn't have much longer," Alex said after catching up with Keith.

"I know."

"Do you know what that means?"

"I'm not sure what you're getting at."

"You have to tell her."

Keith stopped and turned to Alex. "I have to tell her? Why? It's been over ten years. Why can't we just let it go? Let it stop controlling our lives? It's over. Done with."

"Is it, Keith?"

Keith couldn't answer. Not honestly, at least.

"Listen, Keith, maybe it is time for everybody to simply forget about what happened and go on with their lives. That's how it should be, but it's not. You may look at Junie and think she's okay, that she's gone on with her life, but you'd be wrong. She succeeded professionally, but personally she's suffered. I did the best I could to take away the hurt, but I couldn't take it all away because I didn't cause it. Keith, she's spent every day since you left trying to figure out what she did wrong and she blames herself. I don't know why you ran away, but I know it wasn't because of something Junie did. Am I right?"

Keith didn't respond.

"You don't have to answer, but I know it wasn't her fault. And that's why you have to tell her. She needs to know the truth."

"What if there's nothing to tell?"

"Something happened, Keith. You didn't walk away for no reason. I don't know you that well, but I know Junie, and you couldn't walk away from her like you did. I've been with her. I've loved her. I know what her love feels like and how it makes you feel. It makes you feel big, special, like you've been blessed. There's no way, man. You had to have a reason to walk away. And for the life of me, I can't understand what could've happened that was so horrible that everybody in this town is too scared to acknowledge it. Nobody knows what you're hiding, but they're all frightened to death of it. Why?"

Keith wasn't ready to stare the truth in the face all those years ago and he still wasn't ready. "People in towns like this paint pictures," he tried to explain. "They paint pictures in their minds of who they are and what they represent. Everybody knows their place here. Look around you, Alex. If Hampton Springs and Bacon Street seem like picture perfect places to live, it's because that's the picture everyone here has painted. They keep secrets around here. They hide the ugliness, and they never tell."

"But—"

"No buts, Alex. Tell me, what would you do if you found out life wasn't as pretty as the picture you've grown up with? What would you do if you learned that the people in that picture weren't who they appeared to be? Would you keep it to yourself or would you destroy everyone's life along with yours by telling? What would you do, man? Tell me. I'm listening."

Alex shrugged his shoulders. He didn't have the answer to Keith's question, but finally he understood the reasoning behind June's decision to hide the cancer from him and everyone else. Like Keith, she did it to protect the people in the picture that represented her life.

"Are you okay?"

"I'll be fine," Keith replied. "Do me a favor and tell Junie it wasn't her fault."

"It would mean more coming from you."

"Maybe it would," Keith said, "but I can't." Keith knew the consequences of coming back here. Hiding away on Philco Road allowed him to eradicate the indelible images that sent him running. But now, being back in Hampton Springs with June, he felt compelled to unlock the door and walk inside that room again with her.

It's okay to touch me.
Touch you?
Yes. Touch me.
Hold up a second.
What's wrong?
Nothing. I just need a minute.
So do I.
Don't do that.
Sshhh.
Please. Please don't.

It was her touch this time. Her touch felt like someone else's. Hers was softer. Sweeter. Gentler. Still, it reminded him of the nights, mornings, and afternoons he was forced to pretend he was outside of himself to escape the deplorable assailments he'd hidden for more than two years. When she kissed his trembling lips, he felt another pair of lips. Not hers. And, it wasn't June who took him inside of her, who he surrendered to underneath the green comforter that night. He loved her and making love to her should not have felt like that.

June loved him, too, and she had loved him since the first time she saw him get out of his parents' car and then climb the chinaberry tree in the yard next door. Now they were graduating from high school, preparing for college, and a life of perpetual bliss. This night was their beginning. She was ready to give herself to him. No one told her she was making love to a damaged man and that getting too close to a man who'd been touched by unwanted hands could sometimes be the worst thing a woman who loves him can do.

"Junie, I just wanted to say thanks for covering for me the other day when I missed baseball practice," June read one of Keith's old letters aloud as she sat on the couch in her mother's living room. "Coach Rickards was really upset and going to suspend me for a game, but when you told him that you were sick and that I was with you because your mother was out of town, he excused me. You know, Junie, I don't understand why Coach gets so mad with me about little things. He doesn't get mad with everybody else like he gets mad at me. I think it's because he lives next door to me and knows my folks so well."

June was glad to finally have some time to herself. Kathryn and Lucy Kaye were shopping and planning her wedding, which was set for the following Saturday. Alex and Willie had driven Bernard and Leatrice to Tallahassee to catch a plane back to Detroit so they could deal with the media frenzy surrounding her illness and upcoming wedding. Alex insisted that Joe stay with June and Trevor, even though he knew there was no safer place on the planet for them. Trevor was at Coach Rickards' playing catch with the new glove Coach had given him the day before. And, June had sent Joe to town to get doughnut holes from her mother's bakery.

"Can I ask you something, Junie?" she read from another letter. "That's okay. I better not. It's nothing. I was going to ask if you've ever been to or heard of another town like Hampton Springs. If I had to live somewhere else, it would need to be a town just like this. Everything is so simple, so beautiful here. My only problem with Hampton Springs is some people aren't who they appear to be. I hope they're not like that everywhere."

When she asked him who he was referring to, he told her, "No one in particular." June knew he wasn't being totally truthful, but she didn't push the issue. Instead, she folded the letter and put it with the other letters he wrote. A thousand readings later, she still wondered what he meant when he wrote, "People aren't who they appear to be."

June looked up and stared at the straw pocketbook on the end table. It was overflowing with Keith's letters. She had read each and every one of them more times than she cared to remember hoping to find answers to the question that had plagued her since the morning Keith tiptoed out of the room with tears in his eyes while she lay in bed pretending to be asleep: Why did he leave? However, today, instead of pondering why Keith left, she wondered aloud, "Why didn't I say something? Why did I just lie there pretending not to see his tears?"

The doorbell rang.

June looked up and saw Keith standing at the door. She hid the letters under the crocheted blanket covering her legs and then waved her hand for him to come in. She straightened the pink and green scarf tied around her hair and pulled the blanket up to her lap. When the door opened, she smiled. "Hi."

He smiled back, closing the door behind him. He sat in a chair across from the couch. "I was just dropping by to check on you. So, how does it feel to be thirty?"

"Pretty good, I think," June answered. "How have you been?"

"Okay." Keith looked at the fireplace mantle lined with pictures of June, her mother and father, her Uncle Ben and their prom picture. "I saw you outside this morning. I was going to come out with you, but I figured you already had enough company with your mom, my mom, Alex, Trevor, and everybody else on Bacon Street."

June laughed. "You may not believe this, but I had no idea everybody was going to show up like that. I figured it would be Trevor, Alex and me. Actually, I was a little surprised at Alex, he never gets up with me." She wanted him to turn and look at her, so she could stare into his eyes. She never grew tired of losing herself in his deep brown eyes when they were young and in love. "I was really hoping you'd be there with me. How long has it been?"

He quickly changed the subject. "Alex told me you said yes."

"I know." June tried to gauge his reaction, but his face was barren. There was nothing to go on. No frowns. No smiles. No signs to read. So she inquired. "And?"

"And I think you made a good choice."

"Really?"

"Yes."

That wasn't the response she'd hoped for, but it was the one she expected. "Keith, can I ask a huge favor of you?"

He hesitated. "It depends on what it is."

"It has nothing to do with that," she assured him with a smile.

"I'm sorry. I shouldn't have assumed anything."

"Will you give me away?"

"What?"

"I want you to give me away."

Keith looked confused. "Me?"

"Usually, the bride's father gives her away," June explained, "but my father's not here. And I can't think of anyone else I'd rather have give me away than you. Please."

"All right, I'll do it." Keith smiled. "That is if Trevor doesn't mind. By the way, where is he?"

"Over at Coach Rickard's playing."

"No! No! No! No!" Keith dashed frantically out the door.

The line had been crossed, and until now, June had been too blind to see it in Keith's eyes. Feel it in his touch. Or read about it in the letters he'd written. It was all there in his letters. Suddenly, she felt the enormous weight of realization crashing down upon her.

"Oh God, no!" June struggled to get to her feet and then to the door. The pain was unbearable, but she had to get outside. "Trevor! Trevor!" She pushed the screen door open and fell on the porch. "Keith!"

Keith was running. Running toward the footsteps in the dark. Toward the whispered words. The unwanted touch. Running. Running. Running.

"Somebody help me!" June yelled as she crawled to the edge of the porch. "Trevor!"

Lucy Kaye saw June as soon as she and Kathryn pulled into the driveway. Kathryn saw Keith first and the car came to a screeching halt. They both jumped out of the car.

"What happened?" Kathryn yelled as she ran toward the porch with Lucy Kaye right behind her. "What's wrong with Keith?"

"Keith?" Lucy Kaye stopped in her tracks. "Where's Keith?"

"Stop him, Ma," June cried. "He's gone to Coach Rickards'! You have to stop him!"

"What's wrong?" Lucy Kaye was hysterical now. "What?"

"Coach was the reason he left!"

"What do you mean the reason he left?" Kathryn asked and reached for Lucy Kaye's trembling hand.

"I'll explain later! Just get him!"

Kathryn couldn't hold Lucy Kaye. Like her son, she was running. "Lucy," Kathryn yelled. "Come back!"

Alex had to swerve to the side of the road to keep from hitting Lucy Kaye. When he flung the car door open, it almost knocked Kathryn down as she rushed out of the yard behind her friend.

"Alex!" June was struggling to get down the steps. "Alex!" He started toward the porch, but June waved for him to follow her mother. "No! Get Trevor! Get Trevor!"

"Help her!" Alex instructed Willie before taking off behind Lucy Kaye and Kathryn. "And don't let her out of your sight!"

Coach Rickards was throwing the baseball to Trevor when Keith burst through the gate. Trevor, startled by Keith's sudden and alarming appearance, turned away and the ball hit him on the side of the head, knocking him to the ground.

"Trevor!" Keith ran over to Trevor and kneeled beside him. After making sure Trevor was all right, he turned to Coach Rickards. "Stay away from him! Do you hear me? Stay away from him!"

"Trevor! Trevor!" Alex rushed past Lucy Kaye and Kathryn, through the gate, and over to where Trevor was lying on the ground. "What happened?"

"We were playing catch," Coach Rickards tried to explain before Keith cut him off.

"Tell him what you were going to do to him!" Keith yelled. "Tell him!"

"I don't know what you're talking about, Keith." Coach Rickards' glove dropped to the ground, but he didn't seem to notice. "We were only playing catch."

Lucy Kaye and Kathryn hurried into the yard.

"What did you do to my son?" Lucy Kaye marched up to Coach Rickards and stared angrily into his eyes. "What did you do to him?"

Kathryn tried to step between Lucy Kaye and Coach Rickards, but Lucy Kaye pushed her to the side.

"I'm going to ask you one more time! What did you do to my son?"

Keith walked up to his mother and put his arms around her. "Don't worry about it, Ma. It's okay now," he whispered in her ear. "It's okay."

"No, it's not!" Lucy Kaye pulled away from Keith and stared directly into Coach Rickards' eyes as she spoke. "Your father died thinking he was the reason you ran away! You weren't here to see how much he suffered! Now, Jordan, tell me what you did to my son."

"I didn't do anything," Coach Rickards answered nervously. Then he turned to Keith and asked, "Did I, Keith?"

Fear kept Keith from telling years ago because he remembered Coach Rickards' warning. "If you tell your mother or Reverend, all you're going to do is hurt and disgrace them. Is that what you want to do?"

Kathryn married into the portrait her husband and the others had of their community, and she wasn't ready to see a different, more veracious, picture of her town, her neighbors, and friends. These people became her family when she moved here thirty-five years ago. And now, there was no way she was going to let everything she believed in crumble because of a moment of indiscretion. She couldn't even imagine it. So she backed away from it all, finally coming to rest in the waiting arms of her grandson.

Lucy Kaye didn't budge. She never knew why her son ran away, but she knew it was something horrible, something no one in this town, including her and Reverend Adams, would allow themselves to see. But she was ready to look now. Ready for the truth. She turned and looked at her son. "Keith?"

He didn't answer.

"There!" Coach Rickards was confident Keith would keep their secret like he had for the past fifteen years. "He said no!"

No one noticed Willie walk in the gate with June in his arms. "He didn't say anything!" June yelled at Coach Rickards. Willie, still carrying June, walked over to Keith. June reached for his hand. "How could you?" she asked Coach Rickards. "He trusted you! We all trusted you!"

Alex knew the truth now. "This is your chance to let it go," he told Keith. "If you don't, it will destroy the rest of your life and everyone standing here. They deserve to know the truth, and you deserve the right to finally be free of it. Listen to me, man. It wasn't your fault."

Tears filled Keith's eyes as he recalled the leathery feel of Coach's callous-ridden fingers stroking his private parts; Coach's wet lips pressed against his; the painful jabbing of Coach's rock-hard penis inside him; the unimaginable shame.

"He," Keith responded, locking onto June's hand. He knew she was strong enough to hold him this time because now she knew his secret. Finally, with her beside him, he could utter the words, "He touched me."

Words could describe the horrible act, but they were an ambiguous means of expressing the anguish he felt. What he lost. What they all lost.

"He touched me."

That was the last thing Lucy Kaye remembered about that afternoon. Those three words and then awaking with skin and green cotton fibers under her fingernails. Everything else was a blur, an all-too-real dream that faded when she regained consciousness. She didn't recall falling to the ground or scratching through Coach's socks and drawing blood from his ankles. Or June asking Keith the only question left to ask.

"Why didn't you tell us?"

"I couldn't tell because I was my father's son," Keith tearfully answered. "And I was perfect in his eyes."

"A Song Still Unsung"

(lyrics and arrangement by June)

So long.
Good-bye.
I'll be missing you my friend.
So long;
Good-bye.
Every story has to end.
But saying good-bye
and watching you go,
is more than I can stand.
So I'll say the words out loud,
and watch you through shut eyes.

So long.
Good-bye.
I'll cherish the memories.
So long.
Good-bye.
It's time I set you free.
But setting you free,
and walking away,
is too much for one heart.
So I'll break the ties that bind,
and hold you from within.

So long.
Good-bye.
It's time to let it be.

So long;
Good-bye;
Go on and spread your wings.
But letting it be,
and living without you;
No, I'll never be the same.
But, I'll bid you farewell,
and swear that's what I mean.

So long; Good-bye.
So long; Good-bye. (Repeat to fade)

Chapter 14

I t took more than a century and four generations to create the conterminous lives the seven families on Bacon Street lived. One-hundred and seven years, the majority of which were spent in servitude to the man who built the once-famous hotel at the end of Bacon Street. His death lifted them from their toilsome existence. He bequeathed to each family a beautiful home, 125 rich, fertile acres of land and timber, and a chance to script their own lives and their children's. They vanquished all the memories—the disparity and anguish—of their past lives before stepping into their new ones. The folks who were old enough to remember the travails of hardship and loss simply forgot, and those who couldn't remember were never told. They rewrote their lives and were in control of their destinies. They became decision makers. Business owners. Teachers. Leaders. Dreamers. One even became a star. Finally, they were who they wanted to be. In an instant, three words changed everything: He touched me.

Mr. and Mrs. Whitehurst, the only residents of Bacon Street who were there when the original seven families agreed to forget the past and start anew, now worried that their decision to live apart from the rest of the world had somehow contributed to this horrible transgression. Keith's confession was proof. He ran away to keep from shattering the image his father had of him. If Jordan Rickards had been able to live outside the world his parents and the others created for him, maybe his wife would have stayed and this never would have happened. That's what they concluded, and in doing so, placed the blame on themselves.

No one went untouched.

For the first time in her sixty-three years, Mrs. Blue Hen's faith wavered. She didn't question God when her husband died in a car accident the day after he bought the yellow '55 Chevy he'd worked six days a week for two years to buy. Her faith wasn't brought into question the night her daughter, Wilhelmina, laid her ten-month-old son, Simon, in the bed with his grandmother before she walked out of the front door and never returned. Instead, she told everyone that she had chosen to raise her grandson because Wilhelmina had enlisted in the military and would be serving in Europe. She believed in God's infinite wisdom, despite the imperceptible reasons for her husband's tragic death and for having to be the only mother her grandson knew. But today, she looked toward Heaven and asked what could be right about having to ask her grandson had he been touched.

"I'd give anything to keep from having to ask you this," she told him. And she would have, had she not already witnessed its crippling impact on Keith's life. "Did Coach ever touch you?"

"What?"

"Did he touch you?"

"You mean like?" He glanced down at his genital area.

She nodded yes.

"No," he stuttered. "Why would he touch me there?"

Mrs. Blue Hen watched as his dream of pitching for the Atlanta Braves faded along with his innocence and her faith.

Although it had been forty-six years since Mrs. Rosa Lee married and moved off Bacon Street, she felt the tremors that day. She had not thought about her youngest son since he confessed to murdering a convenience store clerk in Perry seventeen years ago. She went home after hearing his confession and removed every photograph of him, every piece of clothing that belonged to him, and every other sign of his existence. And, she did not speak his name again until the afternoon when the revelation of another unspeakable act forced her to relive the shame.

The picture no longer perfect, their lives no longer theirs, they joined Keith, June, Lucy Kaye, and Kathryn and did the only thing left to do.

"They won't get the police involved if you leave and never come back," Alex informed Coach Rickards later that evening.

"Where will I go?"

"I don't know," Alex answered. "But if you leave, which is in your best interest, they're prepared to make you a very good offer for your house and land."

"My house and land? What's Keith trying to do to me? Take everything I have? Destroy me?"

"Isn't that what you did to him?" Alex turned and looked across the neatly manicured yard. He shook his head in disgust. "You really don't get it, do you?"

"I said I was sorry! What more does he want from me?"

"He wants you to leave. And so do the others." Alex stared at Coach, who sat in his porch swing. The reality of what had occurred earlier that day had not fully settled in.

"This is my home and these people are my family," he said. "Why do they want me to go?"

"You molested one of their children!"

"No!" Coach objected. "That's not what happened. That's not how it happened. You have to believe me."

"Keith trusted you!"

Coach stood and walked toward Alex. "Please," he said and reached out to Alex. "Help me. They'll listen to you."

"Don't!" Alex stepped back toward the steps. "Don't expect any sympathy from me because I don't have it to give. When you molested Keith," he said, "you ruined June's life. She wouldn't be with me now if you hadn't done what you did to Keith, but she wouldn't be dying! And another thing. Count yourself lucky. Because if you had put your hands on my son, you wouldn't have to leave. You'd be a dead man right now. Now accept Keith's offer or we're calling the cops."

"Why can't we discuss this?"

"Accept or decline!"

"Why?" Coach sat back down. "Why is he doing this to me?"

"I'm only going to ask you one more time. Do you accept or decline?"

"I'll go," Coach reluctantly answered. "I don't know where, but I will go."

Alex walked off of the porch and didn't look back.

The following Friday, two moving vans pulled out of Coach's driveway. Kathryn and Lucy Kaye were assisting a crew of florists and decorators as they hastily prepared her house and yard for June's wedding. June's condition had worsened, so Kathryn moved the wedding from the church to her house. She and Lucy Kaye were stringing a wreath of golden oak leaves, ornamental berries, and magnolia blossoms across the porch banister. They tried their best to ignore the vans, but it had only been seven days and that wasn't nearly enough time for them to forget and to forgive.

Kathryn nudged Lucy Kaye, whose eyes were filled with tears, to the door. "We will be inside," Kathryn signed to Inez, who she'd asked to assist her in coordinating the wedding.

Lucy Kaye went inside but Kathryn couldn't walk away. She had to wait long enough to watch the two vans drive past her house. They were transporting more than the well-kept furniture, heirlooms and keepsakes of one of the first families to settle into the Quarters and the first to move into their new home on Bacon Street. The van pulled around Sheriff Walker's blockade at the corner of Bacon and Willow Streets, carrying the banished memories of four generations of Rickards.

The living room, the dining room, and the hallways were filled with bouquets of hydrangeas, sunflowers, roses, orchids and an assortment of other seasonal flowers.

Everyone saw the tears in Lucy Kaye's eyes when she and Kathryn walked through the living room and up the stairs, but they pretended to be so involved in what they were doing that they didn't notice. June, more peaked and emaciated, was lying on the couch staring blankly at the television while Alex, Keith, and Trevor installed a new ceiling fan in the living room. Her health was failing more rapidly now, and she was taking more and more medicine to make her condition tolerable. Everyone, including June, had accepted the inevitable, but they were still struggling to come to grips with the abeyance of their lives without her.

Keith stood on a footstool holding up the ceiling fan while Alex stood on a small ladder and attached it to the wires. "Trevor, hand me a screwdriver," Keith said.

"The big one or the little one?" Trevor asked.

"The little one."

Keith handed Alex the screwdriver and Alex used it to tighten the last screws.

"What do you think so far, Junie?" Alex asked.

"It looks good," she answered without turning away from the television. A television special devoted to her and her music was airing on BET, and the show's host was reflecting on June's early years as a youngster in Hampton Springs. There were pictures of June singing at age nine in Mt. Nebo's adult choir and pictures taken from her high school yearbook.

"What are you watching?" Alex asked.

Despondent, she answered, "Another one of those tribute shows that's talking about me like I am already dead. She was a shooting star! Did you see her? Did you spot her before she burned out?"

Alex stepped down from the ladder and sat down next to June. "They're just trying to show you how much they love you," he told her. "They want to make sure you know."

"Her latest CD, *The Pages We Forget*, is still riding the top of the album charts after eight weeks," Roxie told viewers. "The title cut from the CD is also number one on the singles chart. Personally, I think this CD is June at her absolute best. If you don't believe me, check out the video to the album's title track, 'The Pages We Forget.'"

Trevor closed the toolbox and walked over to the couch so he could watch the video. "Keith, have you seen Ma's new video?" Trevor asked.

"No." Keith shook his head.

"Yesterday's songs. Some live forever," June sang as she walked up the stairs of a Victorian-styled inn, which was an exact replica of Mildred's Bed and Breakfast. She stepped lightly, hand-in-hand with no one, but in her mind, holding onto a man whose face she hadn't seen in seven years. "Their rhythm and their rhyme, still playing melodies in our minds."

Keith stepped down from the footstool and walked over to the couch. He stood slightly behind June, Alex, and Trevor.

"A story behind each, of a love we both promised to keep," June sang as she remembered touching and kissing her lover. "So many, many years of lonely nights filled with tears."

Keith remembered the night depicted in the video.

"Our eyes tell stories of how we used to be," June sang in the video and, in her mind, undressed her lover. "Memories locked inside, never to be free." They were there again. "And now after all this time, we pass like we've never met." June stood alone at the window, wrapped in a green comforter, solemnly staring out into the rainy night. "Neither wanting to remember the pages we forget."

Keith knew June was still feeling the hurt he caused her when he walked away that morning. It was etched across her face and he could hear it in her faint sobbing as she watched the video. "I'm sorry," he said and placed his hand on her shoulder.

"I know," she replied and wiped the tears from her eyes. "It wasn't your fault."

Although she had said yes to marrying him, Alex was still uneasy about June's relationship with Keith. He knew this moment was theirs, one that he had no place in, so again he buried the envy and jealousy and did what he thought was best for her. "Trevor, I need you to help me in the kitchen," Alex said.

Trevor knew what was going on, so he followed Alex into the kitchen, being careful not to look at his mom or Keith as he walked out of the living room.

"The years have healed the pain," June sang as she made love to her imaginary lover. "We've learned to love again."

Keith sat next to June. She reached for his hand and he placed his hand in hers. Once again, they watched their lives change forever.

"Junie, if I could turn back the hands of time, I would never have left you."

She placed a finger across his lips and nodded her head in agreement.

"You asked me if I still loved you," Keith uttered, moving her finger from across his lips. He stared into her eyes. "I—"

"Please don't," she begged.

"I have to, Junie."

"No, you don't. Please." Since the morning he left her in bed pretending to be asleep, she'd dreamed of one day hearing him say the words that she could not allow him to say now.

Keith reached around her and then took her in his arms and held her close to him. He still loved her. But she was right. It was too late. He ran too far and waited too long. Still, that didn't stop him from asking, "May I kiss you?"

"Please do," she answered without hesitation.

Tenderly, affectionately, his lips met hers.

"And now after all this time," June sang in the video. She stared out the bedroom window as the rain scribbled her lover's face on the black canvas of night. "We're still feeling the rhythm and hearing the rhyme. Will we ever remember? Why don't you want to remember the pages we forget?"

A peculiar calm followed; June was ready now. All her questions had been answered. Her life redeemed. Lived. There was only one thing left to do before saying good-bye. Marry the man who saved her, who stood beside her and loved her even when she wasn't able to love him back.

Trevor lit the first candle and began the sunrise ceremony to unite his mom and dad. He walked over to light Simon and Lucy Kaye's candles. They in turn, lit the candles of the people behind them, and when all the candles were lit, they placed the candles in the holders that lined the aisle. The forty guests included Delaine, president of Antmar Records; their Grosse Pointe neighbor and friend, Anita Baker; Susan Taylor, the former editor of *Essence* magazine; and the rest of June's Hampton Springs' family.

Keith was inside waiting for the door of the study to open and for June to step out. He paced the hallway, pausing as he turned around each time to fidget with his boutonniere. Keith stopped pacing and walked to the window and stared enviably at Alex, who wore an identical tuxedo with a boutonniere of five mini-spray rosebuds framed in a spiral of white silk. He tried not to, but he couldn't help wishing he was the one standing at the altar waiting to take her as his wife instead of the one giving her away. Alex had been right. He couldn't walk away after loving her. For more than ten years, he ran from her. But now, the thought of facing the rest of his life without her cut deeper than anything.

Inside the study, Kathryn's eyes were fixated on her daughter as Inez arranged June's ballerina-length silk-tulle veil.

"You're beautiful," Kathryn remarked.

June tearfully stared back into her mother's eyes and responded, "I love you so much."

"And I love you. Now stop that crying." Kathryn reached under the veil and wiped June's eyes with a handkerchief. "You're too pretty for that."

Inez opened the door. "It's time."

Keith's heart raced.

Kathryn pushed June's wheelchair into the hallway. The sequined flowers appliquéd to the elegant white gazar sheath shimmered beneath the silk veil.

"You look good," Keith said and smiled. "Actually, better than good. You're beautiful."

June exhaled. "Thank you."

Kathryn turned the chair around to Keith. "I'll be watching," she told June and kissed her on the forehead. "Let's go, Inez."

"Ma," June called. "Do you still want to know why I didn't tell you?"

Kathryn looked at June and coerced a smile. "I know why," she said, "and I understand. You're like your father, baby. He didn't think I was strong enough either." She and Inez hurried to take their places outside.

"I'm ready," June said and reached for Keith's hand.

Leatrice was June's maid of honor. Dressed in a white gazar sheathe dress accented by an organza wrap, she stepped out of the darkness and began the bridal march. As she glided down the aisle, the soft light of the flickering candles highlighted the glistening pearls that Inez had woven into Leatrice's stacked locks.

Leatrice took her place across from Alex and his best men, Bernard and Trevor, who wore white Hugo Boss tuxedos.

June's elegant voice harmoniously joined the song of the redbirds perched in the magnolia trees. The recorded song blended perfectly with the silence of the dawning morning. "Yesterday I was at my end. I didn't know broken hearts could mend. But today you're here and you love me so right. I know tomorrow will come, and it's going to be bright," she sang. She had written this song, "Because I Love You," for her *Pages* album, but decided not to use it because it didn't fit the album's overall tone. She felt it was better suited for an occasion like this, a wedding instead of a quest to find a lost lover. "Because I love you, and my love is true. I love you. No one else will do. Because without you, I cannot see. Who would I love and who would I be?"

June gripped Keith's hand tighter as they waited in the darkness for the cue to start down the aisle. "Keith," June whispered. "I don't want to go down the aisle in this wheelchair. Will you help me walk?"

"Are you sure about that?"

"No, but at least let me try."

He helped her to stand, but her feet gave even before they felt the full weight of her ninety-five pounds. "Dammit!"

"That's okay," Keith consoled her. "I'll be your feet." He lifted her in his arms and stepped out of the darkness. Everyone stood as Keith, carrying June, started up the aisle. Tears flowed from Keith's eyes as he whispered in June's ear, "I love you, Junie, and I'll always love you."

June stared into Keith's eyes and silently replied, "And I love you..."

Keith stepped up to the altar. Reverend Diggs stepped forward. "Who gives this woman's hand in marriage?"

"I do," Keith answered and placed her gently in Alex's arms. "Take care of her," he told Alex.

"I will," Alex replied.

The first rays of sunlight crept across the gray sky as June and Alex exchanged vows. They promised to love, honor and cherish each other forever. He was a man of his word.

Alex was sitting with her in the windowsill of her bedroom two hours later when her song faded. She gazed into his eyes, as he cradled her in his arms.

"Take care of our son," she told him.

"You know I will."

"And yourself."

He nodded.

"Thank you for loving me, Alex," she said and stared into his eyes for the last time. "I thank God for you, Alex," she said.

When everything that was needed to be conveyed was said, she let go.

"Junie, I love you." He pulled her closer to him and tearfully said good-bye as the melody in his life ended.

Trevor and Keith were horseback riding in their white tuxedos when the last notes began to play. June, knowing the end was near, had asked Keith to take Trevor riding.

"Well, let me go change," Keith replied.

"No." June hesitated before asking, "Why change?"

She paused for a moment before answering her own question. "I bet you've never ridden a horse in a tuxedo. Now have you?"

"And I don't plan to," he responded.

"Go ahead, Keith." She urged. "Live a little."

Keith and Trevor were riding along the pathways of the old hotel when Trevor heard the music end. Frantic, he took off for the house with Keith hurrying behind him. Except for Bernard, everyone else was in the yard or the house. Kathryn and Lucy Kaye were outside saying good-bye to the last three guests. Inez and Leatrice were straightening up the kitchen, while Willie and Joe cleaned the yard.

"Ma!" Trevor screamed and jumped off the horse. "Ma!"

"Trevor!" Keith hurried off his horse and ran behind Trevor.

"Trevor!" Kathryn yelled and ran toward the back yard with Lucy Kaye, Joe, and Willie right behind her.

"Ma!" Trevor called as he ran through the house and up the stairs.

Leatrice and Inez raced out of the kitchen and rushed up the stairway behind him. Trevor pushed his mother's bedroom door open and burst into the room. "Ma?"

There was only silence.

My God...the silence.

"Because I Love You"

(lyrics and arrangement by June)

Yesterday, I was at my end.
I didn't know broken hearts could mend.
But today you're here,
and you love me so right.
Tomorrow will come
and it's gonna be bright.

CHORUS:
Because I love you,
and my love is true.
I love you.
No one else will do.
Because without you
I cannot see.
Who would I love?
And who would I be?

I was dreaming
and found that dreams do come true.
I was praying for someone like you.
To hold me and show me love
I knew you were my answer
from Heaven above.

CHORUS

BRIDGE
Forever,
is what we have.
Together,
we will make this last.

CHORUS
(repeat to fade)

About the Author

Anthony Lamarr grew up in North Florida, where he still resides. He is a novelist, screenwriter, playwright, and Florida Press Association award-winning newspaper columnist. *The Pages We Forget* is his second novel. His first novel, *Our First Love*, was also published by Strebor Books.